HOUSE

OF

SHADES

Also by Lianne Dillsworth

Theatre of Marvels

HOUSE

OF

SHADES

LIANNE
DILLSWORTH

HUTCHINSON
HEINEMANN

1 3 5 7 9 10 8 6 4 2

Hutchinson Heinemann
20 Vauxhall Bridge Road
London SW1V 2SA

Hutchinson Heinemann is part of the Penguin Random House group of companies
whose addresses can be found at global.penguinrandomhouse.com

First published by Hutchinson Heinemann in 2024

www.penguin.co.uk

A CIP catalogue record for this book is available from the British Library.

ISBN 9781529152159

Typeset in 14/18.25pt Dante MT Std by Jouve (UK), Milton Keynes
Printed and bound in Great Britain by Clays Ltd, Elcograf S.p.A.

The authorised representative in the EEA is Penguin Random House Ireland,
Morrison Chambers, 32 Nassau Street, Dublin D02 YH68

www.greenpenguin.co.uk

Penguin Random House is committed to a
sustainable future for our business, our readers
and our planet. This book is made from Forest
Stewardship Council® certified paper.

For Mama

Contents

I

A row of spiked railings

Did you know that a deathbed promise has a sort of power? Words spoken with a dying breath bind like a spell. They change you. As a doctoress, I've seen plenty. As a daughter, I made one of my own. It took me to a place called Tall Trees. A place that part of me has never left. Let me tell you of what happened there and you can judge for yourself whether the promise I made was kept.

Doctoress to Gervaise Cherville. A rare chance for a woman like me, but as I turned the corner into the square, the misgivings I'd suppressed on my way here welled up. I'd been so enamoured of my good fortune at landing this job I'd not asked enough questions. What did I know about treating swells? My usual patients were the streetwalkers of King's Cross. If only they could afford to pay for my services, I'd be with them now, but there was no use in harping on it. Two hundred yards ahead of me, set back from the road behind a row of spiked railings, Tall Trees lay in wait. Half past nine and I wasn't due to arrive until ten. Nothing wrong with being early. It could only speak to my sense of duty, but the closer I got to the house, the more my confidence ebbed. Jos had offered to walk me here; perhaps I should have let him, but a final parting when I was already worried about being away from home for four weeks would've only made me blub and the last thing I wanted was to turn up looking weepy. I'd got this job on the strength of the vicar's recommendation. It was unlikely I'd keep it if I made a poor first impression.

Tall Trees took up one whole corner of the square, so large I wondered if it had once been three separate houses, the strongest devouring the two either side of it. Dark curtains, half-drawn, gave it a baleful look as though it watched through narrowed eyes. When I passed through, the gate slipped from my hand, and I flinched as it clanged shut behind me. For two, three seconds the wrought-iron sound reverberated, but there was no one near to be disturbed by it, only a crow that took off with a resentful caw. The meal it left abandoned was small and furry. I averted my eyes and, hurrying along the path and up the front steps, I yanked down hard on the bell pull. A doleful chime tolled through the house and sweat prickled on my palms, forming dark patches on my gloves. Half my life had been spent walking into strange houses, knowing that inside dwelt blood, disease and even death. In all that time, I'd not been daunted. Tall Trees should be no different, but as I waited for an answer I couldn't shake the sense of dread I'd felt as soon as I'd laid eyes on it. Only time would tell if my past experiences had prepared me for what I might find in a house like this.

At last, there was a scraping of metal on metal as, one after another, a series of bolts were pulled back. The heavy door swung silently inwards and I peered uncertainly into the gloom beyond. I'd have given my eyeteeth to be able to walk away, but a young maid around fourteen years old stepped forward and there was no time for bargaining.

I'd expected a stern, hawkish-looking matron, but this girl was more like a dove, with wispy tow-coloured hair which she blew from her eyes with a huff.

'Sorry it took so long. When you rang, I thought Madam would get it. She must've popped out and Spinks won't do anything unless she's here. He's lazy as anything.'

Save for her uniform, she could easily have been one of the bargee girls I saw every day as I walked along the King's Cross towpath, yet her familiarity wrong-footed me.

'I'm Hester Reeves, here to nurse Mr Cherville,' I said, wanting to be sure she hadn't mistaken me for someone else.

'Yes, I know all that. The vicar told me to look out for you. Are you coming in or what?'

The entrance hall was dimly lit, a space large but somehow close thanks to the panels of reddish wood that lined the walls. The narrowing effect was heightened by a cloying scent that hung heavy on the air and caught in the back of my throat. I traced it to a thin-legged table – again, that rich dark wood – where a small lamp glowed over a bowl of dried rose petals. The girl held out her arms and I shook my head when I realised she was expecting to take my coat. It was far too threadbare for that.

'You're right, it is a bit chilly,' she said, mistaking my hesitancy. 'The range is on all day so the kitchen's much better. I'm Jenny, by the way.'

She wiped one hand down her apron and held it out for me to shake.

'Mr Bright said he was trusting me to make you feel welcome, seeing as Madam's not the friendliest.'

There was no lady of the house, so she must mean the housekeeper. I knew little enough about what working in service was like, but surely the housekeeper didn't merit a title.

'Is that what you call her?' I asked.

Jenny giggled at my puzzlement.

'Not to her face, silly. Only behind her back.' I'd known her five minutes, and though she was almost ten years my junior, already she was teasing me. Her easy manner reminded me of my sister Willa at that age, and a little of the apprehension I'd felt as I waited on the doorstep lifted.

'Come on,' she said. 'Leave that big bag here, I'll take you straight upstairs and get it brought up later.'

She moved off to the right, turning when she realised I hadn't followed.

'Did you not say we were going to go upstairs?' I asked, looking up the thickly carpeted staircase that curved around to the floor above.

'I did, but that means back stairs for you. That way's just for the family. You shouldn't let Madam catch you at the front door neither. We're supposed to come and go by the kitchen entrance. Not that you'll be needing it much.'

I frowned, not understanding.

'The master likes us to be at his beck and call so it's best if you keep to the house.'

It wasn't unexpected considering what Cherville was paying me, but the thought of a whole month bound to this strange place was unnerving.

'Your face. You didn't think you'd be free to come and go as you pleased, did you?'

It made me seem foolish when she put it like that, but seeing me crestfallen, Jenny patted me kindly on the arm. 'I know it's a lot to get used to. You'll feel better once you're settled.'

No fine papers had been used to decorate the back stairs and the walls were the colour of unbleached cotton, their only decoration a criss-cross web of hairlines cracks. Just as well Jenny had warned me to leave half my things behind in the entrance hall. The way was so narrow I had to hunch my shoulders and hold my bag out in front of me. As we made our way upwards, I touched my hand to the wall from time to time to keep my balance. I must've caught one of the cracks at the wrong angle, for it splintered and a chunk of plaster fell to the floor. A black beetle crawled out of the hole it left behind and I gave a yelp, that was half-surprise, half-disgust.

'I'm always doing that,' Jenny said. 'Sometimes it feels like the whole house will come crashing down around me.'

'Honestly? I'd expect that from a rookery tenement, not somewhere as grand as this.'

'Looks can be deceiving. My da knows a bit about building and the last thing he said the day he left me here was the way it was listing meant the foundations were rotten.'

Was it better to think of Tall Trees as crouched down ready to pounce or on the verge of collapse? There was no time to decide before we moved on again, talking less as the stairs steepened. Even so, Jenny was out of breath when we reached the top. Milk of meadowsweet. That's what she needed for her lungs, and if I was going to be stuck indoors most days, it sounded as though I had plenty of time to brew her some.

The fourth floor was one long corridor with six doors off it. It was lighter and less oppressive than the family's quarters thanks to the whitewashed walls, which felt far more familiar than the rich papers and gas fittings of the entrance hall. The first room was reserved for linens and smelled strongly of starch. A large tablecloth had been laid out to dry and I guessed that two cloth bags leaning against the wall contained the household's soiled sheets and delicates. The remainder of the rooms were for sleeping in, all identically furnished with a small cot, a chair and a chest of drawers. Jenny stood to one side while I poked my head into each in turn. How lively it would be if there were servants enough to occupy them all, but for now the rooms had the melancholy feel that came with being out of use.

'It's only you and me up here,' Jenny confirmed. 'Margaret sleeps along the corridor from the master, and has her own room down by the kitchen, besides, on account of being housekeeper, and Spinks – he's the driver I mentioned – lives over the stables and does for himself. Mr Cherville is on the second floor, and when he's here Mr Rowland takes the first.'

'They each have whole floors to themselves?'

'It's probably just as well. They're not as close as a father and son should be.'

I tried to keep the hope from my voice. 'You said when he's here. Does that mean Rowland Cherville's not home often?'

'Very rarely. About a month ago he moved into his club, but when the master goes to the country I think he'll come back home. I'll be out of a job if he doesn't. Look at you, though, your eyes just flashed. Do you know Mr Rowland?'

'Sort of,' I said. What I'd really been thinking of was how well my sister did.

Two months earlier, Willa had started at the Cherville factory, around the same time as Rowland had stepped in to take charge while his father was ill. I'd thought a steady job would help keep her out of trouble, unluckily she'd caught Rowland's attention. To stop him from ruining her, I had to get my sister well away from King's Cross, but fresh starts did not come cheap. That's why I'd put my all into earning the money I needed and why I'd been so grateful when the vicar, Mr Bright, had recommended me for this role. Now here I was at Tall Trees, in the heart of the lion's den.

'You'll have to fill me in later,' Jenny said, bringing me back to myself. 'Will you pick a room now, though? It can be any one of these.'

The room closest to the stairs followed the shape of the eaves, with the bed tucked into the corner where the roof sloped down. There was every chance I'd bump my head if I sat up too quickly on waking, but of all those I'd seen it felt the cosiest. I went inside and put my bag on the bed to claim it. Handed down from Mama, it clinked with bottled tinctures and vials of tonic. The one I'd left downstairs contained my few clothes, grey with washing and much-mended.

'I won't be a moment,' Jenny said and disappeared down the hallway leaving me alone.

The bedroom window overlooked the square and I tugged at the sash. Fresh air, that's what was needed in here to blow away the mustiness. I wanted to feel the wind on my face, but the frame resisted stubbornly despite my efforts.

'You won't get out that way,' Jenny said at my ear and I jumped back, bashing my side on the bed frame. 'Sorry, I didn't mean to startle you.'

'I know you meant no harm, I just wanted to open the window,' I said, giving the sash another jiggle to loosen it.

'It's hard when you live on your nerves,' Jenny sympathised. I wanted to correct her. I wasn't naturally nervous – a doctoress couldn't afford to be – but ever since I'd entered this house I'd felt uneasy, and I rubbed the tender spot on my hip.

'Look what I went to fetch for you.'

She held out a black dress much like the one she wore, but longer, so it wouldn't come up too short on me. There was a pale blue apron, too, with a tree embroidered on the pocket in gold thread – the Cherville family crest. I measured it against myself.

'Where did you rustle up this from?'

'It belonged to Bridget, but she left a few months back.'

'Was she Cherville's nurse before me?'

'Not her,' Jenny said with a laugh, making me think that the Bridget whose uniform I'd inherited was less than kind. 'He hasn't needed that sort of care until now, so you'll be the first.'

'How come she moved on?' I said as I turned to one side so she couldn't see my whole body while I changed. All I'd wanted was to make conversation, but Jenny's silence told me I'd struck on something, and when I popped my head through the neck of the black dress she was wringing her apron in her hands. She might talk a mile a minute but there was a keenness of feeling in her, too. That was like my sister also, or rather as she used to be before the grief of Mama's passing had swamped her.

'Will you help me with the buttons?' I said, to break the awkwardness, and Jenny stepped forward swiftly, fastening them with nimble fingers.

The dress was more fitted than I'd first thought and I pulled at the seams to loosen it.

'I can let it out if it's too tight?'

'I'm just not used to it, that's all,' I said, looking down regretfully at my well-worn dress discarded on the bed. I'd have little chance of rolling or lifting my patient when I could barely raise my shoulders but that wasn't my only concern.

'You ready?' Jenny said. 'Margaret's always telling me off for jawing and I don't want you to get in trouble for being late on your first day. If you promise to tell me what you think of him at dinner, I'll show you to the master's room.'

'You've got yourself a bargain. Lead on,' I said, and together we made our way downstairs to the second floor and Cherville's bedroom.

II

The smell of the sickroom

When I was called out to see my regular patients among the bawds of King's Cross, I knew what to expect. A thick lip or cut eye; maybe even a broken rib, depending on how hard they'd been punched or kicked by a punter. Often there were injuries to their insides, too, and the pox was more or less a given.

Gervaise Cherville was different, not just because he'd insisted I move into Tall Trees in order to tend him, but because he was rich and had promised to pay me handsomely: ten pounds in total, the same amount for four weeks' work that Jos could earn in a year.

'What's he like?' I said to Jenny as we walked along the landing.

'Old. I don't have too many dealings with him, honestly,

and lately he often stays abed. There's been doctors in and out ever since I started here, but never someone on call around the clock. Whatever he's got, it's worsening.'

Mr Bright had not said exactly what was wrong with Cherville – only that he thought I'd be well placed to treat him. Wishing I'd asked him why, I seized on what Jenny had said.

'Cherville can't walk?'

'Oh yes, he walks well enough. Only a few months back, he was going off to his factory every day, but then he started having trouble sleeping and after that he lost the stomach for it and asked Mr Rowland to take over.'

There wasn't time to learn more. We'd reached Cherville's door and Jenny tapped on it lightly with her knuckles.

'Enter,' came the reply and she stood back to let me pass.

'One last thing, he often complains about too much noise so make sure you speak softly and remember, straight down to the kitchen once he's let you go.'

Gervaise Cherville's bedroom was as gloomy as the entrance hall, despite the high ceilings. As I stepped inside, the smell of the sickroom was strong, and strewn herbs crunched beneath my boots. I let my eyes flicker around, taking in the rich curtains, the desk, and the otherwise puzzling lack of furniture, before lighting on the canopy bed in the centre of the room and the wasted figure sitting in it.

'So you're Hester Reeves?'

Gervaise Cherville was about seventy years old – more, perhaps – with a white beard and pale blue eyes that had a glassy look to them. In the half-light, I didn't see his arm reach out and I gave a cry as his hand closed on my wrist and pulled me forward.

'Don't writhe like that. You have to come close so I can see you properly.'

I stopped struggling. In turn, he slackened his grip; now it was his eyes that held me.

'Yes, yes, you will do very well,' he said, and the self-satisfied tone in his voice made me uneasy.

He placed a small wooden ball into my hand. 'What do you make of that?'

The strange request nonplussed me. Nevertheless I made a show of weighing the ball, holding it up to my eye while Cherville watched me intently. It was dark and smooth, the same mahogany colour that lined the walls, and that his bed was carved from. The grainlines were akin to veins in skin, surely that wasn't what he wanted to hear from me?

'Well?' Cherville pressed, but I wasn't quick enough to come up with something, for a moment later he snatched the ball back. Without knowing how, I'd managed first to please, and now to disappoint him.

'You come highly recommended by Mr Bright. I've known him from a curate, thirty years and more. He must have been impressed by your skill, to be so fulsome in his praise,' Cherville added. His tone had a searching quality to it and the last thing I wanted to do was explain that the vicar only knew I was a doctoress because I'd told him so. He'd taken pity on me one day in the churchyard when he'd seen me crying over Mama's grave and I'd admitted how much I needed a job that would pay enough for me to buy my family a new start away from King's Cross. I'd be forever grateful for the unexpected kindness he'd shown me.

'Will you tell me what it is that ails you, sir?'

'It should be you telling me, if you're half the doctoress he says you are.'

A test of my ability and the perfect chance to settle my nerves and assert my credentials. There was nothing obviously wrong, from what I'd seen so far; I would have to take a closer look. I gestured to the candle on his bedside table. 'May I?'

'By all means.'

The light flickered across his face. Eye whites bloodshot; nose collapsed, the bones softened and wasted like his frame; hair yellowed and wispy. Some might say he was suffering from old age, but I knew there was more to it than that. For all his money, Gervaise Cherville wasn't so different from my regular patients after all.

'You have syphilis, sir.' No need to beat about the bush. The best way to prove I knew what I was doing was to confirm the diagnosis I was sure he'd already been given. 'It's a complaint I see often in the course of my work with the streetwalkers of King's Cross,' I said, trying not to think of

Willa's crush on Rowland and how the disease ran in families. 'There's a tonic I can make up for you. Ground rosehip and poppy have been shown to be most efficacious and—'

He held up a hand and cut me off, clearly not as interested in my plant lore as I'd thought.

'Give me whatever potions will help. I don't need to know the ins and outs of it. Tell me, though: you discern nothing else?'

Had I missed something obvious? Not in his looks, that was certain – which left only one possibility, and here I had to be more careful. He'd challenged me but did he really want to hear what I would say? There was only one way to find out.

'A disorder of the mind, perhaps? I gather you have not been sleeping well. It has made you tired, irritable maybe?'

He nodded, apparently satisfied, and I felt my shoulders relax, sensing I'd passed his initial scrutiny.

'In four weeks' time I'll go to my estate in Sussex where I expect to live out what little time remains to me. Until then, I'll be relying on you to keep me well. There are things, important things, I must do before I leave London for good. I'll be needing every ounce of my strength.'

'I'll make a start on that tonic I mentioned.'

I was rummaging in my pockets for my seeds and powders, regretting not having brought my whole bag, when there was a knock on the door and a woman dressed in black swept in. Lean and pinch-faced, she was what I'd been expecting when I first arrived – the Margaret who Jenny had warned me of.

'Sir, I came to . . .' she began and stopped short when she saw me step forward. 'Forgive me, sir. I did not realise you had a . . .' She hesitated again, not knowing how to refer to me.

'This is Reeves. For now, let us call her my nurse.'

Margaret's lips thinned as her eyes flickered over me. 'I'd come back later, sir, but I have your letters here ready for reading out to you.'

Cherville considered for a moment then said, 'You'd better leave us, Reeves. Spend the remainder of the day learning the ways of the household and we will speak further tomorrow.'

A smirk of triumph tugged at Margaret's mouth – *I've seen you off*, it said – and, brushing past me, she sat down in the chair by Cherville's bed and produced a bundle of letters and a silver paper knife from beneath the folds of her dress.

'This one is from Viscount Wesley, sir. It'll contain reference to some private matters. Very private.'

Her implication was clear: it wasn't for the likes of me to hear, and Cherville waved a hand to shoo me away.

'Get along then, Reeves.'

I turned on my heel and bowed my head before withdrawing. He didn't see, his attention already on Margaret and the news she carried. For herself, the housekeeper ignored me, but she had the awareness of a cat because it wasn't until I'd stepped out and closed the door softly behind me that I heard her begin reading.

I'd made it two paces down the corridor when she followed me out and called, 'Reeves, you forgot to take this with you.'

In her hand she held the twist of paper that contained my poppy seeds, but when I reached for it she let it fall to the floor. 'Silly me,' she exclaimed as if she hadn't done it on purpose.

I knelt down and dabbed my finger on the carpet to collect the scattered seeds. Margaret crouched beside me and, in a lower tone meant for my ears only, said, 'We don't need any nurses here. I can look after the master well enough.'

'That's not what Mr Cherville thinks. He's hired me for the next four weeks, until he goes to the country.'

'What could he possibly want from you when he has me to tend to him?'

I had no answer for her, and Cherville's voice intruded into the silence between us. 'Margaret,' he called fretfully.

'One moment, sir, Reeves dropped something,' she said, but though she stood up she wasn't quite done with me yet. 'I don't know exactly how you've managed to inveigle your way in here, but believe me, if there's anything untoward I'll find it out,' she hissed.

Cherville called out to her again, his voice more impatient this time. She couldn't resist a parting threat.

'I'm watching you,' she said and hurried back through the door into Cherville's bedroom, leaving me staring after her, troubled. All I'd done was accept a job that would help me protect my family, yet here she was acting like a jealous sweetheart. This morning my heart had lightened when Jenny had told me Rowland was seldom home. It turned out there was an enemy waiting for me at Tall Trees after all.

Ten pounds, though, I reminded myself. Enough for me to get my whole family away from King's Cross. For that sort of money I could endure any number of hostile house-keepers, and strange patients – even the unsettling effect that being inside Tall Trees had on me – couldn't I?

I got to my feet and returned the seeds to my pocket. Jenny had demanded my immediate thoughts on Gervaise Cherville, but that was before Margaret's appearance had cut short my first meeting with him. At this time she'd still be busy with her chores and I didn't want to distract her. Margaret's voice floated down the corridor from Cherville's room where she continued to read out his letters. Her country tones were warm, even soothing, no trace of the venom with which she'd addressed me. What on earth could account for it? If I wanted to avoid a further clash, the best thing to do would be to stay out of her way. I'd go to my room, make up my medicines. First, though, I wanted to get my bag. The rocky start to my time at Tall Trees had me rattled, but if I had my things about me I knew I'd feel better. Deliberately, I took the main stairs. A risk for certain if Margaret insisted they were for the family only, but after the way she'd treated me I couldn't resist the chance to cock a snook at her.

The stairs were wide enough to accommodate at least five people walking abreast. I went straight down the middle, partly because I could and partly so as not to leave fingerprints on the polished wooden banisters. Was everything in this house made from mahogany? On the first floor – Rowland's floor – I paused on the landing and looked down the corridor in the direction of his apartments. It was an unexpected piece of luck that he was often from home. Perhaps he wouldn't remember me and the run-in we'd had a few weeks back, but I'd discerned a cruelty in his eye that suggested he was exactly the type to hold a grudge. Handsome or no, I'd have thought Willa would have been sharp enough not to fall for him.

I was about to carry on, when a large painting hanging on the wall arrested me. It depicted a white house, surrounded by lush green grasses. Had I been coming up the stairs, it would have been the first thing I saw. A gas lamp had been installed to light it, and because mere daylight was not enough to penetrate the Tall Trees gloom, I turned it up to get a better look. I knew nothing of paintings, had barely seen more than a handful in my life, and definitely none like this in its imposing gold frame. Still, I knew instinctively that the scene before me was not

English, and now every detail I spotted confirmed it, from the piercing colours to the series of dark figures at the edges of the picture. Seeing them as nothing more than their labours, the artist had given them tools – spades and hoes and a wheelbarrow – but no faces. I took a step back and saw another, lighter-coloured than the others, perched on the house's porch with a bowl in her hands. For a long time I stared at her, but it didn't matter how hard I looked: I couldn't conjure the detail I craved, the eyes and expression that would give me a sense of who she was.

I reached out and my fingers found the frame and an inbuilt plaque at the centre of its long edge. I leaned down to read the crabbed title: *Our plantation, Honduras*. The house depicted belonged to the Chervilles and no doubt they thought the people working in and around it did, too. My new employer was a slave owner.

III

Old wives' tales

I spent the rest of the day mixing up remedies in my room. Again I'd tried the window in the hope of letting in some air, again it resisted; so though I'd come prepared with my bag full of ointments and powders, I ground up fresh to shift the stale smell that lingered. Mercury was what the apothecaries prescribed for syphilis, but from what I'd seen among the streetwalkers I treated it harmed as much as it healed, loosening their teeth and bowels. Tincture of feverfew and marjoram was what Cherville needed and I ground up some lavender to help him sleep, too. Using Mama's tried and tested recipes meant my mind was free to roam where it would. Unfortunately, like the rest of me, it was held fast at Tall Trees and the painting on the first floor. So Cherville's money came from slavery. It was no surprise, really. Only the trade in human flesh brought the sorts of riches that built houses like this. It also explained why Cherville had felt so comfortable around me. On the way here, I'd wondered if Mr Bright had described me to him, had worried he might turn me away because he thought I wasn't English. As a slave owner, he'd have been accustomed to people who looked like me. Or would he? His plantation was in Honduras, but that didn't mean he'd been there. Plenty of owners had never set foot on their slave holdings. It was how they fooled themselves that keeping people in bondage for the sake of their own comfort was justified. And then I wondered: had there ever been slaves *here*?

I looked around the little room, with its cot and chest of drawers, and then down at my dress and the blue apron with its gold embroidery. My outfit had been Bridget's once, was there a Black woman who had worn it before her? With a determined effort, I put the thought aside. *No use dwelling on it*, I told myself. However distasteful Cherville's source of wealth was, I couldn't afford to walk away from this job.

It was a relief when the clock struck six. Here was permission to put down my worries, even if only for the time it took to eat my dinner.

The kitchen was warm as Jenny had promised, made cheery with a big fire and a hand-knotted hearthrug. Copper pots hung from hooks on the wall and there was a tall dresser filled with blue and white patterned china. Jenny was busy at the range when I slid into a chair at the large wooden table. A booklet had been left half-open on an illustration of a woman at the gallows and I pushed it away.

'Don't tell me you don't like *Lives of the Most Notorious*,' Jenny said as she brought over two steaming bowls of soup and placed one of them in front of me.

'I see blood enough in the course of my work without wanting to read about it.'

'You're right, I suppose. This one is good, though,' she said, untying her apron and taking a seat opposite me. 'Leek and potato,' she added as I took my first sip. Though it was warm, creamy and comforting, Jenny's poorly disguised impatience prevented me from lingering over it. I'd barely eaten half when she burst out, 'Tell me what you made of him, then?'

Despite my worries, I couldn't help but smile. 'He was very direct,' I said, fishing for the right word and not sure if I'd caught it.

'Did he ask you lots of questions? The first time he called me in, it was like being back at Sunday school. I was worried he'd cane me if I didn't know the answers.'

'He wanted to be sure I knew my business. I suppose it's fair enough, seeing as he didn't hire me himself. From what I understand, it was mainly Mr Bright's doing, but I wish he'd told Margaret. We had a bit of a set-to.'

'She came down earlier muttering to herself about char-latans and clattering about. If she's in a pet, it's always the crockery that feels it. Shame, really,' and Jenny's eyes flicked sorrowfully to the dresser.

'She's taken against me, that's for sure.'

'I wouldn't worry about that, it's nothing personal. Madam's down on everyone except the family. You'd think she was one of them, the way she carries on – at least that's the rumour,' Jenny said with a smirk.

'Are you saying she's his . . .' I let my voice trail away, not wanting to say *bastard*. Such an ugly word. I hadn't noticed a resemblance when I'd met Margaret this morn-ing, but it would explain why she'd been so possessive when Cherville had told her he'd hired me to nurse him.

'She's been with the Chervilles from childhood, at their country house as well as here. Come to think of it, she'd know about . . .' Suddenly, Jenny was very interested in her own bowl of soup.

'What is it?'

She spooned up a mouthful and took her time about swallowing it. 'Ignore me, I shouldn't have said anything.'

'Well, you have now, so out with it.'

'You promise not to laugh?' I nodded and she leaned for-ward conspiratorially. 'They say the Cherville family is cursed.'

Her voice was so solemn and what she'd said so ridicu-lous that I couldn't hide my smile.

'See, I knew you wouldn't take it seriously,' Jenny said indignantly.

'I'm sorry, but you must know these things are nonsense?'

'It was Cook next door that told me. I didn't believe it myself at first, but when you start to think, it all adds up. How else can you explain why no one quite knows what ails the master, and how Mr Rowland lost his wife and why they can't keep any servants?'

'You're here,' I pointed out, 'and Margaret.'

'We don't count. Madam would work for old man Cherville for free if he asked her to – and me, well, I've nowhere else to go.'

'I reckon you could go far if everything you cook is as good as that soup,' I said, but she waved away the compliment and I could see she needed more persuading on the curse, too.

'I know what's wrong with Cherville and surely you know why Bridget left?'

'Something to do with a poorly aunt, she said. I always thought it sounded like an excuse. If it was the curse, though, she wouldn't dare speak of it, would she – and I almost forgot: there was a fire at their plantation in Honduras, too. To hear Mr Rowland talk, you would have thought he was there to see it. What happened to his wife was the saddest thing. She was called Mae; I'm not sure how long they were married. There was a boy too, Osbert, and he died as well. There's pictures of them upstairs in his rooms, and one of the plantation, actually, on the first-floor landing.'

She didn't need to tell me that. I'd already seen the painting for myself and worked out what it meant. I pushed away the remains of the soup, my appetite gone. Meanwhile, Jenny sat back from the table, arms folded as though she'd proved beyond a doubt the curse was real. There was little I could do if she wanted to believe it, but I could see one hundred everyday reasons for what she'd described. The disease that ravaged Cherville was common enough. More likely he just didn't want to admit to any suppositions regarding how he'd caught it. What was more surprising was thinking of Rowland as a widower. Willa was always gossiping. It was a strange thing for her not to have mentioned.

'Exactly when did all this happen?'

'Four or five years ago, I think.'

'All right then, I'll play along,' I said. 'Who do you and Cook think cursed the Chervilles?'

'Someone powerful, must be, for it to be passed down the generations like that. Or maybe one of their ancestors stole something. There's gems and trinkets all over this house. Next time Cook pops over from next door, I'll call you. She'd be happy to tell you what she knows.'

I was sure she would, although I felt a little impatient with the woman for hoodwinking Jenny with her old wives' tales.

'It's bad luck, that's all,' I said. 'You'll see when

Cherville starts getting better. If he's truly cursed, then my salves and tonics won't help him, will they?'

Jenny considered, her head tilted to one side. 'Are you going to cure him?'

There was no cure for syphilis. Cherville knew it himself, and that he'd only get worse; I guessed it was why he was taking himself off to his country house away from the gaze of London society.

Jenny mistook my silence. 'You can't be thinking of leaving already, not when you've only just started. It's what I said about the curse, isn't it?'

'There is no curse,' I said, just as there came a sharp rap on the glass.

A rapid look passed between us and Jenny jumped up so quickly her chair clattered to the floor. She put a hand to her heart. 'What was that?'

'Someone at the door.'

The candlelight reflected off the glass, making it almost impossible to see outside into the darkness. I got up to take a closer look and as I neared the door the shadow of a man loomed.

'Who's there?' I called out.

'You don't have to answer it,' Jenny said, feeling on the worktop for a knife. A sweet girl, but she'd been reading far too many penny bloods.

'Don't be silly,' I said. 'It's my husband.'

★

I'd become Hester Reeves when I married Jos five years earlier, aged eighteen to his twenty. All the girls canal-side had set their cap at him at one time or another. I thought he'd chosen me because it was less obvious that I liked him; in truth I was as moony as the worst of them, only better at hiding it. Now Jos stepped into the kitchen, filling it with the familiar smells of coal dust and horse. He must've come straight from his work loading and unloading the barges that travelled the canal.

His head swivelled round to take in the range lined with copper saucepans, the big table and the dresser filled with china, clearly expensive but homely for all that. 'I didn't like the look of this place from the outside, but this is very cosy.'

'Jos, this is Jenny. She's been doing her best to make me feel welcome.'

'I'm pleased to hear it.' He turned to her and said, 'Jos Reeves, chief docker at the Regent's Canal. I'll hold it a personal favour if you continue to look after my wife. She spends all her concern on others and if I'm not around I need to know there's someone who's worrying about her.'

Jenny had been smiling shyly since he'd first spoken. It was his accent; all the girls loved it.

'I can make sure she's well fed at the very least,' she said, and I rolled my eyes to think there wasn't one woman he didn't have an effect on, though secretly I was gratified by it.

'What are you doing here?' I asked him.

'You refused to let me walk you over this morning. I wanted to make sure you'd settled in.' He looked about him again. 'Do you sleep down here?'

'I've got a room on the fourth floor. I'd show you, but the housekeeper's a bit of a dragon.'

'She seems fine to me,' Jos said with a wink at Jenny.

'I'm only the kitchen maid,' she laughed, knowing he was teasing her. 'Margaret's the one you need to watch out for. She won't like to hear you're married and she's strict on gentleman callers. Don't let her catch you.'

'That's not a problem, I'm no gentleman,' Jos said, but he took a step back towards the door. 'Come outside with me, Essie. Across the road, there's a garden.'

Despite the October cold, the thought of getting out of Tall Trees was tempting. Jenny had said we must stay in at all times, but surely Cherville was unlikely to call on me now? I gnawed at my thumbnail, jagged from when I'd broken it trying to force up the window in my bedroom.

'Go on, I'll cover for you if needs be,' Jenny said and, smiling my thanks, I cast off my apron and went with him.

IV

Beds of flowers

Tall Trees had exerted such a pull on me when I'd arrived that I'd barely noticed the gardens at the centre of the square. Jos jemmied the locked gate with a twig and when it sprang open I cast a quick look over my shoulder before following him inside. If anyone had seen us break in, we'd be in trouble. Even so, without permission and exposed to whoever happened to glance from their window, it was the safest I'd felt all day.

'This is better,' Jos said, and I realised that Tall Trees had the same effect on him as it did on me. Something within the walls of that house made it hard for us to breathe.

The gas lamps from the street beyond gave off just enough light to show a path that wound through beds of shrubs. We walked across the grass instead and sat down on a bench out of sight of the house.

'Anytime you feel low while you're here, I want you to come to this garden and think of this moment,' Jos said.

I was about to ask what made it so special when he leaned forward, put his cold lips on mine and kissed me dizzy.

'I'll remember,' I said as he put an arm around me and I cuddled into his shoulder.

'You should have let me come with you this morning,' he chided.

'It would have made you late for work and the barges won't unload themselves. Besides, I'm a doctoress to the upper classes now. I can't be seen with a lowly dock worker.'

'Nothing to do with the fact you were coming to the house of the man you believe wants to ruin your sister?'

I thought I'd managed to hide Willa's flirtation with Rowland, but I should have realised Jos would find out. Did he know the whole story? I wondered.

Back in August, I'd gone to the Cherville factory one evening to meet Willa once her shift had finished. It irritated her when I fussed, but I didn't feel truly calm unless I could lay eyes on her. It wasn't long since she'd returned to us from wherever she had fled when Jenkins the landlord had evicted her for falling behind on the rent at the house she'd shared with Mama. She'd never said exactly how she lived in the fortnight she'd been missing and I was so relieved to have her back I didn't want to push her. I'd not paid enough attention after Mama died, and when Willa told me everything was fine, I'd believed her. It was a mistake I wouldn't make again.

I'd found a spot on the wall just opposite the factory entrance so I could see her as soon as she came out. Over the next twenty minutes, girls had streamed past in twos and threes, but my sister was not among them. I'd expected her to be one of the first – she wasn't the type to linger late at her work – and so I approached the thickset man who stood sentry by the door to ask if maybe she'd finished early and I'd missed her.

'I'm looking for Willa Martin, has she left yet?'

He spat in the dirt and shrugged. 'Never heard of her.'

'Well, she's been working here for the last two weeks and she's hard to miss. My height, wears her hair in plaits?'

He knew exactly who she was, I could tell.

'Please, she's my sister,' I said, and he leered in a way that made my gorge rise.

'You could try the side entrance that comes out on the road. Sometimes she leaves that way.'

I rounded the building just in time to see the side door open and a gentleman walk out into the circle of light that shone from a nearby lamp. Tall and nattily dressed, he had the sort of showy handsomeness that made men think too much of themselves and I knew him for Rowland Cherville, lately given charge of the family factory while his father was indisposed. He looked up and down the road and a moment later a carriage pulled up alongside him, its driver decked out in pale blue livery. I expected him to climb straight in, but instead he leaned back against the carriage and lit a cigar, his eyes on the door he'd just exited. I watched it, too, my heart in my mouth, willing it to be anyone but my sister who came out. After a minute, the girl he'd been waiting for appeared, hard to miss, with hair in plaits, just as I'd described. Rowland Cherville pulled her towards him by the waist, said something that made her giggle. My stomach roiled to see his hands on her. Jos held me like that, but he was my husband, and I moved forward and called out her name.

'Hester, what are you doing here?' Willa cried, as she stepped back from him smartly.

I cleared my throat and thankfully my voice sounded steady when I said, 'I was close by and knew you were due to finish. I thought we could walk home together.'

Willa turned from me to Cherville. 'This is my elder sister,' she muttered to him. 'I've been living with her and her husband since my ma died.' Judging by the smirk on Rowland Cherville's face, he was not in the least abashed, nor did he attempt to hide the carnal glint in his eye.

'We seem to have had the same aim in mind, madam. I, too, was hoping to escort your sister home.'

Down by her side, Willa's fingers fluttered, shooing me away. She should've known better than to think I'd leave her in the clutches of such a man when she'd not long since returned to me.

'There'll be no need for that, sir. I'm here now, and even if I were not, she's quite able to make her own way.'

'It's no trouble, I assure you,' he said before turning his back on me to address Willa directly. 'We enjoy our little drives, don't we?'

I reached for my sister's wrist and held it tight when she would have shaken me off.

'We'd best let you get on, sir,' I'd said and marched away, pulling Willa along after me.

'Do you know how far it's gone between them?' Jos said, breaking through my memory.

'Nothing's happened yet,' I snapped, hoping it were true. There was a recklessness about my sister borne of grief, but it wasn't too late, not yet. If I could get her away from Rowland, there was still time to divert her from the path I feared she was taking.

Jos stroked my hair, knowing it was worry that had made me sharp with him, and I sat up so I could look him in the eye.

'I'm sorry, I should have told you, but I thought you'd assume I was here for revenge and it's not the case. Rowland's hardly around, anyway.'

'I don't like the thought of you in the company of people like him, and in his house as well. If you're going to run such risks, you can't keep secrets.'

The catch in his voice told me he was hurt. In truth, he had every right to be and yet there was another secret I held from him, something far bigger than Rowland Cherville's living arrangements, that would have made my husband even more convinced I should never have taken the job at Tall Trees. Involuntarily, I pressed my hand to my stomach, firming every day to protect the child I carried. If all went as planned, my job with Cherville would end and I'd be back home before Jos even noticed. I hated to lie to him, though, and he caught the look of regret that crossed my face.

'You know you don't have to be here if you don't like it.'

I resumed my place with my head against his shoulder. 'Don't let's have this again – not when we've got so little time together.'

The tension in his arm told me he wasn't completely happy about it, but he saw the sense in not raking over old ground. The merits, or otherwise, of coming to Tall Trees had been our main topic of conversation since I'd received Mr Bright's letter telling me the job was mine if I wanted it. I understood why Jos was wary. It meant leaving him, and Willa, and my patients, going to a new area and living around people I knew nothing of, but to me at least, the one thing in its favour – the money Cherville had promised to pay me – trumped all.

'It's not for long,' I reminded him.

'I liked your friend,' Jos said. 'It makes me feel better

knowing it's not just you and old man Cherville alone in that house.'

'There's Margaret – she's the housekeeper – and Spinks, too.'

'Now you say it, I did see a man as I came along. Short fellow in livery the same blue as your apron? I caught a whiff of onions.'

'I don't know what he had for dinner – he lives in a room over the stables and eats separately from us – otherwise it sounds like him, from what Jenny told me earlier. She's been so sweet since I got here, just like Willa was at that age.'

Jos humphed. His patience with my sister was running out, but I knew that with love and care she could be her old self again. If she would stay away from Rowland Cherville, if I could find us a new house far from the factory which brought her into contact with him daily.

'I hope you and Willa haven't been fighting already?' I said.

'Don't worry. I told you I'd be on my best behaviour and I meant it.'

'You know how important it is to me that the two of you get on while I'm away. I'm relying on you, Jos,' I said, sitting back again and fixing him with my eyes so he knew that I was serious.

'I only wish . . .'

His voice trailed away. This was a conversation we'd

had plenty of times before, too. He wished that Willa hadn't turned into such a tearaway following my mother's death, that I hadn't offered her a home with us, but he knew my answer. That I had made a deathbed promise to take care of her, and so however hard it was, I could never send her away.

'It'll be different, you know. Once Cherville has paid me.'

'Ten pounds is a lot of money,' Jos agreed.

For a moment we were both quiet, picturing what a sum of that sort could do for us. I peered upwards, imagining somewhere new that offered stars instead of smog.

'What is it that's wrong with him, exactly? You've said so little of what he's like,' Jos said.

It was the house, rather than its owner, that had made the most impression on me in the hours since I'd arrived. I certainly had no intention of telling Jos about Cherville's plantation, though. Growing up in America, he'd seen slavery first-hand in a way that I hadn't. No good could come from reminding him of that.

'I want you to be careful, Essie, that's all,' Jos said.

'You know what I've had to do to treat my ladies in the past. Cajole them out of their mistrust, browbeat their pimps. I can handle one old man who's spent his life in the lap of luxury.'

Jos leaned his forehead against mine. 'I know you don't need me to worry about you. I hope your sister appreciates the lengths you're going to for her, that's all.'

A part of me felt guilty for letting him think this was all for Willa. *He'll understand when he knows about the baby*, I told myself. As for my sister, I suspected she was still too lost in grief to thank me for what I was doing for her. Once we were away, I trusted she'd see I'd only ever had her best interests at heart. We needed this fresh start – all of us.

My husband's stomach rumbled.

'That sounds like time you were getting home.'

'Willa might have a dinner on the table waiting for me, is that what you think?'

The smirk on his face told me he was teasing and I punched him lightly on the arm.

'I wish you could come with me,' he said, pulling me to him for one last kiss before he left.

'I'll be back on Saturday, it's not so very long.'

He nodded, but I wondered if it felt as far away to him as it did to me.

Together we rose and walked to the gate. One more kiss and then Jos slipped through and was gone, claimed by the inky shadows. I raised my hand and waved. Had he waved back? It was too dark to see and I felt a little melancholy as I crossed the road and made my way down the side entrance to the house. For all too brief a time as we'd sat hand in hand in the gardens, I'd been Jos's Essie; now he'd returned to King's Cross, I belonged to Tall Trees.

I let myself back in, surprised to find the kitchen empty.

For a moment, I wondered if Jenny had gone to bed early and then she called out to me. 'I'm in the larder, will you give me a hand?'

I followed her voice through a door and down a flight of steps that led to a room of bare-bricked walls lined with shelving. Instantly, my arms broke out in goosebumps.

'Didn't know about this, did you?' Jenny said through chattering teeth. 'I couldn't believe it myself when Margaret first showed me.'

I looked around, taking in the wrapped foodstuffs and the earthy smell of meat. There was a haunch of bacon and what appeared to be a pork pie, which Jenny sniffed for freshness before handing me a wheel of cheese in a gauzy cotton cloth.

'This'll do for tomorrow,' she said. 'Now let's get out of here before we perish.'

Back in the kitchen, we pulled the chairs over to the fire and made ourselves comfortable. Damp from the grass had seeped into my boots and I slipped them off, holding out my stockinged feet to the flames and wiggling my toes to warm them.

'Sorry to drag you down to the larder. It'll be worth it when we have a decent meal tomorrow.'

'I was happy to help – it's not the sort of place I'd fancy being on my own, though.'

'Don't admit that in front of Margaret, whatever you do. She overheard me complain about how dark it was and threatened to make me sleep there. Apparently, it was a bedroom once.'

Strange – hadn't she said earlier that all the servants apart from the housekeeper slept up on the fourth floor? There was no time to probe further before Jenny added, 'You're a sly one, though. I didn't know you were married.'

'It's not only Margaret that doesn't like the idea of married women working for her.' It was the first time I'd lived in with a patient, but I knew that much.

'Nothing she could do if it was Cherville himself who hired you?' Jenny wondered aloud, except she didn't sound too convinced and neither was I.

'It's probably best to keep it quiet,' I said.

Jenny picked up on the gloominess of my tone. 'You just wish he hadn't had to go again so quickly.'

'It's five years since our wedding. This'll be the first time we've been apart.'

'I don't think I've ever spoken to an American before, although I did get a fright when he appeared at the door like that.'

'It's those books you read,' I said, nodding towards the table where she'd left the penny blood.

'Why don't you tell me how you and him met, then? I bet that's a nicer story.'

A smile played across my lips as I thought of the first time I'd seen Jos. With his bow-legged walk and sailcloth trousers belted with rope, I'd known him immediately for a seaman. What I couldn't have guessed was that he'd arrived in London from America determined to swap life in the navy for a job onshore. I'd been on my way to see a patient when he'd stopped me to ask for directions to the warehouse he now worked in. His accent had been so unfamiliar it had taken me a moment to work out what he wanted. Or maybe it was his looks that had distracted me.

'Well, it's definitely a good story if it's got you all sheep-eyed. Better save it for tomorrow if you're tired – I'd rather that than have you skipping bits,' Jenny said, as she saw me stifle a yawn.

'It has been a long day,' I admitted.

'Go straight up, then. I'll be along myself as soon as I've finished my sewing,' she said, and with a grateful smile I left her to the tablecloth she was hemming.

Up in my room, I slept fitfully, shivering myself awake to pull the covers up to my chin. The down-filled quilt was far more luxurious than the blankets I was used to at home, but somehow the cold from the larder had got into my bones and I missed the warmth of Jos's comforting bulk. Earlier, Jenny had warned me that Gervaise Cherville was sensitive to noise, but it was the silence of this house I struggled with. At the cottage, constant call-outs floated over from the canal as the barges from upriver negotiated the locks to deliver their northern cargo. Jos whistled while he readied himself for work and, since she'd moved in with us five months earlier, Willa had added her own percussion to the morning symphony, barging about her makeshift bedroom in the kitchen for lost items. Would the pair of them manage without me? My worries only stopped with the dawn and the permission it gave me to rise and face my first full day at Tall Trees.

V

Pagan myths

'There's a delicate matter I would speak to you on. One of great importance,' Cherville said as I prepared his sleeping draught on the evening of my second day at Tall Trees. Notwithstanding how he'd made his money, I was already growing used to him, so the formality of his tone struck me. Almost as if he'd rehearsed it.

'The fee we've agreed,' he continued.

'Ten pounds, sir?'

'If you assist me as I direct, I will double it.'

I gave a gulp. The money he'd offered had already been enough to overcome my misgivings about moving out of the cottage I shared with my husband and sister and into Tall Trees for the month. With that amount, we could get away from London completely. Willa beyond Rowland

Cherville's clutches and clean air for my baby. It was a prospect I was willing to do almost anything for.

'Well, girl?'

Cherville's impatience gave me pause. I took in his heightened colour and the feverish look in his eyes. What exactly was it he was asking of me? Nothing that sprang to mind could justify such a sum.

'I'm sorry, sir. My only real skill is in medicine. I'm not sure what more I could help you with,' I hedged.

'No, no, don't give me sorry before you've even heard me out. This service I would ask of you, it is your champion Bright who suggested it. It is surely the reason he recommended you for this position and no other.'

What was this? When Mr Bright had written to say he'd found me this job, he'd made no mention of anything other than medicine. If he'd known about this extra task all along, why not say so from the first?

'Forgive me, sir. A misunderstanding. Tell me, what is it you'd have me do for you?'

Cherville gave a glance over his shoulder and leaned forward, his tone confidential though it was only we two together in the room.

'I've been suffering from dreams.'

'Nightmares are not uncommon in those with your condition.'

He shook his head impatiently. 'They don't only come at night. I've had them in the daytime, too.'

'Would you call them imaginings, then – visions maybe? Help me understand, sir, so I know how best to treat you.'

'The problem is not with what I see, but what I hear. The slaves, girl. They cry to me in their torment.'

I schooled my expression into what I hoped he'd take for sympathy and he continued, 'Bright says the sounds I hear are borne of guilt. I didn't believe him at first – why should I feel guilty for doing something that others have done, and Blacks themselves for centuries? My plantation was inherited from my father, I've not set foot on Honduras so I've never even seen it, and yet every day the cries grow louder. I must take action or I will surely run mad.'

My mind flew to the painting on the first floor. I'd not returned to it since arriving at Tall Trees, but the Black figures it depicted refused to remain mere blots. I conjured faces for them as I went about my work, and lives and plans and fears. For Cherville they had voices.

'What is it exactly that Mr Bright recommends?'

'Atonement. He says I will find no peace in this life or the next unless I make amends for what I've done.'

'How is that to happen?'

'In August next year the Abolition Act will come into effect and slaves throughout the colonies will be emancipated. Thanks to the agitations of the West India lobby we owners will be compensated for the loss of our property. Bright wants me to pass that money on to the slaves themselves, but if I am to rid myself of these voices I believe I must begin at home, and soon. The government will require a loan to fund what is owed and sums of that nature cannot be raised quickly. It is unlikely I will live long enough to receive the payment so in the meantime I must draw down against my own capital.

'Almost forty years ago, I brought two slave women from my plantation to England. For eight years they lived here at Tall Trees as servants and then they ran away. I want you to help me find them and make recompense.'

I'd suspected Gervaise Cherville had slaves here in England as well as Honduras and, when Jenny had said the larder had once been used for a bedroom, I'd been certain of it. My eyes bored into Cherville and when he looked up I cast my gaze to the floor before he could read my disgust.

Amends, atonement, recompense. Did he know the weight of these words he cast so freely?

'You're saying you would give them money?' I asked.

'Once we have tracked them down, you and I would visit them together and I would pay them both for every day they laboured for me.'

Tracked them down. Just a turn of phrase, but what an unfortunate one. My mind reeled with the enormity of what Cherville was asking. Was he genuine? Where would the search begin? And what if they didn't want to be found? He was offering me so much money I'd be an imbecile to refuse and yet, for all that, I hesitated to give him an outright yes. I'd become a doctoress so I could help people and here was a man wanting my assistance, but he was a slaver and what he was asking was not medical. All the while he looked at me keenly.

'Now you've heard what I intend, will you help me? If I visit them alone, they might run again. Having you by my side will ease their concerns.'

To think I'd been worried that at Tall Trees my skin would count against me, and all along it was the reason I was here. In the scheme of things it didn't matter, did it? And yet I wished Mr Bright had just told me. Meanwhile Cherville tapped his fingers on the counterpane. He wanted a swift answer, but despite the amount of money on offer, or maybe even because of it, I needed time to think.

'The women – will you tell me their names?' I said to stall him.

Cherville frowned as if to say: *what does that concern you?* He wasn't to know I'd half-guessed he'd had slaves here.

'I called one Nyx and the other Aphrodite. Now she was a handsome girl.'

I disguised my intake of breath with a cough. Pagan myths had played no part at Sunday school where I'd learned my letters, but Aphrodite was one goddess whose associations I knew. Please God it had no bearing on the treatment she'd received at Cherville's hands.

He was still waiting for my response. Luckily, I was spared the need to give it by the appearance of Margaret.

I visited Cherville three times a day and it seemed she was always lurking close by on some unlikely pretence. On this occasion I was grateful.

'I came to check you were content with tomorrow's menu, sir,' she said, and I seized my chance to escape.

'I'll be along to see you first thing in the morning, sir,' I mumbled and left quickly before he could call me back.

VI

Lamentations

I'd pulled on my uniform and was making my bed the next morning when there was a knock on the open door and I looked up to see the fatherly face of Charles Bright smiling in at me. He was dressed in black with a white necktie, but had he worn the latest tailcoat I would've still known him for a vicar. There was something in his weather-beaten face that spoke of goodness; at least that was how it appeared.

'Sir, I did not expect you,' I said.

Did he notice my greeting was cooler than it might have been? Since he'd secured me this job, I'd felt only gratitude towards him – that was until last night when Cherville had asked this extra service of me. He'd said Mr Bright had known about it all along. If that were true, I needed to know why yesterday was the first I had heard of it. Perhaps that was why he'd come to see me?

'I was here to visit Mr Cherville and I thought I would stop by and see how you were getting on.'

'You find me very well, sir,' I said, smoothing my hands down my uniform with its Cherville-blue apron and nodding towards the chest of drawers where I'd arranged my newly mixed tonics and tinctures. 'Jenny has made me very welcome, exactly as you asked her.'

'A good girl, that one – when she told me where to find you, she insisted on making me a cup of tea before I left. The housekeeper has been less forthcoming, I'm sure. She is quite proprietorial when it comes to her master and so I neglected to tell her you were coming. I hope she hasn't proved troublesome?'

Another thing he'd conveniently left out. I shook my head, glossing over Margaret's threat to watch my every move. Now I had an inkling of why she'd been so hostile. Even if she wasn't his daughter, by running Cherville's house and reading his letters, she'd likely persuaded herself she was somehow in charge. My arrival, managed and arranged without her knowledge, would have punctured that delusion.

'I understand she's been with the family from when she was a girl,' I said.

When he replied, there was no hint of consciousness to suggest he'd heard the rumours. 'Yes, that's right, she grew up in the village attached to their home in Suffolk and has always worked in one or another of their houses.'

It didn't surprise me. In fact it helped me understand her. She was a fixture of the Cherville family and of Tall Trees as much as the wood-panelled walls. No one could live in this disquieting place for so long and not be infected by it.

'Anyhow, now I've seen you're well settled, I won't keep you,' Mr Bright said. 'I can show myself to the kitchen.'

What? He was leaving already? I couldn't let that happen, not before I'd had the chance to ask him what he knew of Cherville's request.

'I was hoping you would spare me a minute. To speak privately,' I said.

Mr Bright looked over his shoulder. We were quite alone on the fourth floor. Even so, he lowered his voice. Cherville had done the self-same thing the night before, as if the very walls were listening .

'There's nothing amiss since you arrived?'

'Not exactly, sir. Mr Cherville has made a request of me which might even be a good thing, but I would appreciate your counsel.'

He frowned, seeming reluctant.

'I wouldn't trouble you unless it was important, sir,' I said, and hearing the anxiety in my voice he hastened to reassure me.

'Very well. Let us consider it together.'

Following me into the room, Mr Bright perched on the chair while I sat opposite him on the bed.

'Mr Cherville has asked me to help him find two women he enslaved. He said it was you that put the scheme into his mind after he told you of the sounds that were troubling him?'

A look of irritation flashed in the vicar's eyes.

'Have I done something wrong?'

'No, child. There is no blame attached to you. I had not thought that Mr Cherville would share what he and I discussed, that is all. It was his other symptoms I anticipated you could help him with, on account of your work with the ladies of King's Cross.'

I hadn't liked the idea that he'd suggested me on account of my skin as opposed to my skill. It had made me feel silly for thinking I was here on merit and, feeling warmer towards him again, I explained, 'The two could be related. Syphilis attacks the mind, after all. Is there not more you can tell me?'

Mr Bright rubbed at his face, pulling at the skin. I sensed he was weighing how much to reveal. At last he said with a sigh, 'It was a year ago that Mr Cherville told me he was hearing strange sounds. By the time he confided in me, he'd tried several remedies with no effect and was convinced he was cursed. "Would you perform an exorcism?" he pleaded. Truly, he was desperate; the sounds – he described them as lamentations, sometimes cries – were becoming unbearable. "When did it start?" I asked, and recollected that we'd spent a portion of the date he gave me together, for he was present at a lecture I delivered on my time as a missionary. It was what convinced me the malady he suffered from was guilt.'

'I had not realised you were an abolitionist, sir.'

'No man of God could be anything else, but I eschew that title now we have achieved in large part what we set out to do. That said, I will continue in my task to bring others to our cause, and Gervaise Cherville is ready – he would not hear the voices otherwise.'

Perhaps he was right but I'd detected more of expediency than true remorse when Cherville had outlined his plans.

'Did you ever visit his plantation?' I said.

'Never. I have been told that where it stood there is only charred earth. There was a revolt among his slaves and they burned it to the ground. On the day of the lecture, he heckled me and spoke in the strongest possible terms against showing the enslaved any mercy. I'd warrant the ghosts of the men and woman punished for the crime of wanting their freedom are among the chorus that haunts him now.'

'I'm sure, but it was not his slaves in Honduras that he spoke to me of. It is the women he brought to England that trouble him most – it is them he has asked me to help find.'

Mr Bright's face reddened. I'd never known him show emotion, so why would this anger him?

'Is finding the women not the idea you gave him? Do you think he is not genuine?'

'I believe he is, but . . .' Mr Bright's voice trailed away and he made an effort to compose himself before continuing. 'I had no thought that he would burden you with this. What are two women compared to all those on Honduras? When I spoke to him of atonement, it was the slaves he kept on his plantation I had in mind.'

'If the women here ran from him, it seems they must have been badly treated, too?'

'Oh, yes. It cannot be doubted they are deserving.'

'Mr Cherville told me their names were Nyx and Aphrodite. I know you were his priest long before you became a missionary. You would have been here at Tall Trees. Do you remember them?'

Mr Bright was already shaking his head.

'Let me see if I can put a stop to this, Hester.'

It was the last thing I wanted.

'Please don't. I confess I have my doubts, but it is a lot of money he's offered me. An extra ten pounds on top of what he has already agreed to pay me for nursing him.'

'As much as that,' Mr Bright muttered to himself.

'Unless you counsel me against it, I think I should go ahead. You know of the troubles with my sister. The sort of money Mr Cherville has spoken of will enable me to get her away from King's Cross. Our whole family can start again.'

'By all means. I would not stand in the way of that,' Mr Bright said, but he looked a little grey. I couldn't make it out. The abolitionist in him should have been rejoicing at what Cherville had planned.

'If you do remember anything that could help find these two women, will you let me know? I thought maybe you might have some old friends within the abolitionist movement who—'

The striking clock cut across me. Before I could start again Mr Bright had slapped his thighs and jumped to his feet. 'Is that ten o'clock? Forgive me, the morning has flown,' he said.

Could he really be in so tremendous a hurry when I was telling him things of such import? Hurt as I was, what could I do but say, 'Sorry to have kept you, sir. If we go straight downstairs, I'm sure Jenny will have readied your tea by now.'

'I will have to disappoint her, I'm afraid. There are several parishioners I am promised to.'

'What a shame. Another time, then?' I said even though he'd mentioned nothing of any appointments when he'd first appeared.

'Yes, another time,' Mr Bright said, glancing towards the door.

He would have made his own way downstairs. I insisted

on accompanying him hoping he might relent and explain his strange behaviour, but he was almost tripping over his feet in his haste to get away. Back in the entrance hall, Jenny had hung his black coat on the stand by the door. He pulled it on, followed by his gloves. If I thought he would tell me, I would have asked him outright what the matter was, but he was halfway down the path before I could work out what to say without seeming impertinent.

'A good day to you, Hester,' he called over his shoulder. 'Tell Mr Cherville I will find some time to visit him tomorrow.'

I stared after him as he hurried off, at a loss for why our conversation had so thoroughly discomfited him. All I could think was that he wanted to help as many people as possible, and he thought Cherville wasn't going far enough. Two women brought to England wasn't very many after all; but despite his strangeness, I was starting to think I quite liked the idea of playing a part in getting Nyx and Aphrodite what they were owed.

I arrived in the kitchen at the same time as Jenny clattered in from the courtyard with a pail of water in each hand.

'Where's the vicar?'

'Gone, I'm afraid. He forgot he had some parishioners to visit.'

'I wish he'd remembered before I'd been and fetched the cake,' she said, exasperated, and then brightened. 'Actually, maybe it's no bad thing. We'll just have to polish it off ourselves.'

The dense sponge was sharp with lemon, its two halves sandwiched together with thick cream. Through a half-eaten mouthful, Jenny said, 'I know it's mean to say it, but it was much nicer to share this with you. That palsy he has would've put me right off.'

I shook my head at her and she looked shamefaced.

'You're a kind girl, Jenny, you don't mean that. Besides, illness is not why he shakes. It's because he's not yet acclimatised. While he was in the Indies, his body got used to the sun and now the cold makes him shiver.'

'If you say so. Did the two of you talk before he went? When he said he was looking for you, I thought he might be expecting you to pray with him.'

I smiled at the thought of it. I wasn't as religious as I could've been. Mama had never been one for church-going and it had rubbed off on me, too.

'Nothing of that sort. He came to see I'd landed all right – you know it was him that put in a word for me with Cherville?' I said, deciding not to say anything about his abruptness. I'd already decided not to tell Jenny of the extra task Cherville had asked of me so the last thing I wanted was to pique her curiousity.

'Two visitors in three days to see how you're doing – talk about all right for some. The first was far better looking, though.'

'When I go home for the sabbath, I'll tell Jos you said so.'

It was Wednesday, and I had permission to leave on Saturday at midday; not too long to wait at all, really.

'I can see why you'd want to hurry back,' Jenny said. 'Won't it make the rest of your time here drag, though – to have taken your holiday so quickly?'

She was right, of course; I should have held out a little longer before going back home. My hope was that to see Jos and Willa coping without me would make the remainder of my stay at Tall Trees easier to bear.

'You've got to keep yourself busy. That's how I get through the days,' Jenny said. I nodded along, thinking to myself that searching for the women Cherville had enslaved, on top of my daily nursing duties, would leave little chance for much else.

It was nine o'clock when I tapped on Cherville's door that evening for my third and final visit of the day.

'I wanted to say that I'll help you find the women you told me of,' I said when he bid me enter.

He frowned for a second before nodding slowly, a bemused smile on his face.

All the time I'd been agonising, he'd taken my agreement for granted. How naive of me to think I'd had a choice. He seemed less inclined to talk than previously and his hand trembled a little as he groped in the direction of his bedside table for the douter to snuff his candle. The other day I'd dismissed Jenny's talk out of hand, but if the cries he heard made him scared to sleep that was a curse of sorts. Not that I could feel sorry for him. The people he'd enslaved. It was unlikely they slept well either.

There was a hiss as Cherville finally put the candle out, followed by a rustling that I guessed was him rolling to one side and pulling up his covers. He could not have made it any clearer that he wished for me to go, but the darkness emboldened me.

'The cries you hear. Is it the women you would have me find?'

'They come from more than one soul, but yes, I believe that theirs are chief among them.'

What exactly was it he had done that made their cries identifiable among those that plagued him? I pushed the thought away and asked, 'When they ran, do you know where they went?'

'At the time, I had an idea that a man named Lukes had helped them; he was my butcher and forever talking to the servants when he should have been about his work. I challenged him and he denied all knowledge, even when I made clear I would take my custom elsewhere. I'm convinced he knew more than he was letting on.'

It was enough information to get started on and I withdrew. Yesterday, Cherville had suggested that he and I search for Nyx and Aphrodite together, but I'd begun to form a plan of my own. If I could get to the women before he did, I could explain what he wanted. If they were interested, well and good; and if not, I could feel comfortable that I'd given them fair warning he was coming. I'd been feeling squeamish at the prospect of helping a slaver, at bringing him back into the lives of two women who'd run from him. This approach salved my conscience. It meant I could do right by Nyx and Aphrodite *and* get what I needed for the good of my family.

VII

Receipts for pies and cakes

Cherville had said he wanted to discuss how best to begin the search for Nyx and Aphrodite in a day or two, so I didn't have long if I wanted to warn them of what he had planned. I decided to start by seeking out and speaking to the butcher he'd mentioned. Asking Margaret was out of the question – I sensed the less she knew about the extra job Cherville had given me the better – so although I hadn't wanted to embroil my new friend in the scheme, Jenny was my only hope. When I came into the kitchen shortly after lunch, I found her dusty with flour, a little breathless from kneading the dough before her. She paused and smiled to see me.

'You look a bit perkier today. I told you you'd get used to it here.'

'I do feel better,' I admitted, but getting used to Tall Trees? I never would. My persistent unease was a reminder that I didn't belong here; it would be a bad day if that feeling went away.

I joined her at the table and she rolled two eggs in my direction so I could make myself useful. One by one, I cracked the eggs gently against a bowl, separating out the whites and beating the yolks until they frothed. It felt good to help Jenny after all she'd done to make me welcome, if I was to get what I needed however I'd have to come out with it.

'I was looking for a list of all the tradesmen who visit. Do you keep one anywhere?'

'The ones that come most often, I know them all by heart. There's Heale, he's the cobbler – funny he should be called that, don't you think? And Jones is the chandler and . . .'

She rattled through a whole host of traders one after another and I wondered what excuse I might come up with for wanting to know the name of one from more than thirty years earlier.

'Are you sure they're not written down somewhere? It's none of those you said, but I'm sure if I saw the name I'd recognise it.'

I brushed the egg wash over the rolls Jenny had shaped while she considered.

'Madam has a daybook; it belonged to the previous housekeeper and the one before that. You'd rather not ask her, I take it?'

'If there was another way, it would be better,' I said, letting my voice trail off.

'You'll get me in a world of trouble,' Jenny said, a gleam of mischief in her eye. 'Come with me. She's out at the minute. We'll sneak into her room and get it.'

Margaret's room was just along from the kitchen. It should have been cosy and inviting, but the grate was empty and it gave off the same chilliness as its owner. Opposite a small bureau a picture of Gervaise Cherville hung in a gold frame on the wall. Maybe reflecting on the greatness of the family she worked for was what kept her warm.

'Do you whistle?' Jenny said, and I fluted out a short note. 'That's perfect. If you think you hear anything, anything at all, do that. She's like a cat, and if she sneaks up on us in here, we're both done for.'

Despite the risk we were taking, it was hard not to laugh as Jenny tiptoed over to the bureau looking like she was performing the role of robber at a penny gaff. When she reached it, she rummaged in her hair and produced a clip.

'My brother taught me this,' she said, poking her tongue out in concentration, and a second later there was a click as one of the locks responded to her tweaking. She pulled out the drawer and brought forth a large book in burgundy leather covers. Opening it up, she looked up and down, turning the pages far too rapidly for someone who was taking in the information they contained. After riffling them back and forth, she said, 'Let's switch places. You'll have to find what you need yourself.'

I was very aware of Cherville looking down on me stern-faced as I dabbed my finger to my tongue and thumbed through the pages. Ribbons marked different sections: receipts for pies and cakes, a linen list, the details that I wanted had to be here.

'You won't be much longer, will you?'

'One minute, I think I've found the tradesmen now.'

They were listed by Christian name, then surname, with a third column for their business and a fourth for their address. A previous housekeeper must have been of an artistic nature because in among the entries were small illustrations. I couldn't imagine Margaret doing anything so frivolous. I traced my way down the list, hope dwindling as I went, and then there it was, sandwiched between Leith and Macy.

'Got it,' I exclaimed.

'Then let's go, we're already pushing our luck.'

Hastily, I shoved the book back into the bureau drawer. 'What if she notices its unlocked?' I said, but Jenny only shrugged helplessly. I pulled the door to and followed her into the kitchen just as we heard footsteps on the stairs that led down from the entrance hall.

'That's Madam now,' Jenny hissed, pushing another bowl towards me. 'Quick, stir that.'

There was no need for the tableau as the housekeeper went straight to her room.

We stilled, straining to discern what she was doing in there by sound alone.

'That unlocked drawer is going to give us away,' Jenny fretted.

I put a finger to my lips waiting for the shout that would confirm our trespass had been discovered, but none came and a moment later we heard Margaret's footsteps return to the stairs.

'We were lucky there,' Jenny said. I nodded, not having the words. Had Margaret come in a minute earlier, she would have caught me red-handed and a tingle flowed through me at the thought of it.

'Who was it you wanted, anyway?'

'A butcher by the name of Lukes.'

'We use Bissle for our meat now— Wait, what are you doing?' she said as I stood and stripped off my apron before reaching for my hat.

'I was thinking I might run an errand.'

'You're a live one to go out without permission.' Jenny pursed her lips and jerked her head in the direction of Margaret's room. 'Have you not taken enough risks for today?'

'It'll only be for an hour or so. Besides, it's two o'clock and I'm not due to attend him again until this evening.'

'What if Madam comes asking for you?'

'She hasn't before and Cherville was sleeping when I popped my head into his room on the way down here.' My hand was on the doorknob. 'I'll be back before you know it,' I said, but for once Jenny couldn't summon a smile and I left her looking after me, twisting her apron in her hands.

VIII

Seaside places

The air was crisp as I made my way down Charlotte Street and the further I got from Tall Trees the lighter I felt. Had I been on the towpath, fields to my right, slow-moving water on my left, it would have been enjoyable, but then canal-side was the London I knew. Before I'd gone to work for Cherville, I'd never been near Fitzrovia nor Oxford Circus neither. Not that it was only the place itself I missed and my husband. It was my patients, too. Without me around, there was no one else to care for them. Of all my worries, though, the sharpest were for Willa. I'd said goodbye the night before I'd left to come and work for Cherville. I knew she was still nursing her anger for what she saw as my interference with Rowland when I'd come to meet her at the factory weeks earlier.

'He's gone, you can let go now,' she'd said as his carriage rumbled past us. I'd released her hand and she'd provoked me by rubbing at it as if I'd hurt her. If she'd have come along as I'd asked, there would have been no need to pull her.

'What on earth were you thinking of?' I said as we reached the towpath. 'I thought you'd know better than to be accepting carriage rides from the likes of Rowland Cherville.'

My words were accompanied by a low rumble of thunder. When the rain began to pour we ducked under a bridge to wait for it to clear.

'Happy now? You've made me walk and I'll get wet into the bargain.'

'Stand further in, then,' I said, but she twisted away from my outstretched hand, eyes flashing mutinously, and droplets darkened the edges of her skirt.

I hoped it was a passing shower, but for the minute the rain showed no sign of letting up. It formed a sort of curtain and, though I spoke softly, my words echoed off the moss-covered walls of the tunnel, so I sounded severe when I meant to be sympathetic.

'You've got to be more careful, Willa.'

'What exactly are you accusing me of? He was offering me a lift because he noticed how hard I'd been working.'

'I saw where he had his hands on you.'

Involuntarily, she touched her hip. For a second her eyes softened and I felt a pang of fear.

'How far has it gone? He said he'd taken you on drives before.'

'I've done nothing to be ashamed of,' she muttered stubbornly, her eyes fixed on the ground.

'I'm only trying to look out for you. It's what Mama asked of me, you know that.'

'Here we go. This again,' Willa said, clutching her hand to her heart and mimicking my voice. '"Mama's final words were that I should care for you. I only want what's best, Willamina."'

I let the hurt I felt show on my face, so she knew she'd gone too far. Once upon a time it would have prompted her to apologise; now she chose defiance.

'I won't lurk here any longer like a troll,' she said and stalked out into the downpour.

'You'll come back to the cottage,' I called, but the wind whipped away my words and by then she'd gone too far to hear me. As she disappeared around the corner, the rain eased as though the squall had blown itself out with her burst of temper. Back at the cottage, Jos would be in from work and wondering where I was.

Pulling my coat to me, I'd headed for home, Willa's words playing on my mind then as they did now. She could mock the promise I'd made, but from the moment the words had fallen from Mama's chapped lips they'd had a hold on me. Almost six months since she'd passed and the pain of it was still sharp. Not every day, as it had been at first, but coming at odd moments when I believed I was thinking of something else entirely. I expected to feel teary when I picked leaves or crushed herbs, those were the things we'd done together and I steeled myself accordingly. I was defenceless against the memories that came on me at other times, like an ambush. It stood to reason that Willa had taken it harder – she was younger, still at home – but I would have comforted her if only she'd let me. Even now she said very little and I was loath to push her for fear she'd run off again. Would I ever know where she'd gone for those two fraught weeks? It didn't bear thinking of. The important thing was that she'd come back.

'Watch out!'

I stepped back, mumbling an apology, but the hackney that had almost knocked me over was long gone. The quiet road I'd taken from Fitzrovia had given way to Oxford Street, and the mid-afternoon bustle was a reminder of just how far I was from home. The canal was busy, barges constantly back and forth; here it was all about the carriages, gigs and horse-buses as water gave way to road, meaning the pace was of a different order entirely. The one constant – the horses – reinforced the difference. The ones on the towpath were stoic and faithful, strong enough to do the work of fifty men; the horses that pulled the feather-light carriages here were slender and graceful. The dung they produced was the same, though. I hopped out of the way of a young pure collector and crossed to the other side. The West End was unknown to me but surely I couldn't be too far from where the Lukeses lived now.

I turned off the main thoroughfare into a road with a mixture of shops and houses and a sign that announced it as Ramillies Street. A boy was loitering outside the grocer's on the corner, exactly the sort to give me directions.

'There's a butcher by the name of Lukes who lives hereabout. Do you know where I might find him?'

In answer, the boy stuck out his hand and I fished in my pocket for a ha'penny, which he bit between his two front teeth. Satisfied it was genuine, he said, 'The next road along, take the first left and you can cut through. Halfway down, green door. His wife keeps flowers in the window.'

I set off, repeating his instructions to myself and hoping he was honest. If Nyx and Aphrodite had fled here from Tall Trees as Cherville suspected, I was walking in their footsteps. As I made my way, I felt the discomfort of one or two prolonged stares, but this was 1833 and no one insulted or tried to stop me. How different it must have been for them, on the run and fearful, moving in bursts from shadow to shadow, heads constantly on the swivel to see if they were followed.

I was glad when the twists and turns brought me to my destination just as the grocer's boy had directed. The neat little house with its bunch of freesias in the window held none of the unease that had cloaked me when I'd first approached Tall Trees. To Nyx and Aphrodite it must have felt like salvation.

'Can I help you?'

I started, blushing to realise that maybe ten minutes had passed while I'd stared up at the house trying to see it through a runaway's eyes. I looked stupidly at the grey-haired woman who'd opened the door, wishing I'd paid more mind to what I would say when I got here. Though she'd caught me, a stranger, lurking outside her home, there was no aggression in her tone. It was further proof I'd come to the right place.

'Mrs Lukes?'

'That's me, dear,' she said.

Her simple warmth gave me the courage to come out with it.

'I'm here for Nyx and Aphrodite,' I blurted.

Mrs Lukes led me to a snug living room with a bright crackling fire. She sat me in an easy chair and, as I sank back against a cushion moulded by years of use, I felt a fierce pang of longing for the cottage and the comfort that Tall Trees, for all its luxuries, could not provide.

'You look tired,' she said when she returned with a pot of tea a few minutes later. I couldn't deny it – I was used to walking here and there, but in future I'd need to get more used to making concessions to the baby I carried.

'Thirty-three years ago, I put Dite in that exact same

spot. She sent you to us, didn't she?' Mrs Lukes said as she handed me a cup and saucer.

Her face was so full of hope, I hated to disappoint her.

'I'm sorry, I've never met her. I'm looking for her, and a second woman, Nyx. I'd hoped you might help me find them both.'

A shadow crossed Mrs Lukes's face and her smile was replaced by a grim expression. 'How did you know to come here?'

'Someone gave me your address. A friend,' I added hastily as her eyes narrowed, but her suspicions had been roused.

'John,' she called over her shoulder. 'Get in here.' There was a tramping of boots on stairs and a burly red-haired man in the scarred leather apron of the butcher appeared. 'This woman said she was here for Dite, yet now she claims she never met her.'

John Lukes looked from me to his wife and though the fire still blazed merrily it felt as though the temperature in the living room had dropped.

'Who sent you?' he demanded.

I wanted to tell them of Mr Bright, but our exchange the day before made me think he wouldn't thank me for it.

'Gervaise Cherville,' I said, the name barely out of my mouth before Mrs Lukes cried out in anger.

'I think you'd better leave. You're not welcome here,' her husband said, turning sideways to show me the door.

Mrs Lukes had ushered me in, made me comfortable. Now she looked on me with hatred.

'You don't understand. I come from Cherville, but I promise you I mean Aphrodite no harm. Please let me explain.'

'Shall we hear her out, John?'

He weighed me with his eyes, not sure what to make of me. Sheltering Aphrodite all those years ago, he would have expected a knock on the door. A tracker paid to come and find her and take her back. Cherville had admitted he'd placed an advertisement in anger declaring the women runaways; I had to convince John Lukes that this time around Cherville's motives were purer.

'You've got five minutes. Say what you must.'

A fair hearing. I could ask for no more than that, but it was hard to begin when they watched me so hawkishly.

'Or you can leave right now and forget you ever heard of this address.'

I didn't think it would help to tell them about the twenty pounds Gervaise Cherville was paying me, not when I hadn't earned their full trust. But the money he would pay Aphrodite. Surely they had to believe in that.

'Cherville is ill. He has a care for his soul and wants to atone for the wrong he did.'

Mrs Lukes snorted and her husband put a hand on her arm. 'We agreed we'd hear her out, Flo,' and to me he said, 'Go on.'

'He wants to pay Aphrodite for her labour. He wants to pay all those he enslaved as if he had employed them.'

'All the money in the world wouldn't make up for how he treated her.'

Though it had been my first thought also, I said, 'Don't you think that's for her to decide?'

Mr Lukes tilted his head looking at me as though I were a puzzle to be solved.

'You're happy there, are you, at Tall Trees?'

'I won't be there for long. Cherville plans to leave London and see out his days in the country. He's asked me to help find Aphrodite and Nyx before he goes.'

'Only those two? Not the other girl?'

I looked at him blankly. Cherville had only made mention of two women he'd enslaved and brought to England.

'Dite was one of three of them that ran. They had to split up, it would have been too dangerous for them to remain together. It was only her that stayed with us and she was scared enough as it was. Remind me, Flo, what was that other girl called?'

'Artemis,' his wife replied. 'She was a mite younger than the other two.' Mrs Lukes took over the story; she and her husband were like Jos and me in the way they finished each other's sentences. A formidable pair, providing succour to runaways they would have had to be.

'Dite used to sit behind the curtain, watching the street, and every time someone went past she flinched. Cherville would send someone after her – that's what she most feared. I told her it was unlikely, that no one would guess she was here. Anything to keep her spirits up. You came in the end, though. Albeit more than thirty years later.'

To Mrs Lukes I was an agent of Cherville's, but I wasn't one of the slave catchers that men like him had once employed when they lost their 'property'. This was something quite different. Wasn't it?

'Was she with you for long?'

'She left in the February of 1801 so I'd say about four months altogether. I would have had her stay forever, but she wanted to earn her own way. I got her a job as a char, though I always knew she could do more. She was clever, you see, nicely spoken, and there was a woman who offered her a job as a companion. You should have seen how excited Dite was when she came home that day. They were going to go to Bath or Broadstairs, one of those sea-side places that always seem to begin with a B.'

'She never came back to London, then?' The question hung on the air while husband and wife exchanged looks. 'All I want is to get her what she's owed, you have my word on that.'

Mr Lukes wasn't convinced, I could see, but then his wife said, 'Give her the rest, John, I think it's safe.'

'You know more? Anything you could tell me, I'd appreciate.'

Mr Lukes sat down on the sofa beside his wife and said, 'It must've have been about five years after she left our house and I was over Bloomsbury way, not a million miles from the Chervilles' as it goes. I'd taken a break in one of the gardens and in walks this woman, bundled up in a cloak. I wouldn't have paid her too much mind, but she walked right in front of me and that's when I recognised her. I called out, "Dite. It's John Lukes. You remember me, don't you?" I think she would have preferred to carry on walking as if she'd never heard me, but I was on my feet by then. She apologised for not having stopped at first, explaining she hadn't recognised me. I asked her where she was staying, and said I was glad to see her looking well. When I suggested Flo would love it if she stopped by, she turned chary, said she had to go, she'd only been on her break, and off she went. I was a bit put out, we'd all been good friends, but it had been a long time since we'd seen each other. She darted across the road and I saw her climb up the steps and disappear into one of the houses. I didn't see the number and I've never had call to go back there. If they painted the door, I don't think I'd be able to tell which house it was. That was a good twenty-five years ago, more than that, twenty-seven – we've heard nothing of her since.'

How was it that all this had happened years before I was born and yet sitting in the Lukeses' living room I felt a closeness to the woman they described. Maybe it was because of their obvious affection for her, even after all this time. Bloomsbury Square. That was less than a fifteen-minute walk away from Tall Trees. Surely she wouldn't have settled so close? It seemed a terrible risk after all she'd gone through to get away. I drained my cup.

'Will you go there next to continue your enquiries?' Mr Lukes said. The furrow in his brow told me he was still unsure whether he and his wife had been right to trust me with what they knew of Aphrodite's onward journey.

'You've every reason to be cautious. I wouldn't help Cherville if I thought he meant her any harm. Regardless of his intentions I would like to speak to her first, to prepare her. If she really does not want to see him, I'll say I couldn't find her.'

'I'm glad you have a plan. Maybe she wouldn't need to see him at all if you could hand over the money and a letter he'd written?'

I hadn't thought of that and wondered if Cherville would agree. From what he'd said, I suspected he'd want to look her in the eye when he made recompense, but if he really wanted what was best for Aphrodite, surely he would be guided by her needs, too. It could come as no surprise if she never wished to lay eyes on him again.

I got to my feet and made my farewells before Mrs Lukes led me out into the passage.

'You have a lovely home. I'm not surprised she felt safe here,' I said.

'I wished she'd have stayed for longer. Such a handsome girl she was. If you do find her, you will remember us to her, won't you? Say we still think of her and would love to see her.'

'I will, you have my word.'

IX

A smart blue carriage

Outside, the light was beginning to fade and a chill wind had picked up. I'd told Jenny I'd only be a few hours, but it had taken longer than I'd expected to find the Lukeses' house and, having struggled to gain their trust, it would have been wrong to rush them while they recounted Dite's story. What was the time? Four o'clock? Really, I should go straight back to Tall Trees and resume my search tomorrow, but I felt that while the luck was with me it was right to head for Bloomsbury and make what enquiries I could. It seemed I was at a dead end as far as discovering Nyx's whereabouts went. I didn't want to delay and lose my chance of getting to Aphrodite before Cherville got involved.

I set off, back the way I had come, marvelling at how quickly the roads had quieted. There was no one to be seen when I reached Ramillies Street, not even a beggar, and a smart blue carriage was the only sign of life. Ahead, the grocer's where the boy had loitered had closed, its awning wound up, and the sign offering beef and onion pasties removed. I huddled into my coat, thinking of Artemis, the third woman enslaved at Tall Trees. Could there be a reason Cherville hadn't mentioned her? Even if there was, Mr Bright could surely not have forgotten her? I was wondering if I could broach it with him the next time he was at the house, when I felt a crawling sensation at the back of my neck. Had it been summer, I'd have dismissed it as an insect. At this time of day and cold as it was, there could only be one explanation: I was being watched.

I kept my eyes fixed forward and increased my pace. Oxford Street was only a few hundred yards ahead of me, its lamps already lit. If I could just reach it, I'd feel safe again, but the crawling feeling wouldn't go. Above my rapid breathing I heard the clop of horses' hooves, much nearer than they had any right to be, and though all I wanted was to get back to the main road, I ducked down a side street. It was not one I recognised from earlier and there was no sign on the brickwork to say what it was called. I'd wait a moment, let the carriage pass, then return, but my plan was short-lived when I cast a quick look over my shoulder and saw the driver turn in, too. There could be no mistaking it now. He was definitely following me.

Every fibre in my being told me to run, but I forbore. The West End was a part of town I barely knew. I'd be lost in seconds and then I'd be in real trouble. *Keep going, don't look back.* The carriage must be almost at my heels. I darted out in front of it to cross the road, making the horses that pulled it rear in fright. Behind me, the driver cursed. I'd gained the other side now and doubled back, returning to Ramillies Street, but he wasn't ready to give up. He wheeled round, coming straight for me as I backed away from the kerb. My stomach rolled and then I registered the familiar blue livery and staggered, as relief robbed my legs of feeling. It must be Spinks, the driver from Tall Trees.

He pulled up beside me, the horses tossing their heads. I reached out a hand to the one closest to me, running my fingers through the coarse hair of his mane, partly to soothe him and partly to soothe myself.

'What were you playing at, running out in front of me? A stunt like that could have got you killed,' Spinks said.

The lack of contrition in his tone made me question myself. Had my earlier imaginings about the journey Nyx and Dite would have taken got to me? No. It didn't matter how far the abolitionists had come. Any Black woman chased down in an unfamiliar part of town would have reacted as I did.

'How was I to know it was you following me?'

'You know now, so hop in.'

'I was heading for Bloomsbury Square. If it's all the same to you, I'll make my own way.'

Spinks chuckled. 'You're not going to make me get down, are you,' he said, and it dawned on me that he'd been given express instructions to keep me on watch. 'I thought you'd given me the slip when I got to Oxford Street – one minute you were there, the next I'd lost you. I was going to go back, then I thought it might benefit me to wait a while – better that than a tongue-lashing from Madam, anyway – so I parked up, gave the horses their feed and just when I was about to give it up as a bad job, I spotted you.'

I hadn't led him straight to the Lukeses' door, that was something. If only I hadn't mentioned Bloomsbury.

'Cherville himself authorised my errand.'

Spinks stroked his chin. 'That's not the impression old Margaret gave me.'

'She was the one that sent you to spy on me?'

'Steady on,' Spinks said. 'If you'd have said where you were going, there would've been no need for this, but here we are. Which of these roads was it you came out of?'

I kept my mouth clamped shut and, realising I wasn't going to tell him, he shrugged. 'Makes no difference to me where you slink off to. Climb up now, though, and we'll be home in a tick.'

Tall Trees was not my home. Could never be, but though all I wanted was to continue my search in Bloomsbury

Square, I pulled open the carriage door and climbed in, throwing myself back against the seat. It was padded, luxurious, but as we rattled back towards Fitzrovia I found little comfort in it.

In no time we were back at Tall Trees. In the deepening dark, with the lights not yet on, the house looked little short of malevolent.

I jumped down from the carriage and Spinks gave me a sharp push in the back.

'You'll go straight to her if you know what's good for you. We're all here to do our jobs, aren't we?'

The trouble was, those jobs were nothing like they had first appeared. I'd thought Spinks was Cherville's driver. Now it seemed he was Margaret's spy, too – and what about myself? I'd come here as doctoress, yet today I'd played the part of detective, despite my misgivings. That was the thing when you needed money – it could make you do anything – but even at twenty pounds Cherville had only bought my services not my loyalty. He wouldn't hear anything of what I'd learned today until I'd seen Aphrodite for myself.

The door to Margaret's room was propped open and she was sitting at her desk writing into her daybook. Her face wore a serious expression and the slow movement of her pen told me she was forming her letters with care. I gave a small cough to let her know I was there, but she made no attempt to rush herself. If she thought to provoke me with her rudeness, I was determined not to give her the satisfaction and made a show of looking around, as though I hadn't sneaked in with Jenny that very morning. At last Margaret was finished and closing the book, she locked it away in her bureau drawer. The impression she gave was of a woman engaged in matters of the utmost confidence. Having riffled through the pages myself, I knew it was most likely a shopping list.

'Sit down, Miss Reeves. You and I are overdue a talk,' she said indicating the chair opposite. Not liking the idea of Cherville's painting looking down on me, I perched on the chair sideways on. It felt better to have him in my eyeline.

'Mr Bright recommended you for this job. I wonder if you could tell me why?'

'I've been a doctoress all my life, like my mother before me and her mother before that. Mr Bright said he thought Mr Cherville would benefit from my remedies.' At least I knew now that, from the reverend's perspective at least, it had nothing to do with my skin colour.

'Is it right that all the people you've treated are from King's Cross? You've never worked with a man of Mr Cherville's status?'

She phrased it as a question, but something told me she already knew the answer. If she'd sent Spinks to spy on me this afternoon, I had little doubt she'd also looked into my background.

'It's true that my former patients have been from a humbler station in life –' *and much more deserving*, I thought to myself – 'the thing is, all bodies work the same.'

'I take it that means you've never lived in a house like Tall Trees. We have rules here, rules that must be followed. It is for Mr Cherville to advise when he desires you to attend him, but I am in charge of the household, and if you wish to leave, you cannot do so without my permission.'

'It was on Mr Cherville's business that I went out this afternoon.'

'That may well be, yet you did it without either of us knowing and that cannot happen again.'

I fixed my eyes to the floor so she couldn't see the dislike I felt for her blaze out of them.

'I hope you understand, Miss Reeves, what honour has been bestowed on you here. The Chervilles are a great family. Mr Gervaise is a shrewd businessman and Mr Rowland has great plans to build on what his father has achieved.'

She raised admiring eyes to the portrait and I followed her gaze, marvelling that we could see something so different when we looked upon it. Margaret saw a great man, and I saw a slaver.

'What of the curse that is said to haunt the family?'

'Who told you that? Has that wretched girl been talking?'

I'd meant to jog her out of her complacency, not get

poor Jenny in trouble, so I said, 'It's something I heard before I came here.'

Apart from the way she revered Cherville, Margaret seemed sensible. I expected her to dismiss it as I had, but her face turned grim.

'When a family is on the rise, as the Chervilles are, there are many that are jealous. That's why they gossip of their betters.'

'You think it true?'

'There's no other explanation for all they've suffered; it has made the master very ill.'

Margaret prided herself on how close she was to Cherville. She must know about the cries he heard.

'What of Mr Bright's belief that Mr Cherville's plantations is what troubles him?'

'Nonsense. How could it when he has never even been to the Indies?'

'He brought the Indies here, though, you could say. The women he brought to Tall Trees. Do you remember them?'

'I was working in the country house then. From what the master has told me, I think they were ungrateful, all three of them.'

'All three,' I repeated. It was exactly as the Lukeses had said, so why had Cherville not told me of Artemis?

X

Delicate patterned saucers

Cherville lay in bed, eyes closed, when I entered his room after dinner. Careful not to wake him, I tiptoed over to his desk to prepare his medicine. It turned out he wasn't sleeping at all.

'I called for you earlier. Margaret said you'd gone on a jaunt.'

How she must have loved to order Spinks after me when she saw me walk off down the road. I doubted I'd made it five hundred yards before she came to tell her beloved master I'd left Tall Trees without his permission.

'It was hardly a jaunt, sir,' I said. 'You asked me to help you find those two women. I thought it best to act quickly.' Cherville was unappeased.

'Last night I said I would turn my attention to it in a day or two. Why would you deceive me in this way?'

There was a real anger beneath his peevish tone and I felt suddenly afraid. I'd underestimated the housekeeper's spite – she wasn't only keeping a close eye on me, as she'd threatened; she was trying to lose me my position.

'I was keen to fulfil your wishes, sir, and thought if I could bring you the information before you'd even asked, it would only reflect well on me. Please believe all I wanted was to do a good job for you.'

It sounded plausible enough and it seemed that Cherville accepted it. Thank God. In future I'd have to be more careful. I couldn't afford to give him any reason not to trust me; I had too much riding on it.

'I'll be sure to ask you directly next time I go out,' I added.

'You will, and make sure you always take Spinks with you.'

Cherville levered himself into a sitting position while I stirred powdered poppy seeds into a small cup of water. He dashed it back and I applied the balm of mint leaves I'd made the day before, working it into the skin at his temples.

'You haven't yet said if you met with success in your search,' he said.

'Unfortunately not, sir. There is no sign of Nyx and it seems Aphrodite left London. I'm not exactly sure where she went next,' I lied.

I wanted to ask him why he'd failed to mention Artemis, but saying I'd made little progress had made him peevish again and he pushed me away. That meant he was likely in some pain. There'd be another, better time to press him on the women and what their lives had been like here.

Out in the corridor, I shut Cherville's door behind me, feeling jangled. Though Margaret had failed to get me in trouble this time, it wouldn't be long before she tried again. And if she was watching me doubly close, it would be even harder to make sure I could get to Aphrodite before Cherville did.

'What are you doing there?'

'Jenny, is that you? I was on my way to my room, but I got caught up thinking.'

She walked towards me, balancing two bags of washing, and I took one from her to ease her load.

'You looked like you were in a trance. I called you twice, you know.'

'It's been a difficult day.'

'I thought you were angry because the master learned you'd gone out. I never told, I promise.' Her rounded face was anxious and I reached out to pat her arm.

'There's no need to feel bad; you did warn me, after all. Margaret must have seen me slip out – she asked Spinks to follow me.'

'She never did? I knew she'd taken against you, but even so.'

'The last thing I want is for you to get caught up in it all. You'll be at Tall Trees long after I've gone, so it's important you stay on Margaret's good side.' Jenny made a face at the idea that Margaret might have a side that was anything other than bad. 'I mean it,' I said. 'If she or Cherville ask you what happened today, I wouldn't expect you to lie for me.'

'I would, though,' she said. 'If you asked me to.'

Her eyes were fixed on me earnestly and I felt a burst of gratitude. Despite Margaret and Spinks and Cherville himself, I had one friend at Tall Trees I could count on.

I rose early the next morning, not wanting to give Gervaise Cherville any more reason to find fault with me, and joined Jenny in the kitchen for breakfast. She put a bowl of porridge in front of me but, seeing me green, whipped it away again.

'Is this better?' she said, having exchanged it for dry toast. 'I didn't realise you had . . . you know . . .'

'What?' I said warily.

'Such a delicate stomach. The walls are thin on the fourth floor. I've heard you be sick a couple of times.'

I was glad she'd put it down to poor digestion and not the true reason.

'It must be your rich cooking,' I said. 'I'm sure I'll get used to it.'

Starting my day with Jenny over breakfast had fortified me and I was in a much better frame of mind when I reached the second floor. I tiptoed along the landing, past Margaret's room, and was so relieved to have escaped her attention that I was totally unprepared to see Cherville up and dressed, seated in the chair at his bedside. As soon as I appeared, he got to his feet and rang the bell.

'Be ready to leave in twenty minutes. You and I are taking a trip out.'

'Where to, sir?' He waved a sheaf of banknotes at me, before tucking them into an envelope.

'You cannot guess?'

I shook my head. In truth I was shocked that Cherville looked so hearty, and there was a glint in his eye that showed he liked to see me wrong-footed. Had I somehow misjudged how ill he really was?

'Bloomsbury, girl. That's where we're going. As you yourself would have done yesterday, I believe. I am paying you a lot of money. I expect you to volunteer what you have learned, not leave it to Margaret to winnow it out of my driver.'

So Spinks had reported where I'd been headed when he caught up with me and Cherville had put two and two together. To think that last night I'd been congratulating myself on taking him in, and all along I was the one who'd been bested. I felt sickened, and not only because I had no chance to warn Aphrodite he was coming. Cherville had caught me out in my falsehood. Was it enough to sack me?

'I didn't want to get your hopes up, sir. It was

twenty-seven years ago that Aphrodite was seen in Bloomsbury; she could have easily moved on if it was even her in the first place.'

'Hold nothing back in future, do you hear? I'll be the one to decide if the information is good or not.'

'Yes, sir,' I said, bowing my head and hoping I looked suitably contrite.

Cherville was silent as we drove to Bloomsbury. There was a greyish cast to his face and he blinked continuously, his eyes made delicate by the Tall Trees gloom. Down by his sides he clenched and unclenched his hands. I'd allowed the sense of purpose he'd shown to fool me. He was every bit as ill as I'd always thought, his energy spent by getting dressed and into the carriage.

'It was another difficult night,' he said, putting his hands into his lap when he saw I'd noticed. 'The task I have given you is an urgent one. If I make this payment today, the voices should fade.'

The briefness of our journey made me wonder again if it was credible Aphrodite could have settled here. I wouldn't renege on my deal with Cherville. For my sister's sake, I couldn't. Even so, there was a small part of me that hoped Aphrodite had moved on, as Spinks reined in the horses and jumped down from his box.

'You didn't say which number I should stop at, sir,' he said when Cherville pulled down the carriage window so he could direct him.

'I do not know yet. You're to go to each house, one by one, and ask if they have a Black maid by the name of Aphrodite on their staff.'

Spinks glared at me. It was clear what he was thinking. There were at least forty houses here. He hurried off, not daring to complain aloud, leaving me with Cherville in the narrow confines of the carriage. He was wringing his hands again. Stopping the voices might be his sole motive, but now we were close I saw that there was more to it than he'd been prepared to admit to me and I felt a pang of sympathy for him, despite myself.

'I think this woman was important to you, sir?' I ventured.

'I brought her over to be a maid of all work. She had not one day of ill-treatment at my hands,' Cherville said, 'not one day,' a claim that didn't seem to square with what the Lukeses had hinted at.

'It's thirty-three years since I saw her,' he added, but he was no longer addressing me; I could see by the emotion on his face that he was remembering out loud, when a tap on the carriage window made him start.

'Yes?' he demanded of Spinks.

'I think I've found her, sir.'

Cherville slumped back against the seat. He hadn't expected it so quickly. Maybe, like me, a part of him had been hoping it wasn't really her after all.

'Are you sure it's the right woman?' I said.

'There's only one Black maid on the street; so, if not, it means she's moved on.'

Cherville had placed a hand over his face.

'We don't have to go in right now, sir. You've got her address, you can return tomorrow or the day after,' I urged him. That would give me long enough to warn her he was coming.

'No, no. It must be now.'

'Let me go in ahead of you then, sir. That's why you wanted my help, isn't it – to make it clear that your intentions are good?'

For a moment he considered, but then he barked for Spinks and thrust out his card.

'Send this up,' he said, adding as he turned to me, 'You're the reason I've got this far. I would not run the risk that she flee before I've said my piece.'

Spinks walked towards the house. As he climbed the steps to the front door, it swung back and he reached the top just as a footman emerged with a silver salver. Spinks placed the card on the tray and the footman whisked it away. I pictured the journey that Cherville's card, with its pale blue border, would be taking through the house. So innocuous, and yet for the woman we had come to see it carried all the menace of a noose.

'Sir,' I said, and suddenly desperate, I placed a warning hand on his arm. Cherville looked down at it in surprise and I snatched it back. A second man, more finely dressed than the first, appeared and held open the door to us.

'Lady Raine will see you now,' he announced with a click of his heels.

'Here, come on,' Cherville said, and reluctantly I followed him out of the carriage and into the house.

The butler led us along a corridor into a beautifully decorated sitting room. The walls were clad in a striped paper and every surface bore some sort of ornament. The lady of the house was looking out of the window. Dark hair was piled on top of her head and she wore a dress of the finest lilac silk. Cherville had to clear his throat before she turned around. As she did, it felt as though time had stopped. I was one Black woman looking into the eyes of another. Handsome – it was the one thing everyone had said of her. I should have realised it meant her skin was fair; so fair as to be almost white. Mr Lukes had been hurt by how cagey she'd been when he'd happened across her twenty-seven years before. No wonder she'd not lingered. Lady Raine was Aphrodite.

Beside me, Cherville fidgeted, shuffling his feet. His rapidly blinking eyes were fixed on the floor and when he spoke his muffled voice shook a little. 'I do hope you'll forgive the intrusion, madam. It is an unusual thing that brings us here today.'

He made an effort to compose himself, and as he looked up, I turned away, not brave enough to witness the moment when he would see what I had. The blood throbbed in my ears; I waited for a gasp, an exclamation, none came. For all Cherville had professed to feel, he had not even recognised her. Her rank and money were akin to the stories of faerie glamour my bargee neighbours in King's Cross told. He could not see past them. Only I could.

'Bingham, some tea, please,' Aphrodite said, and the butler bowed and left. How did she sound so cultured, so like one of them? She'd seen his card and yet she took this risk. I felt light-headed with the danger of it all, the feeling heightened by the oh-so-civilised surroundings. Cherville had given the impression that she had been important to him. Over thirty years or no, how was it that he didn't recognise her? And then it dawned on me. Whatever he thought he'd felt for her, she'd been a piece of property. He'd never really seen her.

'I do not intend to keep you long, madam. In fact, it is one of your maids I beg permission to speak to.' Lady Raine's face remained impassive and Cherville carried on. 'Her name is Aphrodite, or at least it was when she was in my employ.'

At the sound of the name she'd once answered to, Lady Raine stiffened, but so imperceptibly only someone who knew her secret would notice.

'I have no one here by that name, but that does not mean the woman is not on my staff. May I understand what it is you want from her?'

This is why she'd allowed him in. The desire to know why he'd sought her out after all this time had overcome her caution.

'I would rather . . . You see, it's difficult . . . The thing is . . .'

Lady Raine stayed quiet while Cherville hemmed and hawed and at last he gabbled it out in a rush.

'If your Black maid is who I think she is, there is a gift I must make her.'

A gift. The money he'd brought was not even half what she was due, yet to hear him speak he was Lord Bountiful. The word hung on the air as Lady Raine motioned to Cherville to take a seat on the sofa, before choosing a chair alongside him. I wondered how she could bear to be so near him and then I realised she'd positioned herself so he could not look at her directly. I took the place she had vacated by the window, turning my back on the view of the square below to face them both. While they waited for the tea things, Lady Raine spoke of the cold and how tiresome she found the rain. Well it was that Cherville continued to mumble his answers into the floor. Surely if he studied her for any amount of time, the game would be up. After ten minutes, the door opened and the butler appeared with a large tray. On to the crisp white tablecloth he laid out delicate patterned saucers, dainty cups and spoons of solid silver with infinite care; and yet I twitched uncontrollably, hearing the words 'it's her', as each one landed with a muffled *thunk*.

'Pour it,' Lady Raine commanded him, and I wondered if it was because she feared her hand would tremble.

The tea seemed to revive Cherville, or maybe he felt more comfortable having something to do with his hands.

For a moment they sipped in silence and then Lady Raine said, 'It is a highly unusual request you make, sir. I take it there is time to consider?'

'I wish that were true, madam; unfortunately I am in some haste. It is my health, you see.'

'You're dying?'

It was the first false note she had struck. I feared the way she leaned forward, the eagerness in her tone had given her away. Fortunately Cherville remained oblivious.

'I am ill, yes, and I cannot go to my grave until I have handed over her payment.'

She beckoned the butler and whispered into his ear before he left the room.

'Bingham will bring the woman up from the kitchen to speak with you.'

'You cannot allow me to address her alone?'

'I think it would be best if I were present.'

Cherville nodded, disappointed, but accepting.

'I'm grateful to you, madam,' he said, and she returned his smile with one of her own. What control she had. I didn't know whether to be appalled or fascinated.

'You did not introduce your companion,' Lady Raine said as the wait for the maid to appear stretched. When she was produced would Cherville still be fooled?

'This is Reeves. She has been caring for me of late. It is she that has been helping me with my atonement.'

'Indeed.'

Lady Raine's face was as blank as if they'd continued talking of the weather. Like a mask, I realised; a mask she had been wearing for many years. When had she struck on this approach? I wondered. And how often had she been forced to hear her race derided for the privilege of passing? When I'd realised who she was, I'd felt apprehensive, but Cherville's attempt at recompense would likely be the least of the indignities that she'd had to sit through, even joined in with for the sake of preserving her cover.

'I should have sent Reeves down with your butler,' Cherville said. 'That is why I brought her, to make Dite feel more comfortable.'

Dite? On his lips, the nickname made me queasy and once again I marvelled at Lady Raine's self-possession when she did not react.

The door swung open and the maid shuffled into the room, smoothing down her apron. She was the right age and, like her mistress, she was fair-skinned, but her heritage was more obvious. Cherville jumped to his feet and I held myself taut. This was the moment he would look into her eyes. If he was to discover Lady Raine's secret, it would be now.

'Aphrodite, is that you?'

The question made my heart plummet. The maid, too, showed some confusion; her eyes flicked to her mistress and she received the slightest of encouraging nods.

'My name is Gervaise Cherville, do you remember me?'

It was the question you would ask an old schoolfellow, someone who had been a friend. He seemed sincere and yet how could he think she would not remember the man who had stolen her freedom and presumed to own her? Cherville reached out to take her hand and, from the corner of my eye, I saw Lady Raine flinch as though she felt Cherville's touch on her own skin.

'I wanted to say . . .' His voice was so low that Lady Raine leaned forward to hear it. If she expected real contrition, she was to be disappointed, for all Cherville could muster was, 'I've brought this for you in recompense.'

When it came to it, he'd only completed half the job, and the easier half at that.

The maid took the envelope he proffered, but let the hand that held it fall limply to her side.

'You can count it,' Cherville said.

Is this what he would have said to her in private? These functional words that contained only fact and no feeling?

There was a swish of skirts and Lady Raine stood.

'Forgive me, this *is* a private conversation and I must

shortly away to Bloomsbury Hall where I am due to meet some charitable ladies. We're planning a bazaar to raise funds for worthy causes and it is our custom to meet weekly of an afternoon.'

She swept out before Cherville could respond and I followed, leaving the maid to play her part. Heaven knows what the butler had told her. Both must be in on their mistress's secret – would have to be – and that would have bonded them all, elevating their relationship far above the usual ties that existed between servants and their employer. Out in the hallway, Lady Raine was almost panting. She made an ineffective fumble at her back and, realising what she needed, I stepped behind and tugged at the ribbons lacing her corset. She exhaled slowly and some of the pink came back into her cheeks.

'How can you breathe in that man's company?' she asked.

I wanted to excuse myself, to explain that I'd intended to warn her first, but my plan had failed and so the words didn't come. Since Cherville had asked for my help, I'd managed to keep my misgivings at bay. Now I must confront them and I felt the creeping warmth of shame wash over my body.

'I can't go back in there,' she said. 'I thought I could do it, but I can't. Did you hear him when he handed over that money? Does he truly believe such a payment would absolve him for what he's done to me?'

'Talking with his priest has led him to seek atonement.'

'Church meddling – I should have guessed,' Lady Raine said, and her voice dripped with disdain.

In the sitting room, Cherville was still talking. She cocked her head, but no individual words were discernible from where we stood. 'I never thought to see him again. When that blue card appeared on my tray, I almost vomited,' she said half to herself. She stepped back towards the door as if she intended to re-enter, at the last second she wrenched herself away. It was heart-breaking to see her torn like this, needing to hear what Cherville had to say yet not being able to bear it. I bitterly regretted my part in it.

'He is genuine in wanting to make amends. That I can assure you of.' I'd realised it on the way over in the carriage. If his only thought were to stop the voices, he would not have been so nervous.

'That's what he brought you with him to say, is it?'

'He was concerned he wouldn't be given a hearing,' I said, unable to utter his name out loud in her presence.

Lady Raine gave a mirthless laugh. 'Yes, of course. Now he is feeling the consequences of his actions, we must all listen. I wonder if he felt such remorse when the trade was still profitable?'

'I don't know about that. I only joined his household this week.'

'You live at Tall Trees? That place still haunts my

dreams. The basement so dark and icy. It was as though he hated us to see the sun.'

So she and Nyx and Artemis had been kept in the room that now served as a larder.

'I am on the fourth floor; my room overlooks the gardens in the centre of the square,' I said. Why was everything coming out so wrong? It sounded as though I were saying things were better now, and they were, but my fingertips still bore the scabs from where I'd made them bleed in my efforts to open the window; and we were only in her house because Margaret had had me watched and followed. 'Will you tell me what happened to the others?'

She closed her eyes in pain and when she opened them they were wet with tears.

'After what has happened here today, you would expose more of us. Who are you?'

Her words dripped with contempt. It was not what I'd intended, but to her my actions were betrayal. I cared little for Cherville's soul; his money, that was the thing. She might not need it, but what if these other women did? I opened my mouth to explain, but she shook her head to silence me.

'You should leave now. Bingham will show you out, before he does, I must ask you to make me a promise.'

'I wouldn't dream of revealing who you are,' I said emphatically.

'It wasn't that, but it is just as important. Never ever come here again,' she said.

I felt so ashamed at what I'd become embroiled with that I wanted to disappear inside myself. As she stalked away, the worried glances she threw back over her shoulder belied her haughty posture. Beneath the fine clothes and the polished accent, she was still the enslaved woman who had fled Tall Trees in the dead of night, and I had brought it home to her.

Cherville had been silent on the way to Bloomsbury. Now we were on our way back to Tall Trees, he couldn't stop talking.

'I expected her to say more. The amount I gave, it will provide for her for life. I imagine it was the surprise of it that got to her. There can't be many who would do as I have done. A shame – she was coarser than I remembered. I thought she would have wanted to count it. As soon as she has done, she can't help but be grateful.'

He was so complacent, I felt sickened. In his delight at how good he thought himself now, he was oblivious to the wrong he'd done in the first place.

'Reeves, did you hear me? I said you did so well to find Dite, it is time we turn our attention to Nyx. Whatever you need to hasten the process, it is yours: a man or two to help, perhaps? What do you say to that?'

I wanted none of Cherville's congratulations for the

role I'd played in finding Dite. It was further grist to the mill of self-loathing that was eating me from the inside, but I forced myself to respond. I'd be damned if I let things go the same way with Nyx.

'Leave it to me, sir. It will be better if I work alone.'

'You're sure? Remember you have Spinks at your disposal.'

I gave a false smile as he talked on, my mind whirring. I had to continue the search for Nyx. If not, Cherville would never pay me; and it was likely he'd track her down anyway, but it couldn't be like this.

When we arrived back at Tall Trees, Margaret was waiting on the front steps and came down to meet us as Cherville climbed out of the carriage.

'Sir, where have you been? I thought you said you weren't well enough to venture far?' she said, shooting me a baleful glare as if I'd lured him into danger.

'Don't fuss, Margaret. I went to Bloomsbury and look at me. I was never better.'

He might feel well, but his colour was too high and his hands shook. The best place for him was bed, but I doubted he'd agree to that.

'Lean on my arm, sir,' Margaret said, and he looked down at her indulgently.

'Very well. You may escort me to the library.'

Margaret stopped me when I would have followed on. 'I

think you've done enough today, Reeves. I will tend to the master this afternoon.'

It wasn't for her to be giving me orders and she couldn't know better than I what Cherville needed. Still, I found myself nodding. Exhausted by his excitement and the part I had played in it, I dragged myself up to my room. And as soon as I shut the door behind me, the tears came.

XI

Marble statues and stone obelisks

I awoke to pitch-darkness. My uniform had twisted around me and my head ached where the pins that bound my hair dug into my scalp. The grandfather clock chimed as I sat up. Only nine o'clock. I would've sworn it was the early hours. Slowly I made my way downstairs and there was Jenny in her usual seat. Despite the turmoil of the day, she remained a constant.

When she saw me, she jumped to her feet. 'I didn't think you'd be down tonight. I poked my head into your room an hour ago and you were out like a light. I thought you'd sleep right through.'

How dearly I wished I had. As exhausted as I'd been earlier, I was wakeful now and that meant for the rest of the night I'd be thinking on Lady Raine and the secret I'd stumbled upon. What would the Lukeses think if they found out that helping me had almost led to her exposure? The thought made me shudder.

'I know what'll cheer you up,' Jenny said. 'Sit down, it won't take a minute.'

I watched as she put some milk to heat on the stove before scraping a square of chocolate and dividing the shavings between two large mugs. When the milk was ready, she poured it on top with a dash of hot water. I took a sip and realised that after the trials of this day, the comforting richness was exactly what I needed.

'Uh oh,' Jenny said and, when I stilled in alarm, she laughed. 'Look at your face. We're not in trouble – I'd forgotten the finishing touch.'

I put the mug down and from the cupboard she produced a nutmeg and grated it on top.

'There, try it again now. It's a bit cheeky, but I think we deserve it.'

It was even better than before, the nuttiness leavening the sugary sweet, and Jenny looked on, nodding with pleasure to see my enjoyment.

'What happened when you went out earlier? You came back exhausted, and the master was like I've never seen him.'

In handing over the money to the woman he believed to be Aphrodite, it was as if all the weight of what Cherville had done had lifted, and found a home in me. I looked up from the greasy dregs of my hot chocolate to find Jenny watching me closely. She wanted to help, I could tell, but the enormity of it was too much. I simply couldn't face it.

'It's too long a story for now. All I'll say is that when I walk out of here tomorrow, I won't be looking back.'

Jenny went pale. 'You've never been fired, have you?'

Wouldn't that be the easiest way out of it all? I shook my head.

'It's Saturday, I'll be going home before returning on Sunday evening, remember?'

'Yes, of course. There's something about this place sometimes, all the days seem to roll into one another. It makes you feel . . .'

'Trapped,' I supplied.

'You're well out of it, I reckon, if Madam's on the war-path. It's not like her to be angry when the master's in a good mood. Either way, I bet you'll be glad to get home.'

'I will,' I said, so emphatically that Jenny blurted, 'You are coming back, aren't you?'

If only walking away was a choice I could make. I knew the anatomy of every single hour I'd spent at Tall Trees and wanted nothing more than never to come back again, but where then would that leave us? As though she knew I was thinking of her, my baby kicked at that very moment.

'It's not so bad, is it?' Jenny persisted, looking crestfallen.

'You've made it much more bearable,' I said, reaching over to squeeze her hand. 'I miss my family, that's all.'

'Your husband especially? I can tell when you're thinking of him. There's a certain look you get on your face.'

'It's not only him that's on my mind. There's my sister Willa, too.'

'I didn't know you had a sister? You've not mentioned her.'

If I hadn't, it was not through lack of thinking of her – specifically, how I was going to broach with her my worries that Rowland had inherited syphilis from his father. Poor Willa. She was the reason I'd come here in the first place, but with Cherville's offer to double my earnings things had spiralled. I'd expected it to be hard here – hadn't I said as much to Jos? But the events of the last two days had made everything that much more difficult. Hearing from the Lukeses, and then seeing Lady Raine herself, had forced me to confront the true cost of how Cherville had made his money.

'Seems the best thing for us both is bedtime,' Jenny said as she stood and reached for my mug. 'You all done?' I nodded and she swiped it away and put it in the sink along with her own. 'If I go up now, I can get a good few hours in. I'll leave this for the morning.'

'Go on, you get to bed and I'll rinse them. I'm not sleepy.'

I shooed her off, washing and drying the mugs before I put them away. There. No sign we'd used them and no need for Margaret to suspect we'd helped ourselves to a treat that was surely intended for Cherville alone. A yawn stole over me and, folding the tea towel into a neat square as I did at the cottage, I made my way upstairs.

Saturday dawned and as soon as midday struck, I was out of Tall Trees as fast as my legs could carry me. All week, I'd been counting the hours until I had the chance to return home, but there was someone I must visit before even Jos and Willa.

The churchyard at St Hilda's was home to at least one hundred souls. They lay buried in uneven rows, their passing marked by wooden crosses, marble statues and stone obelisks. I picked my way past the beloved wives and dearly departed sons to the foot of the tree where Mama had been lain to rest. Some leaves had fallen from its branches and I brushed them away before kneeling down to say a prayer, grateful to be back in the old dress that was so much more comfortable than my Cherville uniform.

'I won't be able to do this for much longer, it's getting too hard to stand up again,' I said as I crossed myself and sat back on my heels. It was our daily conversations about the mundanities I missed the most and so it had become my way to come here and talk to her. 'She's feeling heavy now I'm almost four months gone.'

When I told him, Jos would be the second person to know about the baby. Of course I'd come to Mama first.

'Willa is well, I think. The charge you gave me, though, Mama. I do struggle with it.'

I got to my feet, just as Mr Bright came out of the vicarage and headed into the church. I was already going to be home later than I wanted, but now I'd seen him I must talk to him.

As I stepped inside St Hilda's and closed the door, it felt as though I was shutting out the imperfect world behind me. I breathed in the calm stillness, but it caught at the back of my throat. Dusty books, and wood and leather: that was how Tall Trees smelled, too.

Mr Bright was kneeling at the altar. As I walked up the aisle, I saw his hands move in the sign of the cross that signalled the end of his prayers. He swayed slightly as he got to his feet and I rushed forward to help him.

'I thank you, Hester. I'm not as young as I used to be.' His eyes took in the quiet church. 'You're a little early for evensong.'

'I'm not here for the service. I stopped off to visit Mama's grave on my way home from Tall Trees.'

'Your new job prevents you from coming as often as you would like, I'm sure.'

'It does, but I've been able to clear away the leaves and lay some flowers.' I wanted to add something about how grateful I was, how the job would change my family's fortunes. After yesterday's events my mouth refused to shape the words and Mr Bright sensed that I was struggling with something.

'This extra business Cherville has put you to troubles me. Truly, I had no idea of what he was planning.'

His sorrowful tone sparked my impatience. I was at fault for leading Cherville to Lady Raine. Surely Mr Bright saw he bore some responsibility, too?

'Is there nothing you can do to help?'

'Come to the sacristy. You must tell me exactly what has happened.'

The small room Mr Bright led me to was just behind the altar. It was hung with vestments, shelves lined with chalices and candles.

'If I move these parish registers, you can take a seat,' he said, and I waited for him to clear a space on what looked like an old pew.

Once we were both seated, he said, 'I confess I have been most worried since you told me of Cherville's scheme. On Thursday morning I sent him a note to see if I could turn his attention to the greater cause. I fear I was not successful.'

'We found Aphrodite.'

Mr Bright closed his eyes, looking pained.

'So it has begun,' he said.

'She lives in the square at Bloomsbury, but not as herself – she goes by the name Lady Raine now and is passing as white. I think it was only Mr Cherville's ailing health that stopped him from recognising her.' That and perhaps a latent shame he felt but could not express.

'Lady Raine the philanthropist? It cannot be. I have never met her in person, but I know of her works. She has been at the forefront of many causes. My goodness, what a risk she runs.'

'Mr Cherville has been very pleased since he spoke to her – well, the maid she put in front of him. He vows he will now find Nyx, the other woman who ran from him. I found out there was a third woman, too. Her name was Artemis – do you remember her?'

'I do not,' Mr Bright said, his tone clipped, 'between us we must put a stop to this.'

'Is that not what you tried when you wrote to him the other day? I'm afraid there is nothing that can hold him back now.'

Mr Bright uttered an oath and slammed his hand down on the table so the pieces of altarware jumped. 'I knew no good could come of this.'

If he was angry, it could only be at himself. He might not have intended that Cherville would take his exhortations to mean tracking down the slaves he had brought to England rather than helping those on his plantation in Honduras, but Mr Bright had been the one to plant the idea. He should have done more to think it through and, though it hurt to admit it, the same was true of myself. I'd got caught up in the idea that Cherville money meant freedom. For those he'd enslaved it could never be enough.

'Will you try to speak to Mr Cherville again? I'm scared he'll go back to Bloomsbury and the next time he could recognise her.'

Mr Bright looked grave as he inclined his head. 'The last thing I wish is for you to be worried. Go home to your family and leave Mr Cherville to me. As you know, he and I have been acquainted for some time. If needs be, I will draw on the bounds of friendship to temper his enthusiasm and refocus his attention on the slaves who worked on his plantation. It was never my intention that . . . well, never mind.'

'I doubt you will be able to stop him entirely, but if you can keep him away from Bloomsbury – that'll be something. Besides, if Nyx is poor, she might feel differently to Lady Raine, especially if you can encourage Mr Cherville to own the wrong he has done her.'

'Is that not what he is doing, by giving out these sums?'

Before I'd met Lady Raine, I would have said yes. I saw now it was only one part of it. To her the money meant little without an apology – for true repentance the two must go hand in hand.

Mr Bright put a hand on my shoulder and steered me outside. 'I am glad you stopped by to see me, but it's past two o'clock; you should get along to your husband now and try not to worry your head about this in the meantime. I will continue to think on how I might raise Mr Cherville's gaze to Honduras – you'll remember I always thought that a better outlet for his remorse?'

I nodded uncertainly.

'There is nothing else, is there? Margaret is not causing you misery?'

'She'd do me harm if she could, but it helps that I'm wise to her. When Mr Cherville and I came back from Lady Raine's, he was enervated and she accused me of overexciting him. From the very first day, she set herself to watch me. I'm sure she thinks I am there to do something underhand. She said that Rowland Cherville wouldn't stand for it if he were home.'

'Nor would he. He has no time for the abolitionist cause. I wonder . . .' Mr Bright looked thoughtful for a moment before shaking his head briskly. 'I shall fix this, Hester, I promise you.'

I was pleased to hear it, though not as confident as I might have been. Mr Bright meant well, but I wondered if he had the influence over Cherville he thought he did.

XII

Green shot silk

Candlelight beckoned from the windows of the cottage, and I let myself in, shaking the autumnal mizzle from my coat. Far humbler, but how much more inviting it was, with its cleanly scrubbed table and glowing fire, than the grand entrance hall of Tall Trees. All was tidy and I felt a mingling of pride and gratitude that Willa and Jos between them had kept things going so well in my absence. The two clean plates on the table and the neatly folded dishcloth were no competition for the bowl of roses and ornate hat stand, but for all that they were homely and I gusted out a sigh. At Cherville's house I felt I must hold myself tautly. For the first time in a week I was able to let go.

I hung up my coat on the peg by the door and went in

search of my sister, disappointed she hadn't come to greet me. The cottage was too small for her not to have heard me arrive and I felt frustrated to think that, even though I'd been away for almost a week, she was still offish with me. Well, I was back now and determined to bring her around.

'Willa, I'm home,' I called out.

I found her in the room I shared with Jos, sitting with her back to her bed, a shard of mirror in one hand while she rouged her face with the other. She turned the mirror first this way, then that, to see herself from all angles. She'd always been beautiful, right from the day when I'd been at Mama's side to help bring her into the world. That's why it had hurt so much when she'd returned from wherever it was she had been after two weeks missing, cheeks hollowed, and eyes dimmed. What she had been through in those days when she was almost mad with grief, distraught at being evicted from her home, I could not bear to think of. She had made it back to her family, though. That was the important thing, and when Cher-ville paid me, I could give her the fresh start she so desperately needed.

'The light's better in here,' she said defensively.

I was too glad to be home to care about her using my room, as long as she tidied up after herself. Not that I was in any rush to tell Jos. He would look less favourably on her coming in here while we were both away from home, but I knew how she struggled in the makeshift space we'd fashioned for her by curtaining off a section of the room we used as both kitchen and living area.

'Are you going out this evening?' I said, walking in and picking my way over the clothes she'd presumably tried on before discarding them on the floor.

'The girls from the factory are going to the Hind.'

I'd hoped she'd want to stay in with Jos and me, seeing as I had only one night at the cottage before I was due back at Tall Trees. She was at least talking to me, though, and that was something I could build on.

'Let me see what you're wearing, then.'

Willa got up and twirled, admiring the way her gown flared out. It was one I hadn't seen before, a tight bodice and full skirt of green shot silk, far more expensive than the usual cotton dresses we wore.

'Here, take this,' I said, digging in my pocket and turning up a farthing.

She smiled, not expecting it, but couldn't help adding, 'It won't stretch to a round, you know.'

That was my sister, full of cheek as ever. I made a playful swipe at her and she dodged out of my reach, laughing; and quick as that, we were back on terms.

'Let me tidy up the back of your hair. You missed a little.'

I perched on the bed and she levered herself up alongside and presented me with her tightly bound curls. She'd not been wrapping them as I'd told her and at the ends the hairs were breaking.

'Stay there a minute,' I said, and went back into the other room to fetch my bag.

'What's that you're putting on my hair? It smells nice,' she said as I returned with a small pot and scooped out a fingernail of balm.

'I made it the other day with some bear's grease I found in the cupboard at Tall Trees. See how I'm thinking of you even when I'm away?'

Would she say she had thought of me, too? It hurt that she'd not yet asked how I'd found my first week at Tall Trees, she'd hardened since Mama's death. All I could do was show her as much love as possible and hope that eventually she would thaw and I'd have my old Willa back again. Not quite the same as she was before Mama died – the loss had been too great for that – but something close would do. For now I warmed the balm I'd made between my hands before smoothing it through her hair, twisting section after section into thick sausage plaits that I pinned carefully at the nape of her neck. My stomach lurched a little as I remembered times past when I'd sat in much the same position, plaiting her hair before she went off to play outside, while Mama was in the kitchen mixing up ingredients for her medicines.

'I am sorry, Willa, about what happened when I came to meet you at the factory that time. I only asked you to stay away from Rowland Cherville because I care for you.' In actual fact it had been seven weeks since it happened, but she'd been too angry for me to bring it up. She still was.

'You do realise I can look after myself?' she said, shuffling forward a little. The motion took her just out of my reach and my fingers snagged on a curl. She gave an accusatory yelp as if I'd done it on purpose. 'Thanks, but I think my hair's fine now.'

Seven weeks hadn't been long enough after all, and I sighed, feeling deflated. Willa, oblivious to my mood, took one last look in the mirror and smiled at herself, before rising to her feet and heading for the door. I trailed her into the kitchen, watching as she pulled on her coat and gloves.

'What about your hat?'

'And spoil my hair after you've spent so long doing it? No chance.'

I should let her go, but there was one question that plagued me. 'Will Rowland Cherville be there tonight?'

Her shoulders stiffened ever so slightly, and when she replied her voice was light and innocent. 'I told you already, I'm going out with the girls. I haven't spoken to him in a month.'

This was some reassurance at least and knowing it might be my only chance to broach the subject with her for another week I ploughed on.

'When I warned you off him before, it was because of his position, who he is, and that would have been reason enough, but now I suspect he is diseased also. His father has the lovers' disease and it's possible that Rowland has inherited it.'

'You're trying to scare me.'

'I wouldn't, not with this – it's too serious.'

'If he was ill, I'd know it,' she insisted.

'Not if he's had it for a while. It can be dormant for years, but it's catching all the same. Has he thin hair, soft bones, does his mind wander?'

Willa's lip trembled. 'You say you're not trying to scare me and then you throw this at me just as I'm going out?'

'When else would I tell you? I've been away at Tall Trees all week.'

'I don't believe you. All you want is to spoil my night. I should never have let you talk me into living here. You make me feel like a prisoner and Jos is even worse.'

'All he wants is for you to be safe.'

'Go on, defend him, why don't you? Can't you ever be on my side?'

Her voice was rising and I could see she was frustrated; so was I. She made it so that everything had to be a fight all the time. Couldn't she understand I was only trying to help her?

'I'm always on your side, Willa, always looking out for you. Why would I have spent all the time you were missing searching for you? Why would I have invited you into my home?'

'Invited me in? You make it sound as if I was some sort of waif or stray. I'm the only natural family you have left.'

We stood glaring at each other and in the tense silence we heard the click of Jos's key in the lock.

'What on earth is going on? I could hear you both shrieking from five hundred yards away,' my husband said as he walked through the door.

He couldn't have come in at a worse moment, and as he shrugged off his coat and stood alongside me, Willa's face hardened. For the first time I saw it through her eyes – the two of us ranged against her – and I gave Jos a little push to one side, softening my voice.

'Rowland Cherville is not for you, Willa,' I said, reaching out a hand, but she twisted away before I could touch her.

'That's where you're wrong. You don't know him.'

Was that love for him in her voice? How could she be so naive?

'Please tell me you haven't lain with him?'

'I can't believe you would ask that,' she cried and, pushing past me, she wrenched open the door and stalked out, slamming it shut behind her.

'How's that for temper,' Jos said, going over to the window to look out after her. 'I pity anyone who runs into her on the towpath – if they don't get out of the way, I wouldn't put it past her to knock them down.'

'It's my fault we rowed, I should have chosen a better time to speak to her. I was worried that meeting Rowland

Cherville was the reason she'd got all dolled up. Now I've riled her, she'll probably seek him out just to spite me.'

'That's exactly the type of thing she'd do,' Jos said with a bitter laugh, but as he turned around he saw how upset I was and opened his arms to me. 'Poor Essie, this isn't the welcome home you wanted, is it?'

I cuddled into him, the circle of his arms giving me the strength I needed to step back and wipe away my tears. 'I'll be all right in a minute.'

'You will, but let's make sure of it, shall we,' he said. 'The main thing is you're home now, and whatever's gone wrong we can work it out together.'

XIII

Care and tenderness

An hour later, we sat at the kitchen table opposite one another. Jos had cleaned up while I splashed my face and changed into the old shawl of Mama's that I always wore around the house. He smelled of soap, the coal dust he'd been covered with gone, bar the thin lines around his nails and on his palms, too deeply ingrained to go away.

'How's it been at Tall Trees?'

Just hearing the name of the Cherville house felt like an attack. At all costs I wanted to keep my two worlds separate and yet Willa's affair with Rowland, and the disquiet I'd carried with me ever since agreeing to help Cherville find the women he'd enslaved, meant they grated against each other. I had to share the weight of it, before it wore me down completely.

'There's something I have to tell you.'

Jos frowned. 'He wants you to stay longer?'

'It's not that. He's still planning to move to the country, but there's something extra he wants before he goes – help to find two women he enslaved and brought to England.'

'Slavery's been abolished, remember.'

It hurt to hear the bitterness beneath his words, but I understood it. We both knew that laws were one thing and personal experience quite another. Abolition Act or no, it would be some time before the enslaved were truly free.

'This happened in 1792,' I explained.

'What can he want with them after all this time?'

'That's the good bit – he wants to make amends.'

Jos whistled between his teeth. 'You think he's genuine?'

It was the question I'd struggled with more or less since Cherville had told me of his plan. My conclusion was he was acting for himself more than the women, but if he was willing to pay for his crimes it had to be worth the risk, especially if he apologised, too.

'He's been hearing voices, cries, that mean he cannot find peace. That's what's driving him first and foremost, but if the action is correct I can overlook the motive.'

Jos listened closely while I told him exactly what Cherville had asked of me. Though he was careful not to interrupt, he couldn't help another low whistle when I told him what I'd been promised in return. His eyes glazed and I could tell he was thinking of plentiful food, a roof that didn't leak, fresh air free of London smog. That had been my mistake, too. I'd been so focused on how the money could help that I'd glossed over what I'd have to do to earn it. The fear of those few seconds after Lady Raine had turned around and before Cherville looked up. It would live in me always.

When I had finished recounting what had happened at Bloomsbury, Jos rubbed his hands against his cheeks, pulling at the skin. 'You have no idea where Nyx might be?'

'Nor Artemis. After what happened with Lady Raine, I'm wondering if I'm doing right by trying to find them, but if I don't Cherville will do it without me.'

'Maybe they'll welcome the money. It's unlikely all three of these women have been living as aristocrats.'

'Does the money count if it doesn't come with an apology? Without it there's no acknowledgement of harm.'

I wanted his view on it, but I could've guessed he wouldn't answer my question. Jos never talked directly about his life before he'd come to England. He shook his head, sympathy brimming in his dark brown eyes. 'You'll tie yourself up in knots and you can't think of everything. You weren't to know that Aphrodite had become Lady Raine. Long ago she made her choice to live like that. It's not for you to feel responsible; she could have run into Cherville at any time.'

That was right, wasn't it? I should have thought of it earlier when I'd spoken to Mr Bright. What had happened with Lady Raine had made us think we needed to find a way to put a stop to Cherville's scheme, but lightning was unlikely to strike twice. Thanks to her ability to pass as white, to marry into the aristocracy, Lady Raine could afford to reject Cherville's overtures – literally. Nyx and Artemis, named for darkness, would not have that privilege. Was it a privilege, though? Standing in her beautifully furnished sitting room, witnessing her forced to smile in the face of her enslaver, it hadn't felt like it.

'What do you think I should do?'

'I say you should leave and never go back,' Jos said.

It was not what I'd expected, but as he took my hands in his, I realised I should have known him better. He always said our family was his first priority – this was the proof of it. Even though the money Cherville was offering was life-changing, hearing the toll it was taking on me, Jos was willing for me to walk away.

'I'd love nothing more than to leave, but I can't.'

'It's only money,' he said, and I loved him all the more because we both knew that wasn't true. When you lived as we did, money was security, protection, opportunity, everything.

'If it were just about the cottage, I'd agree with you, but there's someone else we need to think of.'

Jos frowned, and it pained me to realise it was because

he was thinking of my sister – if only he could extend to her a fraction of the love he felt for me.

'Not Willa. Someone else we haven't met yet.' I placed our joined hands over my stomach.

What joy to watch the realisation of the baby move across his face. He leaned his forehead against mine and through the connection between us I felt all his care and tenderness.

'So you see that, however hard it is, I must finish what I started?'

'Our child will be your strength. From this moment, everything we do is for their sake.'

In our bed, amid the rumpled sheets, I lay within the crook of Jos's arm, watching as he trailed his fingers across my belly, tracing the path of the veins that had begun to show through my skin. Being at Tall Trees, I'd spent little time thinking of how my body was changing. Now I saw it through his eyes, the way it was changing him too, and allowed myself to feel his sense of wonder.

'How is it you're so convinced it's a girl?' he said.

'You doubt my intuition? A woman can tell these things.'

The baby kicked and he withdrew his hand sharply, the shock on his face almost comical.

'See? She is kicking because you question me.'

He returned his hand gingerly and she kicked again. 'It doesn't hurt you?'

I was warmed by the reverence in his eyes, but fearful,

too, to see the worries I felt reflected. There was so much more at stake now.

'I've found it comforting this past week at Tall Trees. When she kicks, it's a reminder of us and what I'm doing this for. It's stopped me feeling so alone.'

'When will you tell your sister?'

'I was hoping to tell her this evening. When she let me do her hair I thought things between us might be mending, but – well, you saw how it was as you came in. This is all because of Rowland Cherville. I'm scared she's walking out with him.'

'It wouldn't surprise me. Some nights she doesn't get home until long after I've returned from work.'

I shrugged off his arm and sat up, drawing my knees to my chest and pulling the blanket around me. 'How is it you're only just telling me this? You promised me that while I was away you'd look out for her.'

Jos sighed and rolled over, reaching out for the vest that had been thrown to the floor during our lovemaking. His voice was muffled as he pulled it over his head. 'Must we speak of her now?'

Moments ago, we'd lain together in the glow of our shared love for the child to come. Now I huddled with the blanket and Jos had stood to finish getting dressed. He'd always complained that Willa came between us, but if we didn't address it now the resentment he felt would continue to fester.

'Willa is as much a part of this family as our baby. All I want is for you to accept that.'

'No, Hester.'

He rarely used my full name, never told me no, and I put my head to my knees, knowing that the row I'd hoped to avoid was upon us.

'Your sister is wild. She has been since you brought her home. Whatever you recall from her childhood, she is not that girl any more.'

'Think of all she's been through. Remember her mother died.'

'It happened to you, too. Everyone loses someone they love at one time or another – and you know what? They continue to work and eat and sleep. I can't understand why you make all these excuses for her.'

'Because I made a promise, Jos. Do we really have to go over this again?'

We glowered at each other, then with a sigh he sat down on the edge of the bed. 'Can't you see what she's doing to us? Think of the baby. Is your sister the sort of influence you want for our daughter?'

This was too much. I knew Willa's ways frustrated Jos, but for him to use the baby against her was unforgivable. 'I think you've said enough for now. Will you leave me while I finish getting dressed?'

He threw up his hands and returned to the kitchen while I pulled on my clothes. When I joined him, he was sitting at the table picking at a piece of bread and cheese. Earlier we'd spoken of a celebratory dinner. Of running out to the chophouse for plates of meat and gravy. What a long way we'd come from that.

'Where are you going?' he said as I put on my hat and coat.

'I need to get some air.'

Another time, he would have offered to come with me. Now he gave a slight shake of his head and trained his eyes on his plate. I'd hoped having it out with him about Willa would help; instead it had made things worse.

XIV

A blast of cold air

The newspapers declared canal-side one of the most dangerous places to be once dark had fallen. I felt perfectly safe there. What did I care if there were no gas lamps? The light of the moon was more than good enough. It silvered the ripples of the slow-moving water as I walked downstream, and a bargee up on deck with his pipe nodded to me as I passed. I thought I recognised him, had tended to his wife or sister. To keep Willa safe, I'd have to leave all my patients behind. Was Jos right that Mama would never have expected me to take keeping my promise this far?

I carried on walking, not realising until it was in front of me that I'd had a destination in mind all along. There it was opposite, on the left-hand bank of the water: a single-storey building with a golden light glowing invitingly from its windows. The sign above the door pictured a pretty red doe with 'The Hind' painted in gold, but everyone around King's Cross called it after its owner. Jos was wrong to insist I let Willa go her own way. As long as I could, whether she welcomed it or not, I'd always be there to watch out for her.

I pushed open the door and stepped into a welcoming fug of warmth and chatter. There were public houses that were bigger, or had a regular band in of an evening, but it was hard to imagine anywhere more cosy or familiar than the single room with its faded red carpet, smelling strongly of beer and worn around the fireplace where the men dragged their stools to yarn to one another. I'd barely been in since Mama died, and yet everything I remembered was the same, right down to Sal in her usual spot behind the bar.

'Hester Reeves! Look at you, stepping in casual-like.'

There was a hint of criticism in her tone and I felt abashed. She was right. I should've made more effort to see her, but Sal was nothing if not generous and when she saw my blush she leaned across the bar to catch me in a strong hug.

'None of that. You're here now and that's what counts.'

The curls in her fair hair had caught the smoke of the men's pipes. She pushed me back, and took me in. 'Attendant to Gervaise Cherville himself, eh?' She laughed at the surprised look on my face. 'You should know that news travels fast around here. I've had some of your former patients in. Grousing that you've abandoned them.'

'Let me guess. Rosie and Jane, am I right?'

'Correct. Jane in particular has missed you.'

'I hope her John hasn't set about her. I've tried to persuade her away, but she won't listen. Thank God this arrangement with Cherville is temporary and then I can get back to them.'

'I say we raise a glass to that. Perry's your favourite, isn't it? Let me get you a taste.'

Sal turned to the back of the bar. Two shelves-worth of drinks were ranged haphazardly, but her hand went unerringly to the bottle of Norfolk's and she popped off the cork and gave it a sniff. While she poured, I made myself comfortable on a bar stool. Sal placed a half-pint glass in front of me, the drink inside a rich straw-coloured yellow with a thin head of foam. It tasted like the past, when I'd popped in to sit with Sal during the day, when Mama was at home preparing the dinner and all my thoughts were of my patients and whether Jos would propose.

'Your Willa's in tonight, you know.'

Sal jerked her head to the far corner of the room where my younger sister was holding court among a group of women her own age or thereabouts. They were laughing, joking, and I couldn't help but feel a pang that Willa seemed so much more at ease with her friends than she did with us at the cottage.

'She's the reason I'm here,' I admitted, beginning to think it had been wrong to follow her. She'd already accused me of being on top of her, but in refusing to stay and talk to me she'd left me little choice. Tomorrow I was due back at Tall Trees. If I didn't speak to her tonight, there'd be little chance in the morning when she had a head thick with drink.

'Willa's one of my regulars now,' Sal said, and although her tone was light I sensed the warning beneath it.

'You'd tell me if she was any trouble, wouldn't you?'

'It's not her you need to worry about. It's the gentlemen.'

I smirked at the thought of gentlemen in a place as rough and ready as the Hind.

'There's no account to raise your eyebrows at me like that. I'll let you know, we have a wide and varied clientele,' Sal said, but the laugh in her voice told me she wasn't really offended.

An unhappy thought struck me. 'It's not Rowland Cherville that comes in here, is it?'

'It is, as it happens. Sometimes he brings a friend or two – dressed down, of course, but I know a toff in commoner's clothing when I see one. Those girls can't be too careful, no girls ever can.'

I looked over at them again: too much powder, voices a little loud, but they were only young and enjoying themselves. The thought that they might be prey to men like Cherville was a sour taste in my mouth. I took a sip of perry to wash it away and slid down from my bar stool.

'Careful, Hester,' Sal said.

The worry in her eyes gave me pause. 'I shouldn't speak to her?'

'Not in front of all her friends. No good will come of it. Stay here a while with me and when she gets her next drink, you can try her then.'

I'd missed Sal's advice, always good and gently given. There was no harm in biding my time.

The pub got busier as the evening wore on, Sal pulled away by the steady stream of customers. I nursed my perry, not wanting the baby to get the taste of it. Turning so my back was to the bar, I looked out at the men in overalls who'd come straight from their work on the canal, others smarter who clerked in the city, and then in the corner Willa and her group of friends. It was a world away from Tall Trees. It was my world, and I stored the picture before me in my mind, knowing that in the coming days when I was in Fitzrovia amid the silent luxury, the memory of this raucous setting would sustain me until I could return to it. My eyes were drawn back to Willa. She was watching for someone, too. Her head swivelled in the direction of the door every time it opened and let in a blast of cold air, but each hopeful look was met with disappointment before she rejoined her friends' conversation with a frown.

It had been the best part of an hour when at last she got up and came over to the bar. She wriggled her way in between two men already waiting and said something saucy when they complained. This was a Willa I didn't see often. If I challenged her, she'd agree with Jos that she was more than capable of looking out for herself. While I didn't doubt she had all the smarts, she was still a child in many ways, and as she raised her glass in thanks to the man who'd bought her drink, I felt more than a little troubled. I called out her name and she stilled. Would she pretend she hadn't heard me? No. She wasn't pleased to see me, but she walked over and when the man beside me gave up his seat for her she hauled herself up on it.

'What are you doing here?'

'Don't be like that with me, Willa. I'll be away by tomorrow lunchtime and I didn't want to leave before we'd had a chance to speak.'

'You said plenty earlier. Couldn't you have waited until the morning?'

Not likely. She'd taken to having a Sunday lie-in and, from what I could see, she'd definitely be in need of one tomorrow. Already her eyes were glazed and I doubted she had any thoughts of getting in before midnight.

'Say what you have to say, then,' she said impatiently. 'I want to get back to my friends.'

'You could introduce me. Maybe I could have a drink with you all before I go?'

She gave an unkind laugh. 'I don't think so. I'm having to work to get back in with them myself without foisting you on them.'

Coming back hadn't been easy for Willa either. The local girls didn't know what state she'd been in when she returned, but there were rumours about what she'd had to do to support herself while she'd been buffeted by the waves of her grief. How close she'd come to drowning even I didn't truly know, but I saw how some of my patients lived and, while I did not judge them, I was pre-pared to do much to ensure my sister had a different life.

'Let me go, won't you, Hester. I'll get up before you go to Tall Trees, I promise.'

I gave a nod and she weaved away, skirting around tables and patrons, her drink sloshing but never spilling. She'd asked me to wait until tomorrow to pick up our conversa-tion. It was the right thing to do, with her already tipsy and me on the way, unaccustomed to drink since I'd fallen pregnant. Regardless, after a few minutes I got up and fol-lowed her.

Maybe it was because I was older or had lost the knack of it, but my route across the pub was longer than hers, more circuitous, and Willa had already ensconced herself in the midst of her friends by the time I reached her corner table. There was no chance of talking to her without involving the whole group in our business and so I perched on the edge of their circle, sipping at my perry and looking for my opening.

'You're Willa's older sister, aren't you?'

I turned to the girl on my left. I'd not really noticed her when I sat down. 'That's right.'

'You don't remember me, do you?'

I looked a little closer and realised I did. 'Maudie Clarke,' I exclaimed. 'Gosh, I haven't seen you since . . .'

I racked my brain and remembered I'd been with Mama when Maudie's own mother had delivered her ninth child.

'Your sister's very popular,' she said.

'You work with her at the factory?'

'Sort of, but I do the piecework,' Maudie paused, before adding guiltily, 'She gets on very well with Mr Rowland.'

It was the second warning I'd been given about Willa this evening. The first from Sal and now Maudie. Neither of them meant any malice, and it told me that I was right to fear for her.

'Do they spend much time together?'

'I've seen him call her to his office once or twice; often he gives her a ride home in his carriage.'

I'd seen that for myself, of course, and knew it hadn't been the first time. Since I'd moved into Tall Trees there was no way I could put a stop to it.

'If it was one of the fellows who works alongside us, I'd

say they were walking out, but a man like Rowland wouldn't walk out with one of us.'

Of course he wouldn't, but that didn't mean he couldn't ruin a girl all the same.

'Thanks, Maudie,' I said, getting to my feet. The knowledge that Willa had lied to my face had robbed me of the heart to speak to her here. Before I returned to Tall Trees, we'd need to have it out though, and in the meantime I'd have to think of how best to broach it with her. She was volatile. I didn't want to risk losing her completely.

XV

Groaning and moaning

I trudged back towards the cottage feeling out of sorts, the perry swirling uncomfortably in my stomach. Mixed up with my worry for Willa, it was a sickening brew and I leaned over the bridge of the canal, waiting for the nausea to pass. I'd have to do my best to make sure Willa didn't know it was Maudie that had spoken to me, but I could have no doubt now that there was something happening between my sister and Rowland Cherville. Poor Willa. A child all along, however grown up she thought she was. As offhand as she liked to appear, I worried Rowland had become her everything, but to him she would only ever be a bit of fun. Please God he hadn't infected her.

Jos was polishing his boots at the kitchen table when I got in. 'Did you catch up with her?' He'd probably known before I did that I'd headed out to speak to Willa.

'Sort of. We talked a little. Not properly.'

'Why the long face, if you didn't row?'

'She lied to me, Jos. I point-blank asked her about Rowland Cherville tonight, and she said she hadn't spoken to him in a month, yet one of her friends said she was practically stepping out with him, only . . .'

'He wouldn't see it like that.'

'Exactly.'

I sank into the chair opposite Jos. He looked as worried as I did, but there was an underlying exasperation, too. 'I don't want us to fall out, not over Willa, but . . .' he paused to choose his words carefully. 'You must see what bad news she is. Won't you think of . . .'

The look on my face stopped him from continuing but he'd already said more than enough.

'You want her gone – is that it?'

Even to voice it felt like a betrayal, worse still was when my husband said simply, 'Yes.'

It was the first time he'd admitted it so openly.

'You know I can't do that.'

Jos put down the boots and reached across the table for my hand, holding it fast when I would have shaken him off. Rarely did he look so serious and I fought back the urge to scream or shout or sing, anything to block out the hard truths he'd bitten back for so long.

'I know that she's coming between us, that she's bringing you down. Always you give her the benefit of the doubt, but I can see how it affects you.. Can you blame me for wanting her gone when I see how she hurts you?'

'It's not her fault,' I whispered into the table, unwilling to look into his eyes for fear of what I might find there. As a man, he didn't understand the bond between sisters, but it wasn't only that. I'd made a promise.

Mama's face had been sheened with sweat, the beads standing proud against her dark skin. I'd pressed a damp flannel to her neck and forehead, yet still her body burned.

'Take this,' I urged, proffering a spoonful of tonic, but she twisted away in refusal. 'You can't give up.'

'This is one bind I won't escape. No, Hester, no tears,' she said, and I made a determined effort to swallow them back, even to smile.

'Let me make you comfortable at least.'

I smoothed the covers of the narrow bed and moved to the window to pull back the curtains. Silvery moonlight burnished the room and I cracked open the sash to let the cool evening breeze off the canal blow in. There, that was better, and now when she called out to me I was composed.

'Sit with me. In the time I have left, I must tell you things, but first I need you to make me a promise.'

The speech, delivered in short huffing breaths, had weakened her, still Mama's grip was surprisingly strong when I sat in the chair at her bedside and she took my hand.

'Will you promise me, daughter?'

'Anything.'

'Your sister. I need you to take care of her.'

'Of course I will. Jos and I are only round the corner.'

'No, Hester. You're not understanding me,' Mama said, and the intensity in her eyes frightened me. I wished I could tell her there was no need for this talk, that she would grow old to look after Willa herself, but it wouldn't be long now.

'Mama, I promise you. Willa will be my first concern,' I vowed, but while she lay back on the pillow she wasn't wholly pacified, and continued to mutter to herself.

'Take care, she's not cautious. She needs to be more cautious.'

It was true enough. If there was trouble going, Willa was certain to find it, but she was sixteen now and if she hadn't been of an age to grow out of it, Mama's death would give her no choice in the matter.

'Take care of yourself, too, Hester, won't you.'

I nodded, my voice choked up with tears, and another fit of coughing seized her, wracking her body with its violence. There was nothing I could do except watch. All my herbs, all my ointments, they were powerless against the disease that would soon claim her, a flu caught from one of her patients, and I'd never felt more useless. When the fit had passed and she was quiet once more, I sat on the bed and drew up my legs to lie back beside her.

'Do you remember when we used to sleep like this?' She was too weak to answer, but I knew she did. In those days after we'd learned that Father had died at sea, I'd crawled into her bed every night and clung to her. 'That lullaby you sang to me – I know the tune, I wish I could think of the words,' I said.

I cuddled into her side, leaning my head on her shoulder, humming softly, and I must have dozed for I woke to the sound of footsteps making their way down the passage before Willa poked her head around the door.

'Come in and see her,' I said as my sister hesitated on the threshold.

'She's sleeping. I can come back later?'

'It has to be now.'

'Really? It's that bad.'

'Yes, love,' I said gently. She knew herself, really, but all along she'd done her best to ignore the idea that what Mama had was serious. I hadn't blamed her. It had even given me hope on those days when Mama had been at her worst – that time was past, however. Willa stepped into the room, but one glance at Mama sent her away from the bed. I joined her at the window, slipping a comforting arm around her shoulder, and she sniffed, wiping the back of her hand across her nose.

'Try not to take on, Willa. Just think: soon she won't feel any pain. You want that for her, don't you?'

I felt her nod against my shoulder, but she carried on crying for after a while I could feel the wet of her tears as they soaked through the cotton of my dress.

'Come on, you don't want her to see you like this.'

With an effort, Willa stopped and pulled out a grubby handkerchief to wipe her face, properly this time.

'There, that's better.'

'Should we stay with her?'

'Yes, I think she'd like that,' I said.

We sat on either side of the bed, listening to Mama's laboured breathing. Around midnight, Willa's head began to nod and soon she was dozing. Though my own eyes ached with tiredness, I was determined to keep watch. I heard the clock strike for two o'clock in the morning. It must have been between three and four that I succumbed to sleep, for the next thing I knew the light of daybreak was shining through the open curtains. Opposite me, Willa lay with her head on her arms.

Mama's hand was still in mine, and the fingers had already begun to stiffen. I had held on as tight as I could but still she'd slipped away from me. As the light brightened and Willa slept on, I went to the kitchen, and the drawer where I knew I'd find a black cloth. Carefully, I draped it over the mirror by the front door. She'd never been one to speak of the past, but I knew this world had been cruel to Mama. I wouldn't run the risk that her soul could be trapped here.

It was after the funeral when the landlord called in for the rent that Willa had disappeared.

At first I didn't recognise the sound that had woken me. It wasn't Jos, who slept deeply, his chest rising and falling evenly, though his face wore a frown that told of the worries we shared. I plumped up my pillow and rolled over. Soon I would have to leave for Tall Trees. In the five nights I'd spent there, I'd never slept well – there was something in that house that prevented me from achieving peace – but before I could drift away, the sound came again, followed by a low sobbing, and there was no longer any mistaking it. Willa.

I found her in the kitchen, crouching on the floor, her arms cradled around the metal pail we used to fetch water from the pump. She looked up at me, her eyes rimmed with red, but retching overtook her before she could speak. I knelt at her side, rubbing her back and soothing her. When she'd brought up the last of the alcohol, she shook off my arm and sat back, pale and spent. Her pretty green dress was crumpled and flecks of vomit had stained the bodice. Tears streaked through the rouge on her cheeks and I ached at how hard she was trying to be a woman when in many ways she was still so very young.

'You're going to say it serves me right, aren't you,' she said, wiping her sleeve across her mouth.

'I don't want to fight, not when you're unwell.'

'I'm tired, Hes,' she said. How long had it been since she'd called me that? I shuffled across and put my arm around her shoulder and she leaned into me.

'I know you've been seeing Rowland Cherville still.'

She stiffened as though she might deny it, then she sighed and the fight went out of her. 'He says he loves me. Why can't you let me be happy?'

If there had been even the slightest chance the feelings he'd told her of were genuine, in that moment I would have agreed she should pursue him, but it wasn't true. In her heart Willa knew it, too.

'This job I have with his father. It's not just nursing. There's more to it and he's offered me a great deal of money – it will be enough for us all to move away. To start again.'

'I'm already on my second start – that's what you said when I came to live with you.'

'This time we'll do it together.'

'Is that what Jos wants?'

Unerringly she'd struck on the crux of the row we'd had when I got in from the Hind. I'd gone straight to bed leaving it unresolved and so I lied.

'He loves you as I do; the pair of you just need to learn

to rub along together. It's not been too bad this last week, has it?'

Willa shrugged. 'I suppose not.' She lay down in my lap and I eased the pins out of her hair, wishing I didn't have to leave her.

XVI

A model of diligence and duty

From my very first day at Tall Trees, I'd been struck by its malignant air and just one night at the cottage made it harder than ever to return. It was because of what its panelled walls had borne witness to all those years before. Dite, Nyx and Artemis. For years they had patiently plotted their escape. When they'd risked their lives to flee, it felt absurd that I'd come back voluntarily.

"How was it?' Jenny said as I let myself in through the kitchen door on Sunday evening.

When I didn't answer straight away, she looked up from her darning and saw the dejection on my face. 'Not a great visit, then?'

It should have been: freedom from Tall Trees and good

news to share, only it hadn't taken long for things to turn sour. If only I'd made it up with Jos before I left. I couldn't think of that now though. Instead I willed myself to remember lying in his arms after I'd told him of the baby, and of stroking Willa's hair at dawn.

'Tell me what's been happening here,' I said. 'How's Cherville?'

'He's calmed down a bit since Friday, thankfully, but when Margaret tried to sit with him this morning he said he was busy and sent her away. It's made her very low and I'm sorry to say she blames you for it.'

I had no doubt of that, nor that her intention in sitting with Cherville had been to whisper bile about me in his ear.

'I've got some soup for you on the hob if you want it. A lovely pea and ham?'

I sat down at the table while Jenny went to the range and ladled a bright green concoction into a bowl. She placed it in front of me with a hunk of warm bread. 'There, get some of that down you.'

It might have been nectar, but I could barely taste it. It settled on my stomach, adding to the weight of being back at Tall Trees. I forced down another mouthful and another; until, seeing that I meant to eat it all, Jenny resumed her darning. The sound she made as she drew out each stitch and knocked her arm against the table soothed me, but my travails for the evening were not over.

'You're back with us, I see,' Margaret said as she

swept into the room, and didn't she just hate it. I imagined her secretly praying I wouldn't return. All she saw in me was someone vying against her to be Cherville's favourite. For me there was so much more at stake – it was why, however hard I found it here, I could never walk away.

'He's comfortable, by the way,' Margaret said pointedly. 'I've been with him for much of these last two days.'

'I'm surprised you could spare the time – thank you for telling me,' I said, and she bristled before leaving the room with a flounce. I waited until I knew she'd be out of earshot before I said to Jenny, 'So much for absence making the heart grow fonder.'

'There's not many she likes, to be fair. Only the master and his son.'

'Rowland,' I said grimly, wondering if even now Willa was with him.

'You never did tell me exactly how it was you knew him,' Jenny said.

'My sister works at the Cherville factory – he's paid her more attention than I'd like.'

Jenny nodded sagely. 'I see. He is handsome, though.'

'Not to me,' I said, forcefully enough for Jenny to look up from her darning. 'He has the polish that comes from being rich, but underneath he's loathsome.'

Her face fell at my truculence and I added, 'Sorry. You were only saying. I didn't mean to be sharp.'

'I don't care about that. It's just he's due to come back tonight.'

Poor Jenny, she was only the messenger, but the thought of Rowland at Tall Trees was the final straw. The prospect of living in the same house as him had almost stopped me from taking the job in the first place. There was no way he wouldn't recognise me as the woman who'd challenged him, spoilt his fun for the evening. His smirking face loomed before my mind's eye. He wouldn't care that I was here, would he? Chances were I was one of many mothers or sisters who'd tried to protect their own from his attentions. To him it was all just a game, and I pushed away my bowl knowing there was no way I'd be able to eat any more now.

'You going to get an early night?'

'I need to check on Cherville first, but yes, I think I'd better. Thanks for the soup. I'll be more cheerful tomorrow, I promise.'

I lumbered up the stairs, my limbs feeling leaden. All I wanted was sleep and yet I had to see to Cherville and, if I could, extract some of the poison Margaret would have whispered of me to him.

He was sitting up in bed when I came into the room.

'Reeves, there you are,' he greeted me.

'You seem well, sir,' I said, though in truth his colour remained high and his hands still trembled.

'It pains me to admit that Bright was right after all. It is paying Aphrodite that has made me feel better. The voices have quieted. If I can find Nyx, perhaps they will recede altogether.'

'What of the slaves on your plantation?'

'Yes, Bright came by yesterday evening to urge their cause. When the Abolition Act comes into effect next year, they'll be redesignated apprentices. What more could they want than that?'

So Mr Bright had failed as I'd suspected he would and Cherville still hadn't grasped the full extent of his guilt. How alone I felt and things were only getting worse.

'Jenny tells me your son is coming home later tonight?'

'So I am lead to believe,' Cherville said, and his face hardened. If Jenny hadn't already explained there was little love lost between the two men, I'd have known it now.

'You have continued to take the draught I made for you?'

'I have, but do you know I don't think that I'll be needing it for much longer.'

'Very good, sir. In which case, I'll bid you goodnight.'

I'd only been back at Tall Trees two nights before it felt as though I'd never left. Walking the long corridors from Cherville's room to the kitchen to the servants' quarters and back again, the wide-open spaces of the canal receded, my prospect reduced to perpetual gloom, and the smell of wood polish. Jenny, too, seemed down. We were sat together on Tuesday afternoon, she at her sewing, me weighing out herbs, when Margaret waltzed in. The dampening effect of Rowland's return had produced the opposite feeling in her. I even thought I'd seen her smile.

'Reeves, there you are; I've been looking for you.' I braced myself for criticism, but none came. Instead she said, 'I have planned a dinner to celebrate Mr Rowland's return, and you will help me serve.'

She was gone before I could protest. So far, I'd managed to avoid Rowland. Now I'd be face to face with him.

'It won't be that bad,' Jenny said. 'She's roped me in before. All I had to do was put the plates down and go.'

'I suppose I can do that much,' I said.

The food came from a nearby restaurant, Jenny's hearty soups deemed not fine enough for such an occasion. Jenny unwrapped the packages and my stomach shifted at the strong smells.

'You look a bit peaky, are you going to be all right?'

'It'll pass. I'll be glad when this is over, though.'

'An hour, I reckon, no more. They hate each other, don't forget, so it's unlikely they'll tarry.'

Cherville took all his meals on a tray in his bedroom so there'd been no call for me to go to the dining room since arriving at Tall Trees. It was a large high-ceilinged room just off the entrance hall. Inside was cold – I assumed Margaret had attempted to air it, but it still had the stale smell of abandonment, overlaid with the sickliness of rose petals. Cherville was seated at the head of the table, the loose-fitting tailcoat he wore showing how his illness had wasted him. To the left of him Rowland leaned back in his chair, looking as though he'd rather be elsewhere. Seeing them together the resemblance was clear. Were those pale blue eyes the only thing the son had inherited from the father or was there something more? Now he was home, I hoped I'd get to the bottom of whether he carried the pox as I feared.

Margaret attended to Rowland first, placing a veal cutlet before him. I followed behind with a dish of vegetables, holding my breath as I set it down to his left. He didn't look up and I felt relieved. I wouldn't be able to avoid him forever – not even Tall Trees was big enough for that – but the longer it took for him to recall who I was, the better.

I was almost at the door when Margaret caught me by the arm. 'Not so fast,' she muttered. 'Go and stand behind Mr Cherville and be ready to respond if he asks for anything.'

I took up my place behind Cherville's chair. They'd barely finished their first course before my back began to ache. Rowland kept darting quick glances in my direction, a frown on his face as he tried to recall where he knew me from. His smirk told me when he'd got it and I cast my eyes to the floor, but not before I saw him wink. His father must have noticed, for he said, 'I hope you've not let your-self get distracted at the factory?'

'Not at all, Father. I have been a model of diligence and duty.'

False innocence dripped from his voice. It reminded me of how Willa had answered when I'd asked her a similar question. I'd learned better than to believe either of them.

'Profits are down,' Cherville pointed out, and when next Rowland spoke he sounded sulky.

'Customers are worried about their income, Father. I can't help it if the government wants to steal away their property.'

'You know as well as I that compensation has been promised. We'll do better from it, too. There's not so much money in sugar any more, mahogany neither.'

'Railway investments are the talk at the club. When the compensation comes through, that's where it should go. We need to steward our capital carefully. It's not a time to be giving money away.'

Was he talking about Cherville's plans to gift money to Nyx and Aphrodite? That's what his father thought for he said sharply, 'My money's my own to do what I want with, boy,' and the rest of the meal was conducted in silence save for the scraping of their knives on the crockery.

'That went on longer than I thought,' Jenny said when I limped into the kitchen near two hours after I'd left her.

'And I felt every second of it,' I said, sinking into a

chair. 'You were right to say there's no love lost between them.'

'I kept this back for us,' Jenny said, producing a plate of what they'd had upstairs.

'You have it. I don't think I'm hungry.'

'All right, then. I hope you're not sickening for something, though?'

I shook my head, knowing it was the baby and wanting to keep it to myself. It was almost the first thing Jenny had said to me, that Margaret wouldn't stand for married staff. If she knew I was pregnant to boot, it would be the excuse to get rid of me that she'd been looking for.

'Bedtime, I think,' Jenny said, when she'd scooped the last of the gravy on to the flat of her knife and licked it off. 'You turning in, too?'

'Once I've checked on Cherville, I'll be right behind you.'

Cherville stood by the fire in his room, still in his tail-coat, hands clasped behind his back. I sensed he'd been pacing.

'What do you make of my son?' he said.

'You're very alike in looks, sir.'

'Yet not in temperament. I fear the boy is a bounder. His mother spoiled him as a child and this is the effect of it. I thought a stint at the factory would help him, but I've seen the books. His figures do not reconcile and now I suspect he is imposing on my staff.'

Did that mean Willa or some other poor girl? I wouldn't put it past a man like Rowland Cherville to be stringing along two or even three women at a time. It was a timely reminder of why I was here. To earn the money I needed to get her away from him.

'Is there anything you require before I go to bed?'

'I left my book on the chair in the library – will you fetch it for me?'

It wasn't as though I was his servant, but I bobbed my head and made my way downstairs. Book in hand, I was ready to return when I heard Margaret's voice in the entrance hall. I shrank back, not wanting to be seen, and was rewarded for my caution when I heard Rowland answer her enquiry after his evening.

'What are you doing up?' he asked.

'I wanted to see to the table linens before I went to bed. I wouldn't have you thinking our standards have slipped since you moved into your club.'

I couldn't make out Rowland's response and so I edged a little closer to the library door. Now I could see them both: Margaret at the foot of the entrance-hall stairs and Rowland a few treads up, one hand resting on the banister, the other clutching a tumbler of whiskey.

'You will have been pleased to see your father, sir,' Margaret said.

'I've been in no rush to spend time with the old coot, I assure you. Be that as it may, I think it well that I am here.

That doctoress, or whatever she calls herself, looks every bit the troublemaker you described.'

'She's had a great deal of influence over your father since she arrived.'

'He seems to think her potions are doing him good.'

'The master has said as much to me. She prepares an awful lot of draughts for him – who can say exactly what's in them?'

It took all my self-control not to burst out and confront her. She didn't like that having hired me Cherville relied on her less. I could understand that, but to as good as accuse me of poisoning him? That was a hanging offence and I felt a stab of fear in my gut. If only I could see Rowland Cherville's face, I'd get a sense of whether he was taken in by it. She wasn't finished yet.

'I don't like to cast aspersions on a man of the church, but if I didn't know better I'd say she was in league with Mr Bright over the business of the master's atonement. They're devious, her sort. What's to say she hasn't taken in the reverend, too?'

Poor Mr Bright. Even God could not save him from Margaret's spite. He could vouch for me, though. If it ever came to that.

Rowland returned to climbing the stairs. The way he weaved suggested he'd been at the bottle since dinner, and Margaret called out her final shot. 'Perhaps you might speak to your father in the morning, sir? Tell him your misgivings?'

Rowland rubbed at his face. 'I will. Between them, she and that meddling priest would have we Chervilles in the dirt and every sambo from here to Timbuktu dripping with gold and diamonds. Do you think I could persuade the old man to get rid of her?'

'You know the master, he must have his way.' She spoke as fondly as if Cherville were a wilful child.

Rowland was less sanguine and he no longer sounded tired or drunk. 'Tomorrow I will try a different tack with my father. You heard him talk tonight of doing what he wanted with his own money. For now, though, I must get changed for there's some business I would attend to at the club. Until we speak on this again it's imperative you remain vigilant.'

'You can count on me, sir.'

She craned her head in such a way that I could tell she was watching him up the stairs. A moment later, she turned and I caught the satisfied look upon her face as she slipped through the hidden door, towards her room beside the kitchen. Might it be that she'd sent for Rowland? A risky move if so, knowing how little he and her beloved master got along. It was sobering to consider how much she wanted me gone, how far she was prepared to go. If only she knew I'd leave without a backwards glance were it not for the money. That's what it came down to. In the days ahead I'd have to be even more careful to keep my guard up. Could I tell Cherville that his son and his servant were working against him? It wouldn't hurt me to pre-empt whatever calumnies the pair of them might have in store for me, but by the time I got back to his room he was sleeping. I placed the book on his bedside table, disappointed not to be able to speak to him. I'd have to take my chance tomorrow morning, early as I dared, and before Rowland could beat me to it.

XVII

Curtains drawn

'Hester, I need you.'

I sat up, remembering only just in time not to catch my head on the sloped ceiling. Moonlight shone in from the window, and through my sleep-fuddled haze I realised it was Jenny. Clambering out of bed, I crossed the room and opened the door. There she stood, fully dressed and twitching with anxiety. The worry in her eyes cut through my tiredness and I pulled her inside, shutting the door behind us.

'What time is it?'

'Past one o'clock.'

'As early as that? Whatever's the matter?' I said, shivering a little in the thin shift I wore to bed.

'It's the master. I woke and realised that when I came

straight up after dinner I forgot to bank his fire. I knew I couldn't leave it to the morning and so I thought I'd creep in and fix it. I was on my knees by the fireplace when this sound came out of him, as if he were possessed.'

Jenny may have sounded dramatic but she was deadly serious, and, ever the doctoress, I pulled on my uniform.

'What happened then?'

'I came as fast as I could to find you.'

'You didn't rouse Margaret?'

With her bedroom just a few doors down the corridor from Cherville's, she was the obvious choice so it was a relief when Jenny said, 'I thought you'd want to deal with it yourself, first. Did I do right?'

'You did. No need to get her involved. With any luck, it's just one of his bad dreams and he'll be fine. Let's go to him,' and picking up my bag we left the room.

I set off down the stairs to the second floor, Jenny trailing behind me. In the night-time quiet I couldn't help but flinch at every creak of the stairs, but mercifully our bare feet made little sound. When we opened the door out on to the main landing, I turned to Jenny with a finger to my lips to impress on her the need for silence. The worst thing would be if Margaret were to waken, and if Cherville was groaning as loud as Jenny said it was fortunate she hadn't already. We tiptoed past her closed door and down towards Cherville's room at the far end of the corridor. The closer we got the more Jenny hung back.

'What's wrong?'

'Those sounds he made, they scared me.'

Whatever groaning and moaning she'd heard, it was quiet as the grave now. Although that was not necessarily a good sign. Sound meant pain, but death was silent. If he'd died, what then? I couldn't even entertain it. If Jenny wanted to stay out here, let her. I didn't have time to argue.

There were no obvious signs of anything amiss when I entered Cherville's bedroom. The canopy bed, with curtains drawn, and a blanket folded over the chair were just as I'd left them when I'd brought Cherville his book a few hours earlier. The only difference was a bucket of twigs upended by the fireplace. Jenny must have knocked them over in her haste to come and fetch me. I stood very still, ears attentive, not even the faintest murmurings were coming from behind the brocade curtains. I poked my head back out into the corridor.

'It's safe, Jenny,' I whispered. In she came hesitantly, and though she closed the door she kept her hand on the knob so she could make a quick exit should she need to. No matter that talk of the Cherville curse was rubbish, it had got to her.

'See, he's just sleeping, a bad dream, and you were here at the wrong moment.'

'My little brother used to have bad dreams. They didn't sound nothing like that.'

I shrugged, knowing I couldn't persuade her.

'Well, if he starts up again don't scream,' I said. 'I'm going to pull back the curtains so it might disturb him.'

She looked down at the floor as I gently pulled back the hangings.

'Oh my God.'

'What is it?' she said.

I stepped back so she could see for herself, and she paled.

'He's not here,' she breathed, and we looked at each in horror.

Sitting room, dressing room, study. We searched each room on the second floor bar Margaret's, but Cherville was not to be found. We returned to his room, hoping that somehow he'd be there. The bed remained empty and I touched my hand to the wrinkled sheets and found them cold.

'How long was it before you woke me?'

'I came straight to you, so as long as it took me to climb the back stairs,' Jenny said.

'You have to help me find him. Please.'

We started on the ground floor. The entrance hallway with its ever-present scent of roses showed no sign of life. It was icy cold, but the gas lamp shone all the same.

'Do you leave the lights on every night?'

'Not as a rule, Margaret must've done it.'

'Of course,' I said remembering what I had overheard from the shadows earlier. 'Rowland was planning to go out.'

'I thought you said he'd already had a skinful, at dinner?'

'He mentioned having business at his club. If he has to be there so much I don't know why he bothered moving back to Tall Trees,' I said but it wasn't true. He was here because Margaret had roused his suspicions of me. 'He must have been out late before like this. Do you have you any idea when he'll return?'

Jenny wrung her apron as she so often did when she was nervous.

'I've known him roll in at three, even four o'clock. We'll just have to make sure we find the master before he's back.'

It had been enough to think that Margaret might wake at any moment and demand to know what we were about. Now we had to be wary of Rowland, too.

'Think, Jenny, where else could Cherville be?' I said. He hadn't been on the fourth floor, I couldn't imagine he'd gone to his son's rooms on the first or down into the kitchen. He wasn't here in any of the reception rooms. That left only the third floor. Involuntarily, I looked up the stairwell into the darkness above and shivered.

'What's on the third floor, Jenny? Jenny,' I called when she didn't answer. I turned, my eyes widening to see her standing by the open door.

'The bolts were unlocked. I think he's got outside,' she said.

XVIII

Cherville mahogany

The gas lamps that lined the square had been extinguished so all was dark. Quiet, too, save for the faintest rumble of carriages in the distance. The wind was biting and I shuffled from foot to foot to keep the cold from going through me. Thankfully I'd had the presence of mind to pluck my coat from the stand in the entrance hall as we came out. Would Cherville have done the same? It seemed unlikely and I wondered how long he would cope with no protection from the elements.

'Which direction would he go in?' I asked Jenny.

No reason she should know any better than I did, but the feeling of panic that I'd managed to hold in as we searched on the second floor, and then again when we'd got downstairs, could no longer be contained. Right was Warren

Street and beyond that the King's Cross Road. Cherville wouldn't fare well if he'd gone that way. Left was the back streets that led to Oxford Circus. A little better. Please God he hadn't turned off; it might still be possible to see him.

'You go that way, Jenny,' I said, indicating right. 'I'll go left.'

'How long should I look for?'

'If you haven't found him after ten minutes, you must come back and I'll have to explain what has happened.'

'You'll tell Mr Rowland when he gets in? Or Margaret?'

It was a toss-up which of them disliked me more, but maybe, just maybe, Margaret might have some sort of workers' solidarity. Jenny's eyes were round in her pale face, waiting for my answer. I understood why. Confessing I'd lost my patient, whether to son or housekeeper, could only result in my dismissal. The reckless thought re-entered my mind that maybe losing this poisoned chalice of a job was for the best, but despite what Cherville had done in his past, the nurse in me didn't like to think of him out in these cold streets.

'We'll find him, don't worry,' Jenny said.

'You're a good girl. Now go, and be back here in ten minutes.'

I walked swiftly down Grafton Way, straining my eyes to see in the dark. The lamps had been put out here, too, but if he was in his white nightshirt, surely I would see him: it was unlikely that he would have stopped to get fully dressed if he was in the midst of some form of night terror. A carriage trundled towards me. I was about to press myself back into the shadows when it turned and headed for the main road. I peered into every front garden that I passed, down every connecting road, but there was no sign of Gervaise Cherville. The only living thing I encountered was a stray fox that I disturbed as it hunted for scraps, and it wasn't long before I gave up fearing the search was futile.

I was waiting outside the house when Jenny returned and I saw by the dejected set of her shoulders that she'd had no better luck. He could be anywhere by now.

'I'll go in and wake Margaret,' I said. 'You stand here and keep a lookout just in case he comes back.'

I walked up the main staircase towards the second floor. If I was on the verge of being sacked, I might as well go where I liked. Margaret's door was still shut. I raised my hand to knock before thinking better of it. We hadn't searched the third floor. Wasn't it worth one final check? Quietly, I backed away. Likely I was fooling myself, but if I was going to bring down on my head the trouble that would come when the housekeeper knew what had happened, I wanted to be sure I'd tried everything else first.

The third floor was all in darkness, save for a shaft of moonlight that came through an uncurtained window. There was a musty smell and the cobwebs that arced from one corner to the other showed it had been beyond the reach of Jenny's otherwise diligent mop and broom. I spotted a gas lamp on an occasional table and was relieved when it flickered into life. I held it up and its weak beams showed that the layout mirrored Gervaise Cherville's east wing: one long corridor with several doors off it. The walls were painted the pale sky-coloured shade I'd come to think of as Cherville blue. Just another corridor. Nothing to fear, I reminded myself, but the heavy unsettling feeling that pervaded Tall Trees was stronger than ever here. I'd be glad to return to the more familiar parts of the house. Setting off I touched my hand to the first door. It remained steadfastly closed and the second one the same. Margaret would have the keys, not that I could ever ask for them. In any case, I reasoned, if the rooms were locked, it meant that Cherville wasn't in them. Out on the landing the grandfather clock struck and made me jump. I paused to count the chimes. Two o'clock and Cherville had been missing around an hour.

It was the fourth door that yielded to my push. For a moment, I hovered on the threshold, before steeling myself to enter. *You've come this far*, I encouraged myself. Once inside, I called out as loud as I dared, 'Mr Cherville, it's Reeves. Are you there?' I'd told Jenny to tread carefully for fear of startling him, but the time for gentle handling had passed.

The room was a bedroom, or had been once. There was little time to see as the lamp I held sputtered and gave out, leaving me in darkness. As I walked further in, the shapes of the furniture, shrouded in heavy dust sheets, loomed out at me. I skirted around them, not sure where their edges began, until my eyes became more accustomed to the lack of light. That must be the bed – easy enough to make out, after all. A low oblong was probably a chaise, but there was no sign of Gervaise Cherville. I was taking one final look around when Jenny called my name. she must've followed me back into the house.

'Hester, I've found him.'

Jenny pointed me to the next room along. She didn't need to, I could hear him for myself, keening like an animal in pain.

'Fetch a bowl of warm water and some towels, and I'll meet you at his bedroom,' I said. 'If our luck holds for one hour more we'll not be discovered.'

Jenny set off and I stepped into the room. At once the heaviness I'd felt out in the corridor doubled as though I'd finally arrived at its source. A stack of chairs wobbled ominously and I shot out a hand to prevent them from falling. What was this place? A storeroom of some sort? I took in more chairs, an occasional table, cabinets, drawers, piled up higgledy-piggledy and all made from the familiar mahogany. Gervaise Cherville cowered in the far corner, arms wrapped around his knees, rocking silently while the tears streamed down his cheeks. How he'd managed to get there without bringing the whole lot crashing down on his head was a mystery. How, too, I would manage to get him out before I sank under the weight of the atmosphere.

'Mr Cherville, it's Reeves come to help you,' I called. He didn't know me, so deep in his nightmare I doubted even shouting would wake him. I'd have to work this carefully, and I swallowed back the panic that surged inside me. *Get him upstairs, make sure he's wrapped up, go back to bed*, I muttered to myself. The first thing I needed to do, though, was get him warm for every few seconds he shook violently, so I unbuttoned my coat and draped it around his shoulders.

It was a tortuous journey back to Cherville's room, so slow I was convinced we couldn't make it before we were discovered, and yet we did, and I had just tucked Cherville in when Jenny appeared with the bowl of steaming water. I bathed his face and lay the hot flannel over his chest to bring his temperature up.

'That room he was in, what is it? I've never seen so much furniture.' What I really wanted to ask was if Jenny had felt its strangeness, the pressure in the air that was almost physical.

'It must be Spinks that put it there, but he wouldn't have done it without the master's say-so.'

'Or Margaret's,' I added, and Jenny nodded, her face clearing.

'Have you remembered something?' I said.

'A few months ago, Mr Cherville said he'd heard a noise coming from one of his cabinets. I thought it was woodworm or suchlike. There must have been three different craftsmen he ordered Margaret to call in to examine the furniture, but none of them could find anything wrong. I thought that would be the end of it, but the master insisted he could still hear the noise. One night there was a banging and scraping. I put on my shawl and went downstairs and found Mr Cherville in his bedroom. I was so tired I didn't notice what he'd done at first, but all the furniture had been pushed to the back wall. God knows how he managed it. You've seen he's not strong. Anyway, he wouldn't rest until it had been taken out. Seems strange to move it there, though.'

'The only place in the house that no one goes,' I murmured to myself. When I'd first seen how bare Cherville's bedroom was I'd assumed all but the essentials had been packed up and sent to the country house in advance of his arrival. Now it seemed he'd just wanted the items out of his sight, but tonight something had compelled him to seek them out.

Once Cherville was comfortable again, we made our way down the corridor towards the back stairs. I'd just opened the door when I thought I heard a creak and looked over my shoulder into the darkness.

'Did you hear that?' I whispered, grabbing Jenny's arm. For a long moment we stood still, hardly daring to breathe, but it was silent, and doubly careful now, we tiptoed back up to the servants' quarters.

XIX

Treatment for afflictions

Cherville glanced up warily when I went in to see him the next morning. The skin around his eyes sagged and he looked old and frail.

'How are you feeling after last night?'

'I remember little enough of it,' he said, so offhand I knew he was lying.

'The furniture you have stored on the third floor. Is that where you think the sounds you hear come from? Does it speak to you?'

'I am not mad. Whatever Rowland says, there's nothing wrong with my mind.'

I believed it. We had spoken several times since I'd arrived at Tall Trees and there had been nothing in any of our conversations that made me think he was not in full charge of his faculties. I had seen madmen and women. There were plenty of them in and around King's Cross, their wits scattered by the hardship they suffered. Cherville was not such a one.

'You have heard voices, all the same?'

'Not voices so much as . . .' He paused. 'Crying, that's what I hear, a wailing. I've told you that already.'

It was just as Jenny said, and my mind returned to our very first meeting when he had pressed the wooden ball of mahogany into my hand and asked me what I thought of it. When he'd explained he wanted my help to track down the women he'd enslaved, I knew he'd hired me because I was Black. He must have thought my colour would enable me to detect the sounds within the wood, too.

'Are you saying what you hear is something akin to the effect you get when you hold a seashell to your ear?' I said.

There had never been much time or money in my youth for day trips. Maybe it was the rarity of them that made this one stand out in my mind: me and Mama on the Kent Straits with Willa. I'd cried when it was time to go home. That's when Mama picked up a seashell from the ground. Brown and barnacled, it looked rough and felt scratchy.

'Go on, Hester, take it,' she said.

I put my hands behind my back so I wouldn't have to, but she only laughed and tucked it in the front pocket of my dress. Back home at King's Cross, I forgot all about it, and then one day I stuffed my hands in my pockets and felt it there. Turning it over, I remembered what Mama had said: that if I held it to my ear it would take me back to that day at the seaside. Faint at first, the smooth whooshing sound of the sea sharpened when I closed my eyes. I thought I could even hear the orange-billed gulls cawing. The sounds conjured pictures in my mind. Willa laughing as the ice she held melted and dribbled down between her fingers, the white foam waves that had chased me up the beach, and Mama sitting on the pebbles, watching on fondly as we paddled. All that from the whispering of one tiny shell.

Cherville was quiet, caught up in thoughts of his own.

'When you hear the wood crying, is there some place it takes you?' I prompted.

He shook his head, not for no – it was too forceful for that – more as if he were trying to free himself.

'Does it take you to where the wood was cut?'

He shook his head again, vehemently. 'It takes me to the third floor.'

To the room he'd cowered in, I thought, but there was no need to probe him because he was speaking of his own accord.

'Margaret suggested I arrange for it all to be removed – tables, chairs, ornaments, the lot – but when it came to throwing it out, I couldn't. These items were sent to me by my father from Honduras; all were made from Cherville mahogany. Maybe I should have let Margaret do as she would for the sounds still plague me. At first, I thought it was the curse. No doubt the kitchen maid has spoken of it – how it has affected me, my son, even my grandson; generation after generation of Cherville men ruined. But then I complained to Bright and he told me it was because of the men and women I'd enslaved. Why then, even though I have recompensed the woman most grievously affected, do I still hear it, thrumming in my mind?'

Dare I say it was because he'd expressed regret for what happened without apologising? No – it was a realisation Mr Bright must help him to if he could not come to it himself.

'What about the men and women on your estate in Honduras?'

'You would hold me responsible for them, too? When I have never even set foot in the place? Bright is the same, with his tales of overseers and ropes. He brought me testimonies, drawings. I asked him, "Why should I look on these? I have wielded no weapons." Now I wonder if I must see them. If it is they that will bring me peace.'

'Should I fetch them for you?'

'They are long gone. It was years ago when he brought them to me. He was bolder then, though you wouldn't think it to look at him now. One of the foremost abolitionists.'

Cherville still spoke out loud, and when he said the name of his son it cut through my thoughts.

'What was that, sir?'

'I said that if I am to help the men and women on my

plantation, Rowland cannot know it. His conscience has not developed as mine has. I made the mistake of telling him of the cries that I was hearing and he brought in one of his friends. "Let's take a drive out to the country, Father," he says to me one afternoon. "My chum Lewis has a growing concern I'd like you to see."

'I probably shouldn't have gone along with it as far as I did, but his mother always said I misjudged him and I wanted to see if he was the man I feared I was. This "growing concern" was a crumbling pile – I can see you're not surprised to hear it – not one ounce of comfort, idiots in one room, imbeciles in another. "The patients tend the garden. You like gardening, don't you, Father," Rowland says to me. Talking to me louder and slower than he would a simpleton. "Why don't you stay a night or two, see how you find it?" he says, but I was wise to him. I knew if I stayed there, I'd never get out again, I'd be left to rot in my own excrement. He'll have to try harder than that if he wants to get early hands on his inheritance.'

I'd wondered what the root cause of the antipathy between father and son could be and now I knew. There were not many relationships that could overcome an attempted committal. I thought of the sort of place that Rowland Cherville had suggested for his father and tried not to shudder. Treatment for afflictions of the mind was getting better, but I could never understand the desire to take people from their families when they needed them more than ever, how those like Rowland Cherville let the threat of embarrassment triumph over the need for compassion. Or maybe it wasn't that at all and it was as Cherville said. He wanted access to his family's fortune.

'I'm sure your son is concerned for you, sir.'

'Don't you believe it. The sooner I'm gone, the sooner he will rejoice.'

He said it so matter-of-factly, as though it were perfectly natural for a child to want rid of their father. It was my chance to sow the seed that Margaret and Rowland between them were working against him, but something stopped me from ladling it on when he was still recovering from the night's events.

'Busted flush, that boy,' Cherville grumbled on. 'Wants to bring back the glory of the family, he tells me. How, I ask you, with no wife and no son? The Chervilles are finished.' He added under his breath, 'Perhaps that's no bad thing.'

'I don't want another night like that again,' Jenny said when I joined her in the kitchen for breakfast. There were large dark circles under her eyes and it reminded me that I must look just as haggard.

'He doesn't seem too much the worse for wear; I've just come from seeing him now.'

'I suppose that's the main thing. Can't say it didn't give me a fright, though.'

A long silence passed while we both considered what had happened, until a tap on the glass jolted us from our introspection. Willa's grinning face was at the kitchen door and I looked at her stupidly for a moment before gathering my wits.

'Who's that?' Jenny said, her face brightening with curiosity.

'It's my sister, let me deal with her.'

XX

Happy families

I opened the door a crack and slipped outside, holding it behind me.

'What are you doing here, Willa?'

'Is it wrong now to want to see your big sister?'

She seemed genuinely hurt and I felt a pang of guilt. I'd instantly assumed she'd turned up to see Rowland, perhaps I was mistaken. Irrepressible as ever, Willa rose to her tiptoes, trying to see over my shoulder and into the kitchen.

'Aren't you going to introduce me, then?'

I stood aside to let Willa in. Jenny, still finishing her breakfast, smiled at her broadly with a mischievous glint in her eye that told me she'd been earwigging. Willa made a slow circuit of the room, running her hands along the jars of flour and sugar. She tugged at the door of the larder and found it locked. It was on my lips to say she couldn't go down there, but then she moved towards the stairs that led up to the entrance hall.

'Is this the way to where the family live?'

She had her foot on the first tread.

'Let's go out to the gardens, Willa,' I said and, putting an arm around her shoulder, I steered her outside, knowing Jenny would keep a look out for me.

It was the first time I'd been to the gardens on the square since Jos had visited on the day I moved into Tall Trees. Then we'd been alone. Today a young woman played with a small child, catching him up when he would have run from her. He squealed in delight and she sat him gently on the ground, kneeling, with her hands up to play pat-a-cake. Soon that would be me and my daughter, and a smile rose to my lips at the thought of it. I felt Willa's eyes on me.

'How are you feeling, sis?' she said.

'Fine – shall we sit down?'

We walked over to the bench I'd shared with Jos. 'How come you're here, Willa?' I said.

She wrenched her eyes from the young woman and her child. 'I only came to see how you were doing. Anyone would think you didn't want me at Tall Trees the way you bundled me out.'

'I didn't want you to run into Rowland. He's the reason you're here, isn't he?'

Willa looked hurt. 'Don't be silly, Hes. I see him every day at work.'

'And what about after work?'

'Cooled on me, hasn't he. I would have given him up, though, anyway – seeing as you asked me to.' She held out a poorly wrapped package: no string, just brown paper scrunched around something small and soft. 'Open it, then.'

I folded it back to reveal a knitted bunny. She must've made it herself and unexpectedly I felt tears prick at the backs of my eyes.

'The reason I came over was to give you this. Jos told me your good news last night. When I said I wanted to congratulate you myself, he made me promise that I'd ask you not to be angry with him for spilling the beans.'

The stitches that made up the bunny were small and neat; she'd sewn on eyes and nose in black thread and I ran my fingers through its white fluffy tail.

'I'm glad you know. I wanted to tell you myself when I came home for the sabbath, but there wasn't a good time.'

'That was my fault, really,' Willa said, her tone contrite.

'Is it honestly all done with between you and Rowland?'

'I told you it was already. He was supposed to come to the Hind on Saturday, only he never showed, and yesterday when I went to his office he said he was too busy to see me. I know he's back home because the doorman at his club told me. You haven't been telling him to keep away from me, have you?'

'He's only been at Tall Trees since Sunday and I've barely seen him. I'm the nurse in his father's house. It wouldn't be my place.'

I kept my tone level, hating to see her down, but inside all I felt was relief. If Rowland had tired of her, that could only be a good thing.

'Is it really true what you said about him being diseased?'

'I wouldn't lie about something like that. There's no chance you could have caught it?'

She looked at the ground and I remembered how my doctoress ways made me overly direct sometimes.

'None at all. We've only ever had a little fumble,' she said and exclaimed in surprise when I embraced her tightly. 'You'll squash all the breath out of me.'

'When you've seen a disease like that up close, you know how awful it can be.'

'There are cures, though, aren't there?'

'Prevention is the only cure, I'm afraid. But there's no need for us to talk about it, is there.'

She shrugged and shook her head. 'We don't often talk, do we?'

It was true. I'd been so worried about scaring her off again that I was on eggshells around her, and often I was busy. There had been times she'd sidled over as I weighed ingredients for a tonic and I'd shooed her away. I'd been holding her at arm's length.

'When we get away from London, we'll have plenty

of time to spend together. As soon as I'm finished here, I'll return to the cottage and we can find somewhere new.'

'Jos said that's what it was all about – you being here, I mean. I don't know that I fancy living in the back of beyond.'

'We don't have to go too far.' *Just far enough that no one would have heard of the Chervilles*, I thought to myself.

'I bet Jos will love that: the three of us playing happy families.'

'You haven't been arguing, have you?'

'We definitely won't be on Saturday. He's going away, he said something about a job upriver.'

I looked at her blankly, thinking that I must have misunderstood. I'd asked Jos to keep an eye out for Willa and he couldn't do that if he wasn't there.

'Oh dear,' Willa said, seeing my face. 'I hope I haven't got him in trouble.'

'Not at all,' I lied. 'I'm sure he mentioned something of the kind when I was home.'

'Getting extra cash for the baby,' Willa suggested and I nodded.

She looked over in the direction of Tall Trees, taking it all in.

'Jos said the house was huge. It's a shame you couldn't have given me a tour.'

'I would've done if it weren't for Margaret. She's the

housekeeper, a proper dragon, but Jenny the girl I was sitting with in the kitchen when you came in, she's a doll.'

'That's what you used to say about me. Is that what you still think? Despite everything, I mean?'

'Of course it is. You're my sister and I love you. We both have to try a bit harder and we will. And Jos will, too.'

She pressed me into a brief embrace. 'I'll let you get back to your work, then. I'm due at the factory, anyway.'

I held up the little bunny. 'Thanks for bringing me this. I'm sure she'll like it.'

'Jos said you were convinced it was a girl. Might you consider naming her after me? Mina, though, for short so you don't get the two of us mixed up.'

'I'll think about it,' I said with a smile. 'I don't want to make you late, though,' and, waving her off, I returned to the house.

'So that's your sister, then,' Jenny said.

'That's my Willa.'

'You're the elder, though.'

'How can you tell?'

'The way you hauled her out of here, for one,' she said and we both laughed.

'I didn't want her to run into Margaret,' I said, adding under my breath, 'nor Rowland.'

'You're protective of her, aren't you?'

'I made a promise I would keep her safe and I haven't done a very good job of it. When our mother died six months ago, Willa turned a bit wild. The rent was too much for her on her own and after she was evicted she disappeared for two weeks. I had Jos, but she felt she had no one. I used to look for her up and down the towpath, in and around King's Cross every night. She came back of her own accord in the end, but she's never told me what happened for those days when she was gone.'

'Not much good can happen when a girl's got no family,' Jenny said grimly. 'That's why even though Madam is mean, I'm glad of my place at Cherville's.'

As many questions as she'd asked about Jos and Willa, I realised Jenny had never volunteered much about her own people. From what she'd said, I guessed now she was an orphan.

'You've got no brothers or sisters to look out for you?'

'None worth the name. That trick I pulled to open Margaret's desk when you wanted a spy at her daybook, that's about the only thing my family taught me,' she said, and she turned away so I wouldn't see the gleam of tears in her eyes.

'Would you want to learn how to mix Cherville's tonic?' I said. 'I picked some nightshade when I went back home for the sabbath, but the leaves will need to be boiled first before we can use them.'

She lifted her apron to her face. 'You'd show me that?'

'Why not? Maybe we'll make an extra-strong dose and then he'll be less likely to wander the house at night,' I said and we both giggled. 'Before we start, though, I must write to Jos.'

'Would your sister not have taken a message?'

'I'm sure she would, but this one is for his eyes only.'

'Ooh,' Jenny exclaimed, a pink blush creeping up her face. 'I'll make sure it gets taken when Cherville's letters go.'

If only I was sending him that sort of note. I scribbled: *Willa says you're going away for a few days. Assume she's got the wrong end of the staff. Please come to Tall Trees to explain.*

In case there was any doubt in his mind, I signed it Hester rather than Essie so he knew he was in trouble. I'd made one request of him while I was away, that he look out for Willa. If he thought he could slink off without me knowing, he was very much mistaken.

XXI

A reverend and a quack

As ill as his father was, I'd expected Rowland Cherville to give him some grace, but there he was standing by his bed when I came in on Friday morning.

'And here she is,' he said, leaving me in no doubt that they'd been talking about me – rowing, probably, from the looks on their faces. Rowland had told Margaret he'd speak to his father on Wednesday morning. As far as I knew, however, this was their first interview.

'Nurse Reeves, my dutiful son tells me you'd met even before you came to Tall Trees,' Cherville said as I stepped forward to bolster the pillows behind him.

Had Rowland told his father I'd confronted him at the factory? To do so would have meant acknowledging his dalliance with Willa, and after what Cherville had said the other night at dinner about distractions, I couldn't imagine Rowland wanting to admit to interfering with his staff.

'Her sister works for us,' Rowland cut in, proving he feared I might say too much.

'Reeves came highly recommended by Mr Bright. I have been very pleased with her work,' Cherville added.

If only I could be as pleased. Lady Raine and what she'd had to go through was still on my mind; so, too, the other women. Thankfully, Cherville's relapse had slowed his plans and given me a bit of breathing space to work out how best to get to Nyx before he could.

'You're taking recommendations from a reverend and a quack when you could have an Edinburgh man for the asking?'

'I've told you before, Rowland, I'll have none of your prying into my care. Who treats me and how they do it will remain my choice as long as I am head of this family.'

They glowered at each other, so intently it was as if they'd forgotten I was there.

'This is my house, Rowland, and I'll be making the decisions about how it is run. Do not get carried away with yourself while you're at the factory. I've been feeling better of late so I won't be needing you to stand in for much longer.'

Rowland blanched with fury and I took an involuntary step back, colliding with Margaret, who'd stolen in behind me. A quick glance at her face showed me she too was worried and, sure enough, she pronounced, 'Best not to be making too many decisions, sir. Not when you're in the midst of your recovery.'

Knowing how faithful she was to her beloved master, it was clear to me that Margaret had only Cherville's health in mind, but he, already irritated by Rowland, burst out, 'If I'll not take orders from my son, no servant will gainsay me.'

Margaret, dismayed at angering him, rushed to excuse herself, but it was the worst thing she could have done for it only angered Cherville the more.

'No. I will not have it, no more from you. Get out!' Tears flooded her eyes. 'Get out!' Cherville bawled again and, with as much dignity as she could muster, she turned and left. Wanting no part of this row between Cherville and his son, I would have given anything to have been able to follow her and yet I dared not go without Cherville's permission.

'You can get out, too,' he said to Rowland.

'I've not finished.'

'But you see, *I've* finished with *you*. You come in here criticising my arrangements, questioning my judgement. You'll find I've been doing a lot of thinking over these last two weeks.'

'What exactly am I to infer from that?'

'I suppose I should tell you, seeing as you've been so

concerned about my financial arrangements. You're aware that I have been receiving counsel from Mr Bright?'

'On how to give away my inheritance? Those slaves that burned down our plantation, they should be lynched not rewarded.'

Cherville carried on as if his son hadn't spoken. Only the other day he'd said he wanted to keep his atonement plans secret; now he laid them all out. 'There were two women – slaves from the plantation – who I brought to London to work at Tall Trees. They ran away and I've been haunted by them ever since. Reeves here helped me find the first of them at the house of a Lady Raine. Last week I paid her for the years of service she gave me and I've never felt better.'

'You're spending my money on the say-so of this charlatan?'

'Bright had been trying to involve me in his abolitionist schemes for some time, but the idea to find and pay these women was all my own.'

'The same Bright who recommended her? Can't you see how it sounds? He advises you to atone, then she's here and all of a sudden you're talking about giving away yet more of my fortune?'

'It is my fortune.'

'It is my inheritance.'

So much enmity between them, and I couldn't tell who would come out on top. Then came a turn I wasn't expecting.

'You will have plenty, Rowland. If what I hear about your antics to capture Miss Hawkins is correct,' Cherville said.

'Miss Hawkins is on the verge of accepting my proposal. Part of the reason I came home was to tell you.'

Rowland about to be engaged? No wonder he'd lost interest in Willa.

'Well, I knew already, so it seems you've had a wasted journey.'

The two men glared at each other once more and then Rowland turned on his heel and stalked from the room, slamming the door shut behind him.

'Whiskey,' Cherville demanded. His face was danger-ously red, but knowing that to refuse would only excite him further, I went to his desk and poured from the decanter. He threw the drink down and signalled for another, which this time he sipped.

'Is there anything else I can get to make you comfort-able, sir? Some lavender, perhaps, if you're minded to lie down?'

He looked up at me, his eyes bright. 'By no means. My son seeks to order me, and that I will not have. As you know, I had thought to hide my plans from him, but why should I dissemble? My illness makes him think me weak; a show of strength is what is needed here. Away down-stairs. Tell Spinks to prepare the carriage for two o'clock. I wish to return to Lady Raine – she should have her

charitable ladies with her at Bloomsbury Hall, they're holding a bazaar. I will give her whatever she wants for her
causes, Rowland be damned.'

The morning's scene had sparked that frenzied energy
he'd had on the way back from our first visit to Lady
Raine's. Unwittingly she'd become a pawn in the power
struggle between Cherville and his son. It did not bode
well, yet what could I do but obey his command?

As the time neared for our departure, my mind running
on how I might dissuade Cherville from this path, I made
my way down to the entrance hall just as Jenny opened
the door to Mr Bright. He shook the rain from his great-
coat and greeted me cheerfully, but his tone changed to
one of concern when he saw the expression on my face.

'Whatever's the matter, child?'

'Mr Cherville has called for the carriage to take him to a
bazaar held by Lady Raine.'

Mr Bright looked every one of his sixty-odd years as he
absorbed what I had told him. 'He cannot be put off?'

'No, he cannot!' Cherville's voice boomed behind us,
and there he was lurching his way down the stairs. 'You
should be pleased that I am slowly submitting to your way
of thinking. Come – we have a bazaar to get to.'

XXII

Each spoonful of sugar

We made a strange trio sitting in that carriage as it headed towards Bloomsbury, Cherville almost bouncing with excitement and Mr Bright and I wishing we were anywhere else. Pressing myself into the corner of the seat, as far as I could get from Cherville's volubility, I trembled as though I had the ague and sat on my hands to hide it. On the bench opposite, Mr Bright looked worried, too. Perhaps we need not fret. Cherville had failed to recognise Aphrodite before, so why should he this time? But I saw how much control had been needed for her to meet the man who had enslaved her face to face. To see him again would be an intolerable pressure. How many times could she stand it?

'I'm glad you're both here to accompany me,' Cherville

said. 'Meeting Aphrodite last week spurred me on, but when I had that episode the other night, I realised that while paying her had helped it was not enough; even if I were to find Nyx, too. Bright, you have harried me to look to the men and women who work on my plantation in Honduras. Soon, I will contact Wheeler to put things in motion. In the meantime, I want to help other slaves, not just my own, and it will put that puppy firmly in his place.' He frowned a moment at the thought of Rowland and then his face cleared. 'Lady Raine is a philanthropic woman, as you know. Reeves here saw how well she and I got along, and today I am hoping she will advise me on how best to take the next step.'

'That is wonderful to hear,' Mr Bright said, his pained grimace showing he thought it was anything but. 'I would be happy to advise you myself, though, perhaps—'

He'd been about to suggest we return to Tall Trees, but Cherville held up a hand to stop him.

'You've done a great deal to influence my thinking and I thank you. But if it's all the same to you, now I've come around, I'd prefer to talk about it with the lady.'

He slapped his thigh with a guffaw and Mr Bright nodded faintly. His eyes caught mine. *I tried*, their expression said. I'd tried, too, the first time Cherville had insisted on going to Lady Raine's. Both of us had failed her, though. All we could do was hope that once again her secret would remain intact.

Outside Bloomsbury Hall there was a well-dressed young woman directing two porters who carried large boxes. 'Are you here for the bazaar?' she said as we climbed out of the carriage and assembled on the pavement. 'I'm afraid it doesn't start until tomorrow; today we're making our final preparations.'

Cherville looked crestfallen and then he rallied. 'You say "we". I assume Lady Raine is among your number?'

'She is the head of our committee.'

'Excellent. I was hoping to make a sizeable donation to her cause. I trust there is no reason I cannot make it now?'

The young woman smiled. 'She's always happy to meet anyone who is willing to help the needy. Come with me, I'll take you to her.'

The hall had been decked out with garlands of fresh flowers. They were hung from walls and looped around the rows of stalls erected for the society ladies to sell their fancy goods. The one closest to me had been arranged with doilies of lace, finely crocheted collars and embroidered handkerchiefs.

'Very pretty,' Cherville remarked.

'That is Mrs Jarlin's handiwork,' our guide said. 'She'll be gratified to hear how impressed you are by it.' She looked around, as perturbed that Lady Raine was not visible as Mr Bright and I were relieved, and then she spotted her. 'There she is. I should have guessed that she was seeing to the luncheon. Why don't you join us?'

A table had been assembled on a dais at the back of the hall. On it had been placed a huge array of tartlets, cakes and jellies, and the committee members were in the act of taking their seats. Lady Raine stood when she saw us and I stepped back behind Cherville to shield myself from the flash of fury that blazed in her eyes before her mask came down. At my side Mr Bright mumbled something about needing to see a parishioner.

'You can't go,' I hissed, but he was already making his excuses to Cherville and a moment later he'd slunk out. Anything might happen at this meeting and I'd been counting on him to help Lady Raine and me to get through it. How could he abandon us like that?

Cherville made a small bow to Lady Raine as she stepped forward to greet him.

'So we meet again,' he said. 'A shame Mr Bright had to leave. I wanted to introduce you, but duty called.'

'Who are we to stand in the way of the Lord's work?' she replied before turning to a footman. 'Edwards, a chair for our guest.'

I took courage from how unruffled she was. If she, who had everything to fear from Cherville, could look him in the eye, perhaps I was underestimating her.

'I did not mean to disturb your labours, madam. I believed the bazaar to have started and I was keen to make a donation,' Cherville said.

'I don't think we can call these labours,' she said, glancing at the table and giving a tinkling laugh. 'These sweetmeats will be on sale tomorrow and we thought it only right that we should try them first. I hope I can prevail upon you to join us?'

In her house at Bloomsbury Square I'd wondered how she kept up the facade. How she could have hidden in plain sight for so long. Here, then, was my answer. Her voice, her tone – had I not known her true identity, perhaps even I would have been fooled. Cherville sat down in the seat the footman had brought and motioned me to stand opposite him a little away from the group. I looked on as Lady Raine handed him a dish of tea and he made a comment in return. She laughed again, but this time it was too high, too loud. It was a reckless laugh and the trembling that I'd managed to suppress began again with a vengeance.

Were these ladies really so oblivious? Not one appeared to feel the tension that had settled. I felt it pressing down on me until it seemed as though I carried the weight of the whole room on my shoulders.

'Tell us, sir, how we may assist. You spoke of a donation?'

Cherville turned to the other ladies. 'Last week I paid a visit to Lady Raine, and spoke to her maid, Aphrodite, who I confess I once enslaved. I sought her out to atone for my actions and today I would like to continue that with a pledge of funds.'

'Bravo, sir,' said one woman, and there was a general hum of congratulation from amongst those present.

'Mr Bright said I must give in order to feel peace.' Cherville looked around, forgetting for a moment that the vicar had bolted. 'I am ashamed to say that he has been trying to persuade me for some time of the wrongness of my actions, but it is only recently that I have come to an understanding.'

'I'm sure you're right, but as a cause it's had ever such a lot of our attention,' a second lady said, looking up from the plate of biscuits she'd been picking at. 'There are so many who are deserving on our own streets, you see.'

'I know little of that,' Cherville said, and now a third lady interjected.

'It does feel as though we've made a lot of sacrifices and the cause is won, is it not, now that they are freed – and at great cost.'

'You will be compensated, sister, do not fear,' the lady at her side said before turning to her host. 'Lucilla, I seem to recall this was a pet cause of yours at one time, but even you have moved on. Only last week you were telling us of those matchstick girls. Should we not see if we can convince Mr Cherville here to give his money to them instead?'

Lady Raine put down the tea she held, a touch too hard, and the cup rattled in its saucer.

All eyes were fixed, awaiting her verdict.

'There are indeed many worthy causes,' she said. 'Gertrude is right: much has been done over the years to combat slavery, by us and by others.'

'Dame Hiller doesn't eat sugar still,' piped up one voice, and there was a slightly uncomfortable laugh, but I wasn't sure who it had come from.

'I remember the days when we were urged to boycott sugar,' Lady Raine said. 'There was a pamphlet that went around. With each spoonful of sugar we stirred into our tea, the pamphlet said, we were swirling around slave blood.'

As she spoke the ladies stopped eating. One by one cakes were put down and plates pushed away.

'That's a vivid memory you have, Lucilla,' said the lady who had consoled her sister with talk of compensation. What she really intended was to embarrass her hostess into silence. It didn't work.

'I remember very well,' Lady Raine said meaningfully. I dared a look into her face and saw that it was no pamphlet that she recalled, but a time before Cherville had brought her to England. 'Those sugar slaves, hard as they laboured, were not rewarded for their work. Who can blame them for trying to escape their masters? But they rarely got too far and oh, what punishments awaited them.'

Here Lady Raine got to her feet and her voice rang out in the hall. 'To be hanged was a mercy when masters made torture their game.'

Her voice caught and it reminded her where she was,

what she had said. In that moment, any who looked at her would have seen who she truly was. Thankfully, there were only two of us. Myself, and Cherville, whose eyes glistened with unshed tears. My God, he knew. The realisation was plain on his face.

The ladies had bowed their heads. The very first who had spoken was the first to recover. 'A fine speech, Lucilla, hear, hear.'

She meant well, no one could doubt it, but what she'd heard had been no speech. The complacency of her tone. I wanted to shake it from her. Thank God, Lady Raine had regained her self-control. She resumed her seat, picked up her cup and her hand gave not even the slightest tremor. 'It was a fine pamphlet. When I am next in the country, I will look out my copy for you.'

This was safer ground – country houses, libraries, favours given – and the other ladies rallied.

'Mr Cherville, what say you after all you have heard? Is it still the slaves who would receive your mite, or some other cause?' the lady who'd been referred to as Gertrude said.

Cherville pushed back his chair, and got to his feet. A final searing look passed between him and Lady Raine. He had not the courage to address her.

'I will send a cheque,' he muttered into the awkward silence and stumbled from the room in a daze, clumsy as a child awakened from sleep.

XXIII

The hothouse at the
end of the garden

Cherville now knew who Lady Raine was – I was convinced of it. For the first time he had truly seen her, and it
had aged him visibly. His abrupt exit from the hall had
puzzled the ladies. While they'd whispered to one another
of their confusion, I'd stood rooted to the spot, waiting
for the world to cave in, but it had not. The ladies resumed
eating their sweetmeats and drinking their tea and there
was nothing for me to do but follow Cherville outside.
Something of a magnitude had passed between him and
Lady Raine and only I had noticed.

In the carriage ride back to Tall Trees, I watched the emotions move across his face as he struggled to come to terms
with how enslavement had blighted her life and his own

culpability. I, too, felt raw. To know what she had seen and gone through, how all that pain and anger seethed beneath her measured accent, and fine clothes. Once hurt like that had been acknowledged, the world could only be understood through its prism.

Spinks pulled up outside Tall Trees and immediately Margaret came running from the house heedless of the rain that had persisted all afternoon.

'What have you done to him?' she said as Cherville staggered from the carriage.

'He is tired from his trip to Bloomsbury and will need to go to bed.'

'Tell me why he's weeping?' she demanded, for the tears leaked from his eyes. 'It had better not be anything to do with that godforsaken furniture. I knew I should have destroyed it.'

Taking one arm each, we supported Cherville up the path and into the house. As we stumbled up the stairs in an awkward trio, I thought of a few nights previous when I'd had to coax him back to his bed from the third floor. Then he had seemed numb, in shock, as he rocked back and forth, but today his eyes were not glazed as before. The pain he felt now came from within; it bubbled up and spilled over as though the dam of ignorance that held it back had burst.

'Is there something I can bring you, sir?' Margaret said as he got into bed and she fussed with his covers.

'Leave me. To be alone is what I need.'

Out in the hallway, Margaret rounded on me. 'You've done something to him and I will know what it is.'

'I have accompanied him to Lady Raine's bazaar, as I told you.'

When I made to walk away, she pulled me back. 'Something must have happened there – I'll ask Spinks if you won't tell me – and what of Mr Bright? Wasn't he there with you, too?'

I shook off her hand. 'I owe you no explanations. Please, step aside. There is somewhere I must go.'

'He needs you here.' She ground her teeth; it had cost her a lot to say it, but it wasn't true. There was no remedy for what Cherville was feeling. It was a pain that had to be endured. Not even time could fully heal it.

'There is nothing I can do for him,' I said and, brushing past her, I made my way back downstairs and out of the house. Lady Raine had asked me never to return, but after what had happened this afternoon, I could not rest until I'd seen her. I might not be able to help her either, but I owed it to her to try.

Bingham stood on the front step, resplendent in his green livery. His face wore an impassive look, but his features rearranged themselves into a scowl when he saw me coming towards him. It deepened as I got closer, but when he realised that no look, however dirty, would discourage me, he came down the steps to intercept me before I got to Lady Raine's door.

'My mistress told you not to come back,' he said.

'I came to see how she is. If I'd had any inkling of how she was living, I would never have brought Cherville here.'

'She's only just got in. Be off with you.'

I looked upwards to the first-floor window from where I could hear the tinkling of a piano. 'Is that her? You must let me in, I beg you. He knows who she is.'

Bingham had turned his back to me. I saw it stiffen. 'Will he expose her?'

'I think not, but there are others like her. He will visit them, too, and I want to do a better job of protecting them.'

The butler gusted out a sigh of resignation. 'Go to the hothouse at the end of the garden. I will tell her that you're waiting but I make no promise that she'll meet you.'

I knew what a hothouse was, of course, but had never actually seen one. I peered through its green-tinted glass panels and saw plants inside such as I'd never laid eyes on. On opening the door, I was drenched by a wave of heat. How soupy the air was, thick too, as I fought to breathe it in and felt it settle on my chest. I walked down the aisle, head-height plants with vibrant pink and purple flowers on either side of me, wondering what medicinal qualities they held. Sweat beaded on my upper lip and, swaying a little, I cast around for a seat and put my head between my knees.

'So you came back, even though I told you not to.'

She'd slipped in without me hearing her and I raised my head slowly to manage my dizziness. 'I needed to know you were safe.'

She chuckled and I blushed, hearing how it must sound. As Lady Raine, she was never safe. A word out of turn, even a day in the sun, could give her away. I thought of the effort it had taken me, who had never worked in service, to remember to call Cherville *sir*, something she would have had to unlearn. How did she bear the strain of it?

'Cherville won't share your secret.'

'He wouldn't dare.'

She said it emphatically and I knew she was right. Somewhere along the way, her judgement had become a sixth sense to keep her from discovery. When she'd let her knowledge of and passion for the abolitionist cause show, revealing herself to Cherville in the process, I'd thought it reckless. Now I saw it had been a calculated risk, but why do it at all?

'I wanted him to know who I was,' she said, as if I'd asked the question out loud. 'What he said to Patience my maid, it sickened me.'

'He didn't apologise?'

'Oh, he expressed regret, but he also said that it wouldn't have happened if she hadn't been so beautiful, that he hoped she remembered he'd treated her tenderly. It told me it wasn't remorse he felt, but self-pity. It was all about him, nothing about me at all.'

I thought back to the carriage ride home when we'd first come to Bloomsbury, how proud of himself he'd been. Lady Raine was right: if Cherville's apology wasn't heartfelt, it was better left unsaid.

'He's sorry now.'

'I do not doubt it, but he only saw my suffering because I let myself relive it. Why must we always display our pain for these people? Why must we tell of the bite of the whip and the sting of the lash before they truly believe?'

Her dark eyes challenged me. I had no answer, but I did have one more question. 'When I started working for Cherville, he told me of yourself and Nyx. I've since learned there were three of you he brought to Tall Trees. Do you have any idea of where the others are?'

'Artemis is beyond his reach, and Nyx – even I don't know where she is. I doubt he'll find her.'

'He found you,' was on the tip of my tongue, but I stopped myself. Cherville had only found her because of me. The Lukeses would never have told him where they'd last seen Aphrodite. They'd trusted me and I'd let them down. I'd let them all down, but I could make amends if I warned the others he was coming.

A head had dropped from one of the flowers. Lady

Raine picked it up and pressed it to her cheek before holding it out to me. 'Do you see how the colours of the petals change? As a girl, I picked bunches of these – I'd put them in my hair. Take it.'

I cupped it carefully and put it in my pocket. 'The other women might need the money Cherville has for them,' I said.

'You're not going to let this lie, are you?'

'I can't.'

'Very well, then. I shall tell you of them.'

She joined me on the bench, arranging her skirts so the fine material wouldn't crush. I looked down at her shoes, made of the softest leather. How different to my sturdy boots. She'd taken another flower and I kept my eyes on her hands as one by one she plucked the petals, finding it easier to watch that than the pain in her eyes as she recalled what had happened all those years ago.

'I'd been brought to Tall Trees as a girl. The others arrived in 1792 when I was turning fourteen to act as servants to the family. Two sisters far younger than you are now. Nyx, the elder, was the talker of the two of them. She'd not been here a minute when she declared she would escape, though it took her another eight years to do it. "I will not be Cherville's slave" – that's what she said. So serious she was, and do you know I laughed at her. I had to because she scared me. "There's never been slavery. Not here in the King's England," I told her. Can you imagine? I said it so confidently. I was older, I knew London; she was a child in comparison. I pitied her because she wanted to escape; she pitied me because I didn't.

'Every night she and Artemis would sit at the kitchen table and they would plan. I asked her, "What money will you have? Where will you stay? What if he comes after you?" Nothing I said perturbed her. She had a skill with herbs, she told me – that's what she would use to support herself. I thought her foolish for thinking she could leave. The things the abolitionists spoke of – the shackles and the whippings – I'd seen them as a child, but Cherville did not do those things to us. I'd become inured to my life as it was, you see – numb. The way she spoke of freedom, it made me feel again. I hated her for it.'

The anger in her voice shocked me, and then I thought of what Cherville had said about how she was his particular favourite, the way his hand had shaken when he held the money out to Patience when he thought her Aphrodite. There were so many questions I had for her. I resisted the urge to interrupt, wanting to hear her story as she told it. She may not have worn the shackles, as she said, but there was more than one way to be a slave.

'There was a group of abolitionists Nyx was close to. They were writing letters and holding rallies and making speeches. I guessed that in time they would achieve success, but Nyx said we couldn't wait and whatever happened in the colonies would mean little to us. I started making plans of my own. Mr Lukes, he came by Tall Trees regularly and said that if I managed to get out of the house, he would help me. I didn't want to leave Nyx and Artemis, but we agreed it was safer to go our separate ways. One of the abolitionists had promised Nyx shelter for a week, a month, as long as it took to find somewhere safe. She said it was just long enough to disappear. In London anyone can disappear.

'We said we'd leave on the same night. It was important that I was the first to go. We knew it would throw the house into uproar and then in the confusion Nyx and her sister could slip away. That part of the plan went perfectly, but we'd not been free for a day before the advertisements went up. They gave the names the Chervilles had called us, described what we'd worn on the night of our escape and promised that if we went back of our own volition, we'd receive no ill-treatment. I knew it for what it was, and Nyx too. Lies and nonsense, but one of the abolitionists, he wanted to believe and he persuaded Artemis.'

'Did something bad happen to her?'

'I'm afraid it did and Nyx blamed herself. As the elder she knew it was her duty to protect her sister.'

We sat in silence for a minute. I wasn't exactly sure who Dite was thinking of, but it was Willa that was on my mind and in the moment I would have given anything and everything I had to see her.

'I interrupted you,' I said.

'It's a sad story, not easy to share all at once.'

'I think I must hear it, just the same,' I said. 'You were about to tell me more of the abolitionist?'

'Ah yes, the abolitionist. Nyx thought him a good friend, but I'd seen he was sweet on Artemis. It was him that encouraged her to go back.'

'Back to Tall Trees? Why would she?'

'She believed, and the abolitionist did too, that if she did there would be no punishment. It's what Cherville had printed on those advertisements and the abolitionist was convinced he would honour his word. As I said, he felt strongly for Artemis. He'd told her he would do the right thing and they'd marry. If she'd run, he would have had to run with her, and he was just starting to do well for himself, there was talk of Cherville giving him a living.'

'What happened when Artemis went back to Cherville?' I forced myself to ask. If it hurt me simply to hear it, how much worse it must be for Lady Raine to have lived it, but how could I return to Tall Trees unless I knew all?

'She hanged herself. I imagine that Cherville sought to punish her for escaping in such a way she thought death was preferable. He would know more. The abolitionist.'

Had there ever been someone outside of the West India Interest that said the word *abolitionist* with such venom? She couldn't even bring herself to say his name and, seeing how she hated him, I forbore to ask it.

'And Nyx?' I said.

'After the night I left Tall Trees, I never saw her again. She disappeared exactly as she said she would. As I myself did.'

'Until I came along,' I admitted. I rose to my feet. 'I will leave you now.'

'It is for the best. You understand why I cannot have you here?'

I did. Today had been an exception, she wouldn't reveal herself again. I hoped she never felt she needed to, and I left her to her exotic flowers and the memories that should never have been stirred.

XXIV

A skill with herbs

After the warmth of the hothouse, the cold London air was a shock to the body. With all that Lady Raine had told me, my mind had encountered a still greater one. There remained the mystery of Nyx to solve. Was she alive? Living in London? I needed someone to talk it through with, to help me find the right path. With a pang, I thought of Mama and how much I missed her counsel. I told myself the cottage was too far away to see Jos; in truth I was still angry with him after Willa had let slip that he had taken a job upriver – he hadn't even bothered to reply to my letter asking him to explain himself. Jenny was closer, though far too young to hear what Lady Raine had told me, and much as I valued Sal she wouldn't understand unless I started the whole sordid tale from the beginning and that I simply couldn't face. From the moment I'd arrived at Tall Trees, I'd sensed it held secrets, but none so devastating as this. To think that Artemis had died under Cherville's roof. After his episode in the early hours of Wednesday morning I could guess where she'd done it. Why else would Cherville have gone to that room on the third floor when he said the slaves called to him?

The thought of going straight back to the house after what I'd learned weighed heavy on me. Reluctantly, I turned in the direction of St Hilda's and Mr Bright. I hadn't forgiven the way he'd left me alone at the bazaar and part of me couldn't help resenting him for the role he'd played in sending me to Tall Trees either. If he hadn't pushed Cherville to atone, none of this could have happened, but I believed him when he said he'd never intended for Cherville to involve me in his schemes. Perhaps we could find a way forward together.

I knocked smartly on the door of the vicarage and stepped back, looking out over the churchyard's uneven rows of graves. The wooden door creaked open.

'I'm here for Mr Bright,' I said, turning and expecting to see Mrs Tull, the old housekeeper. It wasn't her at all; it was the vicar himself.

'Hester,' Mr Bright exclaimed. He wouldn't have expected me at this time of night and my arrival had him flustered. 'Please come in. I must offer you some refreshment.'

I took off my hat and coat and hung them from a hook

in the passage. Through the open door to my left I could see the study, where three weeks earlier Mr Bright had sat me down on a squashy sofa and said he'd heard of a job for me. Doctoress to Gervaise Cherville. That's what he'd told me, if only it had gone no further.

Mr Bright now went straight through to the kitchen. I followed him and took a seat at the table, immediately comforted by the homeliness of it. Meanwhile he assembled cups and saucers to make us tea. His large hands were clumsy over the delicate china and, as he carried the tray to the table, tea slopped over the rims and splashed on the floor tiles. Why was he so nervous?

'Mrs Tull has moved north to care for her sister so I have to do for myself,' he said.

'You'll get another housekeeper?'

'I don't think so. In the ten years I spent in the Indies, I lived simply. I've grown accustomed to being on my own and it suits me.'

I wasn't so sure it did, not while he continued to shiver despite the blanket he'd draped over his knees when he sat down.

'I am so terribly sorry I had to leave you earlier. My parishioners, you see . . .' He wrung his hands together. I remembered when he'd come to see me at Tall Trees not long after I started and had to leave abruptly. He'd blamed that on his parishioners, too. How convenient that their needs arose whenever something difficult transpired. The contrition on his face should have soothed my resentment. In fact it sharpened it and bitterness made me terse.

'Mr Cherville knows who Lady Raine really is.'

'How can that be?'

'It was after you left,' I said pointedly. 'They were speaking of donations, then of slavery. She stood and spoke for . . .'

My voice trailed away. At the time, I'd felt she spoke for me, for her – for us, in fact – yet I had never been enslaved and, to all intents and purposes, she was an aristocrat.

'She spoke of the slaves in Barbados,' I corrected myself, 'but she did it with such passion it forced Mr Cherville to recognise her. It was as though the scales fell from his eyes.'

Mr Bright closed his own eyes and tilted his head back. If he was seeking divine intervention, it was too late now. 'What of the ladies? They remain ignorant?'

'When she described the pain of the slaves, it was too much for them; none could look her in the eye. Perhaps if any had they might have suspected, but they see her as a philanthropist and the prospect is so outlandish that even the slightest suspicion they would dismiss as her vehemence.'

'I should go and speak to him: he can't expose her.'

'She doesn't need your help. He'll keep her secret, she's convinced of it. I admire her.'

'You've spoken to her since?'

'I have. I am come from her house now. That is the other

thing I wished to tell you – she has told me what happened to Artemis.'

Mr Bright rose abruptly and took himself to the window which looked out over the north side of the church. 'How could she know?' he said over his shoulder. 'You suggested the women went their separate ways when they ran from Cherville.'

'I couldn't say exactly how she found out, but she told me Artemis went back to Tall Trees, that she hanged herself.'

'An awful tale. It is unwise to dwell on these things.'

'What I cannot fathom is why she returned to Cherville's house after she'd managed to escape.' I said this half to myself as Mr Bright moved over to the fireplace and poked at the coals. 'She'd lived with Cherville, and knew what he was like. Lady Raine laid the blame at the feet of the abolitionist – she said without him Artemis would still be living. She said he should have known better, that no one could be that naive, that in taking her back he might as well have tied the noose himself.'

'How dare she!' Mr Bright spun round, red-faced with anger. 'She knew nothing of what happened.'

He threw down the poker and, as it clattered to the floor, the pieces of the past clicked into place. His dismay when Cherville had ignored his recommendation to focus on his plantation slaves in favour of those he'd brought to London; the way he had slunk off when he'd come face to face with Aphrodite. The fury I'd seen in her eyes when we'd arrived at Bloomsbury Hall this afternoon. I'd thought it was for me, but it had been directed at him.

'It's you,' I breathed. 'You're the abolitionist.'

Mr Bright hid his face with his hands. No wonder he'd dismissed my questions about Artemis. All along, he'd known that she was dead. Nor had he wanted to find her sister. He must know her fate, too.

'Tell me what happened to Nyx,' I demanded.

Artemis's elder sister was the one remaining piece of the puzzle. What had Lady Raine said of her? That she was confident, forthright . . . and then the one thing that I'd not attended to popped into my mind. That she had a skill with herbs.

'Tell me who Nyx was.'

Mr Bright's mouth formed words, though no sound came out. The truth was deafening, but I needed him to voice it.

'You know her better than you think.'

'Tell me,' I cried and at last he looked me in the eye.

'Your mother is dead.'

XXV

Axe raised

Cherville's room smelled of lavender and the curtains had been pulled around his bed. That told me he was sleeping, but I crossed the room and flung them back, needing to look upon the face of the man who'd enslaved my mother.

How ordinary he appeared lying there, tufts of snow-white hair peeking from his nightcap. He shifted slightly in his sleep and I was buffeted by a wave of hatred so strong it threatened to overwhelm me. It receded, leaving me breathless, only to be followed by another and another. I reached out to grip the bedpost and steady myself; instead my fingers flexed towards Cherville's scrawny neck. I felt a flush of power – his life at the mercy of my circled hands. With an effort I wrenched myself back and snatched the curtains shut, horrified by the half-thought of what I might have done to him. Still my fingers tingled and, when my legs gave way, I dropped into the chair at his bedside, weeping silently.

One brocaded curtain separated me from the man who had done my family untold harm. For as long as I was too weak to walk away, I wished it a leaden wall – anything to bar the temptation of tearing it back and taking vengeance. As anguish racked my body, Cherville snored softly until I was forced to cover my ears and block out his humanity.

An hour, maybe two, must have passed while I sat there, trying to absorb what I had learned, not only of Mama but Artemis as well. Had she truly taken her life in that third-floor room where Cherville had cowered? At last I was strong enough to stand, but where would I go? I stared at the lost-looking woman reflected in the glass opposite Cherville's bed until my eyes became fixed on the gold embroidered tree on her apron. His trade, his colours – and then I was pulling at my dress, hating the way it contained me. My hands shook too hard to undo the buttons, my nails were too blunt to tear it. I needed scissors, and I hacked at the fabric, heedless that I grazed my skin beneath. At last I tore it off, and was down to my shift. Tears filled my eyes and the reflection in the glass blurred so it was Mama I looked at, or was it Artemis or Willa? Here in this room, distraught and dishevelled while Cherville slumbered on, I was all of us and I blundered towards the door. My room, I had to get to my room. My hand was on the doorknob when I heard a whistle. It was Rowland Cherville, coming this way, and I grabbed my mangled clothes from the floor and dived for his father's dressing room to avoid discovery.

Watching through a crack in the door, I saw how Rowland swayed and the slur in his voice confirmed he was drunk.

'Father, dear,' he crooned. 'I hear you've been giving my money away again. But I'm going to put a stop to it. I'm going to make it so no slave will dare accept even a remorseful *look* from you, starting with your precious Aphrodite.'

A thump followed by a muttered expletive told me he'd barged into the door frame on his way out, but still it was a while before I summoned the will to rise. Crouched down in Cherville's dressing room, my arms wrapped around my knees, I'd rocked back and forth with no notion of what time had passed. I shivered and looked down, realising I was half-naked. There it was: my uniform. I'd torn it off in a frenzy. I reached down to the floor and picked it up, wondering how I'd explain the rents in the material. At the door I took a final look back. Cherville slept on, a line of worry across his face. How much did Rowland know of Lady Raine? Cherville would not have told him her secret, but maybe Margaret knew – and she would have no compunction in revealing it. Rowland's threat had dripped with venom. Whatever he had planned would be Lady Raine's ruin.

★

Cherville was sitting at his desk when I came into his room the next morning, scratching out a letter.

'Good morning, Reeves.'

'Sir,' was all I could manage back. I couldn't even bring myself to look him in the face. However was I to be around him, now I knew what he'd done to my mother, to my aunt? I concentrated on straightening his bed covers while he folded his letter and melted a blob of wax over the join to seal it.

'I'm going to see my man Wheeler over at Lincoln's Inn,' he announced.

Here was my chance to tell him about what Rowland had said, but I couldn't bring myself to engage him in conversation, wishing he was as far from me as possible. He left and I sat down on the edge of the bed, not knowing what else to do. Had Mama ever been in this room? I hated to think of her at Tall Trees, yet now I knew she'd lived here I could almost feel her presence.

Jenny came in humming to herself and pulled up short when she saw me. 'You gave me a fright, staring off into the beyond like that.'

'Sorry, I didn't mean to. I'm . . .' What could I say? I didn't know exactly what I was. Jenny frowned with concern. 'I'm out of sorts, that's all.'

'I saw the master heading out and Margaret's in the courtyard. Why don't you treat yourself to a lie-down?'

I shook my head vehemently. Being awake was my only

defence against the impressions that hovered at the edges of my mind. Mama in shackles, Mama in chains. I dared not lay myself open to the nightmares that would undoubtedly come as soon as I closed my eyes.

Jenny sat down beside me. 'Has something happened? I could've sworn I heard you pacing last night.'

Had I paced? I shrugged, unable to recall how it was that I had dragged myself through the hours since I'd learned that the mother I'd loved had once been Nyx, Gervaise Cherville's slave.

Jenny fidgeted and I made an effort to rally. 'You told me where Margaret was. Have you seen anything of Rowland this morning?'

'At the factory by now, I would've thought. He went off early this morning, very chipper.'

The news roused me. Could Rowland's good mood be to do with the plans he was formulating against Lady Raine? It was hard to imagine otherwise, recalling how he'd sneered down at his father.

'Do you think Spinks will say where he took him?'

'He probably would, but now he's taken Cherville out it'll be a while before he's back. I know what will cheer you up,' Jenny said and rummaged in her pocket to produce a note. 'This came for you yesterday while you were out. I thought it safest to put into your hand in case it was from your husband.'

I'd been wondering when Jos would reply to my note,

and after what I'd learned last night, knowing he was keeping watch over Willa was even more important to me.
Would he really have gone off without telling me? I
unfolded the letter and read it through once, then twice,
before balling it up into my fist.

'What's wrong?' Jenny said. 'I thought it would make
you happy to hear from him.'

'Willa said he was going away for a few days but I was
convinced she was mistaken. Now he writes it's true and
he would leave her on her own. I've got to stop him.'

The warehouse was busy as usual, with men in and out
carrying timbers and bricks on their backs. The northern cargos came in daily and the warehouse was their
home before they were sent on further south or out of
the country all together. Two young boys at the door
nudged and giggled with one another at the sight of a
woman in this most manly of places, where the air was
heavy with brick dust and rich with the smell of toil and
sweat. I beckoned to them and the taller and more confident of the two came over, pulling a straw from his
pocket to chew on and affecting a cocky stance. 'You all
right, missus?'

His bravado would've been comical if I were in the
mood for laughing. 'You know Jos Reeves?'

He shrugged. 'Not sure I do. Is there something I could
do for yer? Harry's the name,' and he offered me his hand.

I reached out and squeezed hard, so he knew I meant business. 'Go tell Jos his wife is looking for him.'

Harry nodded, a little crestfallen. He ran off and I tried to avoid the knowing eyes of the men my own age and older nearby as I waited for him to return. After a minute or two Jos came along, wiping his hands against his mole-skin trousers, before passing a handkerchief across his face.

'You're well?' he called when he was close enough to speak without shouting. I answered with a withering look and his own expression hardened. 'It's the middle of my shift. You do me no favours turning up like this.'

I withdrew the crumpled note from my pocket and waved it under his nose. 'I want you to explain this,' I said, struggling to keep my voice down. 'You didn't even have the decency to tell me directly.'

He captured my hand and gave a quick glance over his shoulder. The smirking men had moved closer, expecting a scene. 'Why are you embarrassing me like this?' he muttered. 'Do you want me to lose my job?'

'What I want is to know why you think it's all right to leave town when the one thing I asked was that you look out for Willa while I was at Tall Trees.'

Another man had joined the impromptu audience that had gathered. 'That's my foreman,' Jos said. He held up one hand to request a short break and on receiving the nod, he steered me outside.

'Let me get this right,' he said once we were beyond sight of the warehouse entrance. 'You sneaked out of work, even though you know that witch of a housekeeper is looking for excuses to let you go, to berate me for trying to earn more money for us?'

In all the time we'd been together, this was as angry as I'd ever seen him, but I was angry, too. Didn't he know what it meant to keep watch? To take care of someone? Mama's last words, Lady Raine's memories, Mr Bright's shame, all whirled around in my head. I was doing everything I could to keep Willa safe. To get her away from Rowland Cherville I was prepared to sacrifice the needs of my existing patients, the home I'd built for us within the cottage, the area I'd grown up in. All Jos had needed to do was stay put for one month and it had proved too much for him. Didn't he realise what was at stake?

'You could have told me yourself you were going away. If Willa hadn't come to me . . .'

'I was wondering when her name would come up. Why do you let her stir the pot?'

'Actually, she visited to give me a gift for our baby. Why must you always think the worst of her? Can't you see she needs our protection?'

'I won't have this conversation with you. Not here,' he pleaded and gave me a shake. The look in his face was no longer one of anger but of hurt. He didn't know what I knew, and there wasn't time to explain, but shouldn't it have been enough that I'd asked him?

'You can't go,' I said flatly.

'I'm going upriver and I'll be leaving in an hour. I'll be back on Tuesday and when I am we need to sit down and talk.'

'About Willa?'

'Yes, and how she's come between us. You must see it can't continue?'

He was close to asking me to choose. I saw it in his eyes and backed away before he could say the words, knowing he wouldn't like my answer.

Jenny was bobbing up and down in the window when I entered the gates at Tall Trees half an hour later. She opened the main door and beckoned me to come in that way.

'I'm so pleased you're back.'

'How come you were watching for me?'

'It's Margaret.'

'Is she unwell?'

'Not exactly. It's just that she's got at the wood.'

I looked at Jenny quizzically. 'What's she doing with it?'

'All those things we found Cherville with the other night – she's taken an axe to them.'

We ran straight up the main staircase to the first-floor landing which looked out on to the courtyard garden below.

Margaret was there amid a forest of broken furniture, axe raised so high I thought she might topple backwards. She brought it down with the full force of her body so the delicate wooden table she'd struck splintered. Up here, behind the glass, the crash of metal on wood couldn't reach me, and yet I felt it – right in the depths of my stomach. I rapped hard on the window with my knuckles, but Margaret only raised her axe again.

'Has she lost her reason?' Jenny said at my shoulder. 'She's been going at it more or less since you went out. It's like those poor chairs and tables done her some great wrong.'

'I'm going to put a stop to it.'

I took the stairs two at a time, making my way across the entrance hall, then down into the kitchen and along. I burst into the courtyard just as Margaret felled the final piece of furniture. I turned away so the flying chips couldn't hit me.

Margaret's face was pink with effort, wisps of hair stuck to her temples, and dark patches blooming at her underarms. Though she looked in my direction, her eyes were hazy as the frenzy that had gripped her began to recede. She watched as I picked my way through shards of chair and table and ornament, scattered to left and right in the fury of her attack so all the glue in the world couldn't put them back together. I looked up at Margaret from the devastation.

'What have you done?'

'Something long overdue. The curse that haunts him lived in this wood; it can't trouble him now.'

Jenny had said Margaret had been awake in the small hours to keep watch over Cherville. The sleepless night had addled her brain.

'What did you tell Rowland after his father came in ill yesterday? You know Cherville wants to help his Honduran slaves. If Rowland interferes, he won't be happy.'

The flush that worked its way up her neck told me she knew what I said was true. 'I told Rowland that the master had sent for Mr Wheeler, his solicitor.'

'Nothing else?'

'The master wept all evening. I insisted on helping him to bed, but he was muttering to himself and quite confused. You should have been there to administer his draught, I didn't know what to do for him.'

That explained the reek of lavender; she must have panicked and given him all I had.

Margaret continued, 'He spoke of Lady Raine and that woman Aphrodite as if they were one and the same. I had to call Mr Rowland in.'

My heart sank. I'd wondered if he knew; now I was sure of it.

'Where did Rowland go to this morning?'

'To his club to see if he could find Lord Raine.'

Good God, he was going to expose her to her husband. I turned back towards the house.

'Wait, where are you going?' Margaret called after me. There was no time to stop. If Rowland knew Lady Raine's secret, I had to get to Bloomsbury. I'd been given a third and final chance to warn her that a Cherville was about to wreak havoc in her life.

XXVI

The open window

Bloomsbury Square was busy with carriages. A line of them stretched one hundred yards from Lady Raine's door and my heart plummeted. I'd hoped to find her alone, but it was clear she had company. I'd walked as fast as I dared without courting attention – if only I'd got here sooner. I fidgeted, not knowing what to do for the best, still fighting to catch my breath. As I shifted from foot to foot, a young boy made his way towards me, a dustpan and broom in his hand. I moved back to allow him to pass, but instead he stopped and hitched up the raggedy trousers he wore. It was me he'd come to speak to.

'You're to move on, missus,' he said.

I looked over to the other side of the street where he

had come from and saw the glaring face of Bingham, Lady Raine's butler.

'That's right, it's his orders,' the boy said, following my glance. 'I can tell him you won't move on unless there's money in it for yer, if you'd like.'

He looked up at me hopefully, wanting a cut from this scheme, but I shook my head.

'Will you go back and tell him that I need to get in and see his mistress? That I have an urgent message for her?'

I rummaged in my pocket and drew out two ha'pennies, clinking them together in what I hoped was an encouraging manner.

The boy was unimpressed. 'He's given me more 'an that to get the pure up from the horses,' he said and shuffled off as another carriage pulled up a little way from the house.

My stomach pitched at the sight of it, until a second glance confirmed it wasn't blue, as I'd feared, but darkest green. This was no good. If Bingham had sent the boy to move me on, it was unlikely he'd let me in, but I had to make the attempt. I had no idea if Rowland Cherville was on his way – at this time of day he should be at the factory – but I couldn't leave it to chance. I'd wanted to warn Lady Raine when the father tracked her down. I wouldn't fail her now it was the son.

I crossed the road and as I approached the house, Bingham came down the steps to intercept me.

'I knew she was wrong to speak with you again, that it

would only encourage you,' he said. 'You can't come in; she's busy with Lady Cecily.'

'Who's Lady Cecily?'

Bingham jerked his head and I stood to one side as the couple who'd occupied the dark green carriage walked up to him and handed over their card. With the merest of glances at the printed letters before him, he led them up to the front door, bowing and scraping before showing them inside.

'What are you still doing here?' he said through clenched teeth when he'd returned to the bottom of the stairs. He stepped in front of me, shielding me from the eyes of another advancing couple. As they passed into the house, the woman glanced back over her shoulder at me before whispering to her partner.

'Please don't make me cause a scene,' I hissed to Bingham in desperation.

It was just the threat I needed to make him take me seriously. Calling to the footman who stood just inside the door, Bingham ushered me to the basement entrance and we traded words back and forth while above our heads the ladies and gentlemen continued to arrive.

'Have you not done enough?' he said.

He'd seemed angry at first; now I sensed a weariness or even disappointment in his tone. 'Is it money you want?'

I recoiled at the suggestion.

'You didn't see her when you'd gone,' he said. 'She's

lived that lie so long . . .' His voice trailed away. I'd been expecting him to say that she didn't know who she was any more, but she knew all right. For all the defiance she'd shown Cherville yesterday, she couldn't forget her vulnerability.

'You've got to let me in. Lady Raine is in danger from the Chervilles.'

'If I never heard that name again,' Bingham said, clenching his fists, 'after what he did to my mistress.'

'It's not Gervaise Cherville this time; it's his son, Rowland. He is hunting down the former slaves that his father has compensated so that he can claw back his inheritance.'

'She got away with it when the man himself came. Must she really fear his son?'

'Rowland is sharper than his father and he wouldn't hesitate to unmask her. Please, you must believe me.'

Despite his obvious reluctance, the need for caution won out. 'What would you have me do? I can't make her leave her own daughter's party.' Bingham wrung his hands. 'Lady Cecily only came out this summer, the house is crowded with her suitors.'

'You must have a signal, a way of letting Lady Raine know she's in trouble?'

'I do, but if he's really on his way, I would prefer to guard the entrance. You go to her. She'll know that I let you past and she'll find a way to speak to you. Her bag is packed, she knows where it is, and I'll get the carriage brought round.'

'It's the right decision.'

'I hope so,' he said fervently.

The footman looked at me askance as I walked in, but made no attempt to stop me. Flowers from her glasshouse had been wound around the banisters and the air was heady with their fragrance.

'I can find Lady Raine upstairs?' I said, and a pall of apprehension crossed his face. It wasn't only Bingham and his mistress. Every servant who knew her secret had lived in fear of this day.

I hurried up the staircase, drawn in the direction of piano music that spilled over the landing from the floor above. The guests were all in the drawing room, which looked even finer than before. The large windows that opened out on to the park had been flung open, despite the weather, and the doors that connected to the room beyond pushed back to create a double space. The rich carpet was rolled up to make space for dancing and the floor had been polished to a shine so the red tones gleamed. Of course it was made from mahogany. Thirty, or perhaps even forty, people were spread around the room: ladies and gentlemen all. They smiled and chatted and simpered to one another, but how their complacency would be shattered if they knew the truth their hostess hid from them.

Oblivious to the calamity that might soon befall her, Lady Raine was in full command of her guests. It suited her, going from group to group: a word here, a smile there. She must have become accustomed to playing the part of hostess over the years and seemed to be enjoying herself. At the sight of me, her face blanched. I jerked my head, indicating that she should join me in the corridor, and backed myself into an alcove to wait for her. A few minutes later, she found me. I'd expected anger or fear, but the look on her face was more akin to resignation, even relief. It told me she'd been waiting for this moment since the first day she'd obscured her Blackness, burying it beneath the neutral accent, the studied lack of emotion, the understated display of the English aristocracy. In response to my appearance, her mask had slipped to the extent that her breathing was up. When she brushed her palms on her silken dress, she left behind the telltale stains of sweat, yet her voice was composed when she spoke.

'Bingham has called the carriage?'

'Yes, it's on its way. By the time you get downstairs it will be waiting.'

'How long do I have?'

There was a tiny chance that Rowland hadn't worked out who she really was, but the risk that he had was too great, and if he'd heard about her daughter's party, the scandal of laying bare Lady Raine's secret before half of London society would be too much for him to resist.

'You should encourage your guests to depart, and leave as soon as you are able. Within the half hour if you can. Do you have somewhere to go?'

She nodded without saying where. I'd unknowingly made her unsafe in her own home and, though I could blame Gervaise Cherville or Charles Bright, it was my fault, too, and now, for the privilege of cleansing a slaver's soul, Lady Raine would pay the price. Sorry or not sorry, conscience-stricken like the father or remorseless like the son, every which way the men and women enslaved by Cherville suffered, and though the impact on me was a mere echo of what they'd had to endure, I too would carry the scars of tending to a man whose actions had blighted the lives of my family. The guilt, the self-disgust of it, had already begun to gnaw at my insides, and in the fullness of time I knew it would slowly and steadily eat away at me until I'd been completely hollowed out.

'I must let my husband know I have been called elsewhere, otherwise he'll worry.'

I watched as she squared her shoulders, put her head up. It was like watching an actress preparing to return to the stage after the interval. That's what she was doing, after all – resuming a role – but how much more she had at stake. Her performance wasn't the work of an hour, a costume to be thrown off when the curtain fell; it was her whole life. She swept back into the fray in a rustle of silk skirts and after a second I followed her, the reluctant audience, sensing the heroine's doom, unable to look away.

Lady Raine walked swiftly through the centre of the room, not stopping until she'd reached a tall grey-haired man who was observing the proceedings with a half-smile on his face. She murmured in his ear and he pouted, but there was no anger there. Whatever excuse she'd given, he'd accepted, but her daughter was a different matter. Lady Cecily, dressed in pink tulle, her brown hair in ringlets, was surrounded by admirers. They swarmed the sofa where she sat, all of them eager to pay court, to draw her attention from their rivals. Lady Raine had to tap more than one on the shoulder to get him to give way before she made it to her daughter's side and leaned down to whisper to her. Again, the pout I'd seen on the face of her father, but unlike him she wasn't going to agree to leave easily, not when this event had been put on in her honour. Back and forth they argued, and I was so absorbed in it that I didn't hear the commotion outside until the raised voices were close enough to compete with the piano music.

Lady Raine discerned it at the exact same moment. From across the room her gaze searched me out. For a split second her eyes held mine with a look of naked fear, before Rowland Cherville burst in, Bingham lagging just behind him. The butler made one final lunge, but Rowland was too quick for him, and in among the crowd of ladies and gentlemen I saw he dare not make another. Lady Raine had only an instant to make her choice. It felt like time stood still; in truth the die had been cast long before this moment. She was going to front it out.

'What's the meaning of this, Bingham?' she said, her clear voice ringing out across the room.

The butler knew the game, knew how important it was that she win it, and bowed his head. 'Forgive me for the disturbance, madam. The gentleman had no invite,' he mumbled.

'An oversight, of course. Rowland Cherville, is it not? You must know my husband? Tell him the name of your club. Is it Hackers? He leaves me alone and frequents them all.'

The ladies near her tittered, exchanging glances of solidarity, and then Lady Raine was walking straight over to Rowland, placing one hand on his arm and shooing Bingham away with the other. It was a bravura performance. *This is my stage*, it said, *these are my guests, my husband is your equal*, and Rowland was disarmed by it. Whatever he thought he knew, he could no longer be sure and it checked him. Lady Raine's confidence, her smooth manner, gave the lie to the accusations he'd come to make, and the conviction drained out of him. The guests who'd turned in shock when he'd forced his way in resumed their conversations. Now he'd been moved on to Lady Raine's husband. This I was not sure about – surely she should occupy him herself – then I saw her speaking to her daughter and knew she was doing what she needed to send the girl from harm's way. She'd almost done it, too, when Rowland's voice cut through the chatter and the tension that had been borne away on a breeze of conversation descended on the room like a London particular.

'You must introduce me to your daughter.'

Lady Raine acted as though she hadn't heard, propelling the girl towards the door, but Lady Cecily hadn't been brought up to read the signs of peril. Whereas her mother looked at Rowland Cherville and saw ruin, her daughter saw only a handsome man with a raffish smile, asking for the favour of being made known to her. A space had formed where the guests, sensing something afoot, had stepped back to gain a better vantage. Swivelling out of her mother's grasp, Lady Cecily stepped into it and offered Rowland Cherville her hand.

'I'm Cecily,' she said.

He took it and used it to pull her to him. The move startled her and she looked over to her mother, recognising there was something not quite right in the gesture.

'Such a beautiful name,' Rowland said, and she blushed. When she tried to disentangle herself, he would not let her go. 'A beautiful English name,' he said, and his emphasis on 'English' brought bile to my throat. My eyes burned with staring at the scene before me so intently. How desperately I wanted to look away but I didn't even dare blink, forced to bear witness to the catastrophe I knew was coming.

Rowland Cherville turned to Lady Raine with a conspiratorial smile. 'I quite understand why you'd want to avoid anything with a touch of the exotic.'

Lady Raine's mouth moved. No sound came out, but from the shape of her lips I knew she'd said 'please'. She knew what he was about to do, was begging him not to, but Rowland Cherville was not a man to plead with. Her mute appeal only made him enjoy what was coming the more. The power in the room had shifted and he was revelling in it. This was no longer Lady Raine's show; he'd stolen it and was determined to eke out every second of drama. None of the guests were talking among themselves any more. Their eyes flitted from Lady Raine to Rowland sensing we were on the cusp of something incendiary.

'You can hardly tell, she's all but white,' he said.

White. He'd thrown the word down like a gauntlet.

Lady Raine's husband broke the silence. 'What is the meaning of this, sir?'

While his tone would have felled another man, Rowland was assured he held the whip hand and Lady Raine's eyes closed in pain for what was about to come next.

'I wondered if you knew what your wife was? You wouldn't be the first. We both know how popular the coloured whores are at the club.'

Lady Raine made another attempt to pull Cecily out of the door. Like the rest of the guests, the girl was transfixed, needing either mother or father to help her understand what was happening, to make sense of what Rowland Cherville was saying.

'Do you know why he is trying to insult me, Lucilla?' Lord Raine demanded of his wife.

The attack was personal, not because of how he cared for her, but because of what it meant for him. If only I'd got here earlier. She and her daughter could have been well away before Rowland even reached Bloomsbury.

'He is saying I am Black, dearest.'

She'd done her best to sound airy, but her husband stepped back as if she'd struck him. I saw him rake her with his eyes, trying to see beneath the glamour. Softly, he swore under his breath. 'Are you?'

Would she brazen it out again? A long moment passed, and then she said simply, 'Yes.'

I thought she'd been courageous when she deflected Rowland's original sally. But that hadn't been real bravery. This was.

For an instant I thought she'd won, and then the woman who'd given her a look of fellow feeling when she mentioned how much time Lord Raine spent at his club, put down her plate and stood. The other guests parted as she walked through them straight to the door. Another woman followed – I recognised her from the bazaar – then the next and the next; and the men were leaving, too. Lord Raine was the last. Cecily ran to him, but he pushed her away with a force that would have sent her flying through the window and on to the pavement below – had it not been for her mother, who stood braced, ready to catch her.

XXVII

Smelling salts

Since I'd learned Lady Raine's true identity, I dreaded that I'd set in motion a train of events that would lead to her discovery. When Cherville had finally recognised her, I'd felt real fear, then sweet relief when it seemed he would not betray her secret. I could not have known that, thanks to Rowland Cherville's avarice, the worst was yet to come. I trudged back to Tall Trees, so bowed beneath the weight of what had happened, it was an effort to put one foot before the other. Lady Raine was exposed, abandoned by her husband and so-called friends, and I had to bear a great deal of the responsibility.

When everyone else had gone, I'd watched as she stood in the centre of her drawing room, turning slowly to commit it all to memory, knowing she'd never return.

Bingham had fetched a bag for her, and a second for her daughter. It was Lady Cecily I felt for most as the two women left the house and climbed into their carriage. I still reeled from what I'd learned of my mother and aunt, and the role that Cherville had played in their lives, but at least I knew who *I* was. Thanks to Rowland Cherville, Lady Cecily had realised today her whole life was a lie. As she gazed through the carriage window looking back at the house she'd grown up in, I wondered if she'd ever recover.

I arrived at Tall Trees at the exact moment that Spinks pulled up in the carriage and jumped down from the driver's box to let out his master. Cherville leaned heavily on his arm as he got out, seemingly exhausted by his journey.

'Reeves, there you are. I am just returned from Lincoln's Inn.'

I looked at him dully, unable to pretend an interest in his concerns when my head was so full of what had just happened to Lady Raine and her daughter.

'What on earth is the matter with you, Reeves?' Cherville asked.

'Your son,' I forced out. 'I've just come from Bloomsbury.'

Cherville shuffled into the library and signalled me to follow him. It was a small square room, with books ranged from floor to ceiling. He sank into a chair before the fire and rang a bell that summoned Margaret like an apparition. While she listened to his orders, I looked around. I'd only been in the library once before, when Cherville had sent me to retrieve a book he'd left behind. It was on the way back that I'd overheard Rowland and Margaret talking and learned of their intention to thwart Cherville's plan to atone for his wrongs. If only I could have stopped them.

'Tell me what it is my son has done,' Cherville said when Margaret had left the room.

'He exposed Lady Raine before her friends; now she and her daughter have fled.'

Cherville nodded slowly in a way that told me he'd already guessed. 'I wouldn't have done it. Nor should my son.' He pulled at the short white hairs of his beard. 'Do you know where she's gone?'

I shook my head emphatically. I'd been the reason he'd found her once; I wouldn't be again.

'Poor woman. I wonder she didn't come here.'

How could he honestly believe she would ever set foot in Tall Trees again? My expression must have spoken for me, because Cherville said, 'Perhaps you're right. After she left, it was a bloody business.'

'With Artemis, you mean?'

'Who gave you that name?' he said sharply. 'No, don't tell me. It is Bright meddling, I presume. I wonder did he tell you of the part he played in the events that led up to that night?'

He looked at me frankly. Until now he'd not been able

to bring himself to mention her name; if I asked him in this moment, he would unburden himself. I sensed a part of him was desperate to; and I badly wanted to know what punishment he'd promised to make my aunt think death was better – just not from him. When he'd hidden his culpability for so long, how could I ever trust what he told me?

The moment passed, and Margaret returned with a bowl of soup.

'You need to get your strength up, sir. It's too much for you to keep going out. If you have any errands, I will run them for you.'

'I met Wheeler to discuss the terms of my will. I doubt you could have done that.'

'I'm sure Mr Rowland—'

'Don't speak to me of that boy,' Cherville said. 'And don't imagine I'm unaware you've been assisting him. I count it most disloyal.'

Margaret's face reddened. He could not have hurt her more if he'd struck her.

'You're as bad as his mother,' Cherville grumbled. 'All his life women have doted on that boy and it's been the ruin of him. From the day he was born, Diana cosseted him. I tried to check her, but she would insist on spoiling him and so her death hit him hard. What choice did I have save to toughen him up? "No Cherville man should be seen snivelling," I'd tell him. "We Chervilles are brave and fearless." I'd show him the paintings his grandfather had sent home from Honduras, the mahogany trees strong and tall, our house set in acres of lush grasses. I'd say, "One day you will own all this."'

His voice dripped with self-pity. I certainly felt none for him. How could he not see it was he, not his wife, that had created a monster?

'Mr Rowland . . .' Margaret tried again. She would have been wiser to keep her counsel because Cherville turned on her.

'I will not listen to you making excuses for him. He has defied me once too often. What he needs is a lesson he'll never forget. Send for the carriage.'

'You can't mean to go out again, sir, you've hardly touched your food,' Margaret said as Cherville staggered to his feet.

'That is exactly what I intend. I was going to reprimand him when he came in the factory. Now I feel it cannot wait. Reeves, you will join me.'

We stood in the entrance hall while Spinks went to bring round the carriage, Cherville leaning heavily on his stick. His face was a greyish colour and he perspired though the day was chill. Margaret was right. A second trip so soon after the first could do him no good, but I could see from the set of his face that he was determined to go. The row between father and son had been brewing for some time. There could be no further delay to their reckoning.

*

Cherville rallied in the time it took to drive to the factory. Throughout the journey he'd been muttering to himself, preparing for the coming confrontation. Margaret, though pale with worry, dared not intervene. When Spinks pulled up at our destination, Cherville lumbered down from the carriage and pushed the driver away when he would have offered help. He tottered towards the front entrance and, seeing his approach, a young boy set off at a run. By the time we'd reached the factory door, a line of Cherville's workers waited to greet him. The heavily-built man I recalled from my visit eight weeks before was the first to step forward.

'Welcome, sir. We were not expecting you. Should I fetch Mr Rowland?'

His bluff manner was worlds away from how he'd treated me. Beneath the deference required to the man who paid his wages, there was an anxiety. He was sharp enough to see there was something not quite right in this sudden advent of Gervaise Cherville, who'd been away from his company for so long.

'That's quite all right. I'm sure he'll join us erelong.'

The factory floor was a vast space filled with row upon row of machines. The men worked on the right, with the women on the left. Cherville strode down the aisle that separated them, Margaret and I trailing after him. The whirring of the machines fell silent as one by one the workers recognised him and paused in their tasks to doff their caps or nod. One or two exchanged worried glances, and well they might. He was clearly ill, his face pallid and shining with sweat.

Cherville struggled on to a pallet, the better to see his staff, and beckoned them towards him. He swayed alarmingly, and from the corner of my eye I saw how Margaret bit her lip, twitching with the urge to catch him should he fall. She wasn't the only one concerned. Her dismay was reflected in the faces of the factory workers unable to understand what was going on. Willa wasn't among them, as far as I could tell, and I cast around wondering where she might be.

Cherville cleared his throat. 'As you know, I've been unwell and during my indisposition my son has taken over.' Right on cue Rowland appeared on the balcony that overlooked the factory floor. Seconds later, he came down the metal stairs, out of puff and red in the face as if he'd run all the way from his office. His cravat was askew and, while he fiddled to fasten his shirt cuffs, his eyes darted to Margaret, seeking an explanation. What could she do except shrug? At this moment only Gervaise Cherville knew what was about to happen.

'Son, there you are, I thank you for your stewardship,' he said, and then clapped his hands together, leading an uncertain applause among the workers. From what Willa had said, they hadn't taken to Rowland much and, standing by his father, he seemed to shrink a little as their feelings showed.

'Thank you, Father, I hope you've been pleased with what we've produced. Sales have started to recover this week and—'

'Yes, yes, very good,' Cherville interrupted. 'You've done well and I thank you for it. From today I am back, however. Consider yourself no longer needed. I do not expect to see you here.'

When Cherville had said he would teach his son a lesson, I would have never dreamed he'd sack him. Not only that: he'd humiliated Rowland in front of the staff he'd been lording it over. They whispered and smiled to one another at the turn events had taken.

'Father, I must speak with you,' Rowland said.

Until this point he'd been trying to project an air of calm, but now his voice was shrill and Cherville stepped off the pallet to hear what he would say.

'You don't look well, Father.'

'Much you'd care if I was about to breathe my last breath. I came to tell you that you've lost, Rowland.'

'What are you talking about?'

'About the slaves. You've been trying to dissuade me from atoning, trying to keep me from doing what is right. You were wrong to expose Aphrodite and, though it hurts me, you must be punished for it. I have lately come from Wheeler's and advised him that when our family is compensated for the loss of its slaves, I will divide what we are given between the men and women that work on my plantation.'

Rowland's face had blanched in fury and was slowly reddening. 'What do you mean you will divide our fortune among the slaves? You are giving away my future. This is *her* doing,' and he pointed an angry finger in my direction.

The metal stairs clanged again and I looked up to see Willa making her way slowly down. By now the staff had broken into groups, seemingly talking among themselves but really trying to listen to the row that raged between their two masters. I wanted to hear it, too, but more importantly I had to get to Willa who was walking towards the back of the room.

I'd started to follow her, when Cherville bellowed, 'Enough. For once and for all, you will not tell me what to do with my own money.'

The hum of conversation among the workers abruptly stopped. The man nearest me was looking at Cherville in horror – and well he might, for his eyes bulged and as he spoke the spittle that had foamed at the corners of his mouth flew, causing Rowland to recoil.

'What is this nonsense talk? You can't do this to me. Soon you'll be dead and everything you see here will be mine.'

Margaret stepped between the two men, only for Cherville to push her aside. 'What have I done to deserve a son that would wish me dead? It's a shame for you I was never better. Reeves, where are you? You come here and tell my son I'm better.'

Anyone could see he was not. The workers parted as he stumbled towards me, none wanting to catch his eye. Maybe he caught one foot on another, or maybe his legs buckled beneath him – however it happened, he was falling, and he hit the ground in front of me with a strangled cry. Instantly, the workers surged around him and I had to fight my way through to reach him. As I dropped to my knees at his side, his eyes had begun to flicker open.

'Loosen his waistcoat, he needs air,' I said, and then to Cherville, 'Lie back, sir.'

I pulled his head on to my lap to spare him the cold concrete floor. His eyes lolled, searching out mine, and for an awful moment it was Mama's face before me. Was Cherville going to die in my arms, too? And in that moment it didn't matter that she'd been enslaved and he was a slaver. My vocation meant I'd do whatever was needed to keep him alive.

'Margaret,' I called out, but the housekeeper was already there, of course she was.

'Talk to him, try to keep him from fainting,' I said. In my pocket, I had a vial of smelling salts. I waved it under Cherville's nose and he sat up sharply with a groan.

'Where am I?' he said groggily.

'At the factory, sir,' I said.

'I want to be home,' he said plaintively.

'We'll get you to Tall Trees right away – can you stand?'

Together, Margaret and I pulled him to his feet. Someone fetched the doorman and, with his help, we ushered
Cherville outside. Rowland was nowhere to be seen.
Spinks, leaning back against the carriage, jumped to attention when he saw us half-dragging Cherville towards him.

'What's happened?'

'You're to drive Mr Cherville home to Tall Trees very
slowly,' I said. 'Watch out for any holes in the road, he
cannot be jolted.'

Meanwhile Margaret coaxed Cherville into the carriage
and climbed up after him.

'Remember, keep the horses steady,' I said to Spinks.

I gave one final look around for Rowland. Whatever had
happened between him and his father, could he not see
we needed his help? Willa was watching on and I beckoned
her over. 'Did you see where Rowland went? He needs to
know his father is very ill.'

'Can't you find him yourself?'

I blinked in surprise at her sulky tone. She'd been so
much more like her old self when she came to Tall Trees
to give me the bunny.

'Is it true? What Rowland said about you coming
between him and his father?' she asked.

Until she was wholly free of his influence, he'd always
be a thorn between us. 'This isn't the time for accusations,

Willa. We must get Cherville back to Tall Trees immediately.'

'Is that not what's happening?' she answered, nodding beyond me in the direction of the carriage. I turned just in time to see Spinks whip up the horses.

'Wait for me,' I called as they jumped into a standing canter, but he gave no sign of having heard me. Within moments he was out of sight as he took the turning that led back to the main road. What was he thinking to leave me behind like that? Margaret's doing, was my first thought. I couldn't blame her for wanting to get Cherville straight back to bed. The fear in her eyes when he'd fallen had been painful to witness.

'Will you take me to Rowland's office?' I said over my shoulder. No answer came and I turned to see my sister hadn't bothered to wait either and was almost back at the factory. Picking up my skirts, I hurried after her. I needed to find Rowland Cherville and explain the gravity of the situation, whether she was willing to help me or not.

XXVIII

A villain to the last

The machines on the factory floor lay idle, left halfway through their cycles when the workers were called together to hear from Gervaise Cherville. Following his collapse, none had returned to their posts. What they'd seen had unsettled them and they huddled in clumps of two and three trying to make sense of what had happened.

I approached the nearest trio of men, who all wore grave expressions. 'Where can I find Rowland Cherville?'

'First floor. His office is halfway down the corridor.'

'Did you see if my sister went that way, too? Willa Wright?' I said, but the one who had spoken only shrugged and his fellows ignored me completely. Quickly as I could, I made my way up the metal stairs. If Spinks had continued at the pace he'd set, Cherville couldn't be far from

Tall Trees. I needed to get back there as soon as I could to tend him, and Rowland had a duty to be with his father in this moment, too. Cherville had overextended himself going first to visit his solicitor and then on to confront his son. The additional fall could only have a grievous effect. He'd already been weakened by his condition – I couldn't afford to spend too long chasing down Rowland. It would take me at least half an hour to get back to Tall Trees even if I hailed a cab.

I jogged along the first-floor corridor towards Rowland's office. Outside, I raised my hand to knock, grateful for the chance to catch my breath, when I heard a giggle.

'Willa, is that you?' I cried, pushing open the door.

Her mouth made a round O of shock to see me, and she turned to the wall, but not before I saw that the buttons of her bodice were gaping. She started to fumble them shut and I turned to Rowland, who leaned back against his desk, fully clothed and smiling at me maliciously.

'Still here, Reeves? I'd have thought you'd have been back at Tall Trees by now.'

'You should be there yourself,' I said tightly. 'Your father is very ill.'

'I find myself quite busy here,' he said and then, turning to Willa, 'I think that's the second time we've been interrupted this afternoon, isn't it?'

I thought back to when he'd come down to the factory

floor all out of puff. I'd assumed he'd been rushing to pre-empt his father; in fact he'd been occupied in quite a different way.

Willa was now dressed. 'Let's leave,' I said, holding out my hand to her, but she left it hanging in mid-air. 'You can't stay with him, Willa. You must come with me now.'

I wanted her as far away from Rowland Cherville as possible, but worry sharpened my voice and made her rebellious.

'You can't order me, Hester.'

Her words snapped like a whip.

'Please, Willa,' I tried in a softer tone, but the effect it had was worse for she put her arm around Rowland Cherville's waist.

'Rowland's told me how you've been working on his father. Persuading him to do things he doesn't want to, like give away his money.'

'You know better than to believe that pack of lies, Willa.'

'Do I? Isn't making everyone dance to your tune exactly how you carry on? I didn't want to come and live with you, but you kept on and on and wore me down. I don't want to leave London, but you keep telling me I must. If he says that's what you've done to his father, why wouldn't I believe him?'

Was this how she really saw me? The pain her words caused me was physical in its intensity. I couldn't bow to it. First I had to get her away.

'You're right that I'd do anything to separate you from him,' I said, glaring at Rowland Cherville. 'He doesn't want you, Willa.'

'It's only that he's been busy, haven't you?' she said, looking over at him. The expression on her face cut my heart. There was so much hope in it, so much love, that for a fleeting moment I almost wished he returned her feelings. 'Just before his father arrived, we'd agreed to start up again. That's what you want, Rowly, isn't it?'

I closed my eyes, not wanting to witness the moment when he let her down once and for all and she finally saw him for who he really was. It was all too obvious what had happened. After humiliating Lady Raine, he'd come to the factory drunk on the trouble he'd caused. Poor Willa had wandered into his path and mistaken his triumph for genuine affection. It sickened me to think that ruining the life of a woman who'd already suffered so much at his family's hands aroused him. Knowing what I knew about the disease he'd inherited from his father, I could only hope things hadn't gone too far.

'Rowly?' Willa pleaded when he didn't answer. 'Tell her what you said, that you wanted us to be together.'

The crack in her voice brought tears to my eyes. Rowland, however, was unconcerned. He let out a wide yawn as if bored by the idea he should care either for his ailing father or a girl he was taking advantage of. A villain to the last, and maybe he'd realised that by toying with her, he could get back at me, too. Willa's face crumpled and she began to cry.

'Come with me,' I urged her.

But again, my sister refused to take my hand. 'Don't follow me, Hester,' she cast over her shoulder as she barged past me, and with that she was gone.

'What did you do to her?' I said.

Rowland Cherville smirked in the face of my fury. 'The question should really be: what did she do to me?' That mocking look he wore, I wanted to slap it off, but if he didn't outright admit he'd seduced her there was still hope.

'From now on, you must leave my sister alone – I know you've inherited your father's disease.'

The mocking expression dropped and he took a step forward, but I held my ground. 'That's why you hate him so much, isn't it?'

He took another step forward and I braced, fearing he would strike me.

'You're fired,' he whispered.

'You can't do that.'

'Complain to my father, by all means, but after today I doubt he'll be responsive.'

'He'll recover. Margaret took him straight home, and once he's rested he'll be back as he was.' I hoped I sounded more confident than I felt.

'I saw a man who was unhinged. Talking gibberish about atonement. You and Bright have stuffed his head full of nonsense. There'll be no more of it. I'll speak to Wheeler; it won't take much to persuade him that when my father came to him he was not in his right mind.'

'You're despicable. You would cheat your own father of his wishes as he's on the brink of death?'

'That is exactly what I'll do.'

I couldn't let it happen. Cherville's remorse had come too late for Mama, and doomed Lady Raine and her daughter. In Honduras it could help, but only if I kept him well enough to confirm his intentions and stop his son from countermanding him. I turned on my heel and Rowland called after me, 'You won't get into the house.'

I ignored him, picking up my pace and hurrying down the corridor back the way I came.

'You were the one that lost, Reeves – to me!' he shouted, following me out. 'You thought you'd got to my father with your talk of atonement and your witch's potions, but I've got a factory full of people who'll say that he's mad and a housekeeper who's been watching your every move. She's been on to you from the start and those slaves you would give my inheritance to – they'll not see a penny.'

His words rang in my head as I reached the factory floor and shouldered my way through the workers to breathe in huge lungfuls of air outside. Poisonous lies. But who would believe me over him? Only Gervaise

Cherville knew the truth of it – he was my last chance to get justice for the men and women on his plantation and, yes, my mother and aunt and Lady Raine, too. I had to get back to where it all started. I had to return to Tall Trees.

XXIX

The end of the alley

Coloured spots danced before my eyes and I clutched at the spiked railings for support. Before me, Tall Trees loomed, dark and forbidding. Inside, Gervaise Cherville was dying and I had to reach him. I hastened down the side entrance, but the kitchen door was locked and bolted against me. Frustrated, I jerked on the door handle, but it only rattled uselessly. I stepped back, unsure of what to do. The blood still throbbed in my ears where I'd run from the factory. Reflected in the glass panes of the kitchen door, I looked like a wild woman, where my hair had loosened itself from its pins. Shading my eyes, I peered inside. The kitchen was in a state of disarray, the table piled high with pots and pans as though a feast were about to be prepared. The fire glowed red, but there was no sign of Jenny in her usual chair. Feeling uneasy, I made my way back to the main road and climbed the steps to the front door. The bell tolled through the house and I tried to stop my thoughts from reeling. I could believe that Jenny had been called on to help Gervaise Cherville, but that didn't explain why I'd found myself locked out.

At last the door opened and there stood Margaret. It was almost three weeks since I'd moved into Tall Trees and she still looked on me as though I were a stranger.

'I couldn't get in through the kitchen,' I explained, making to go past her, but she widened her stance to block me from entering.

'I don't think so.'

'What do you mean? I need to see to Cherville, you know how ill he is – I could have been here much sooner if you hadn't left me behind at the factory.'

And if I hadn't bothered to try and find Rowland first – although thank God I did. Who knew what might have happened between him and Willa if I hadn't interrupted them?

'The master is being very well looked after. By me.'

She'd disliked me from the first. I'd hoped her love for Cherville would overcome her jealousy, but though she knew it was against his wishes, she'd aligned herself with Rowland and meant to frustrate me.

'He would want to see me,' I said.

267

'If he does, it would only be because you've dosed him in some way.'

'You have no right to prevent me from treating him. Cherville himself hired me, not Rowland. I can't be fired without his say-so. I want to see him,' I said, but she stood firm, her face as grim as the house behind her.

Feeling desperate, I stood back from the door and looked up to the second-floor window, calling, 'Mr Cherville, it's Reeves, can you hear me?'

Margaret shook her head sorrowfully as though she were embarrassed for me, but thank goodness, help was at hand.

'Is everything well, miss?' I turned round to see a peeler approaching in his dark blue coat and leather stock, his height improved by a hardened top hat.

'I need to get inside and see my patient. She's stopping me doing my job,' I said, but he was looking past me. It was Margaret he'd been talking to.

'I'm so glad you're here,' she said, as if I hadn't spoken. 'This woman claims to be a nurse of some sort and has been imposing on my master with her tricks. She's a charlatan.'

'I've been living here,' I wailed.

'I'll take her away, miss.'

I looked from one to the other, unable to accept what was happening. Margaret, calm and impassive; the policeman stern-faced. He made a swipe at me and I stepped back smartly to evade him. Again he lunged, but I was too quick.

'Don't let her get away!' I heard Margaret cry, but I had already started to run again.

I was halfway down Warren Street before I slowed, the curious glances of the people I passed forcing me back to a walk. I couldn't afford to draw attention to myself. What if the peeler decided to come after me? My lungs were burning in my chest and when I saw an alley I ducked into it, leaning back against the soot-stained brickwork. Rowland and Margaret thought they could drive me away, but what I'd said to Margaret was true. Gervaise Cherville had hired me; so only he could sack me. *You can't get to Cherville, though, can you,* came the voice in my head. The kitchen entrance was barred, and Margaret's bulk blocked the front door. How would I ever hope to get in?

'Jenny,' I breathed, and there she was, coming down the road in my direction, almost as if I'd summoned her. She was in her black dress with blue apron, no coat, arms folded tight to stop herself from shivering. Her head turned from left to right, she must be searching for me.

'Over here,' I called, stepping out of the shadows at the mouth of the alley, and at the sight of me her face cleared. I pulled her off the street and deeper into the alley. It might smell of urine and excrement, but we could talk away from prying eyes, at least for a minute.

'Oh, Hester, I'm so glad I caught you.'

She cast a quick glance over her shoulder. On Warren Street people were walking past. Though none of them looked towards us, I couldn't blame Jenny for being scared. Not when Margaret had set the constable on me.

'Did you see what happened? Margaret wouldn't let me in.'

'She's been distraught about the master. He was in a state when she and Spinks brought him back this afternoon. What happened? The last I knew he was going to Lincoln's Inn.'

I explained that Cherville had returned around half-past one and then gone more or less straight out again to his factory.

'What happened in Bloomsbury, exactly?' Jenny asked, but I shook my head and she didn't pursue it.

'When Cherville arrived at the factory, he announced to the workers that he was going to return and cut off Rowland, all in one go. Rowland argued back, but Cherville wasn't to be swayed and then he collapsed,' I said.

Jenny frowned, trying to take in all that had passed. 'I guessed something was wrong as soon as they came in. I was in the kitchen and there was such a commotion I ran up to the entrance hall. Margaret was there with Spinks and they were half-carrying the master between them. He was so grey, I honestly thought he'd snuffed it. Madam has had me fetching towels and carrying water and mopping his brow. It's the absolute worst day for it an' all. I'm up to my eyeballs with all the baking. It's Mr Rowland's dinner with Miss Hawkins on Tuesday so I was trying to get a head start.'

In all that had happened, I'd forgotten about Rowland's engagement. It explained why he'd dismissed Willa with so little feeling.

'Should I try and speak to Madam for you?' Jenny said. 'I'm not sure how far I'd get. You should have seen how she was hanging over the master this afternoon. I could have sworn she was weeping.'

Just as a daughter would, I thought to myself.

Her love for Cherville was what I needed to appeal to. In her heart of hearts, surely she would want his wishes respected over Rowland's avarice.

'Where will you go now?' asked Jenny.

'Back home, I suppose.'

'If Cherville's condition changes, I'll let you know. I wouldn't leave it too long before you see him, though.'

It was good advice. I shared Jenny's sense that Cherville didn't have much time left on this earth and I needed to find a way to shore up his commitment to the Honduran slaves before Rowland got to Wheeler, the family solicitor.

'When might be a good time to come back?'

'Do you think that Mr Rowland will obey his father and not return to the factory?'

'I can't imagine it,' I said.

'That means he'll be out during the day, then, but

Margaret will be watching for you and it would be too dangerous.'

Margaret would be a factor at any time of day. I doubted she'd let Cherville from her sight – and then it came to me. There was one occasion when I could guarantee she'd be distracted.

'What about the night of the dinner party?' I suggested.

'Do you think it will still go ahead? Might it not look callous if Mr Rowland is celebrating his engagement when his father is dying upstairs?'

'I can't see him cancelling. He wants the girl's money, remember? Look out for me just after the party's started. I think it will be my best chance to get back in and speak to Cherville.'

'Tuesday evening it is, then. Margaret told me to have the first course ready to serve at seven o'clock, so any time after that and we'll be in all sorts of uproar. You'll be able to slip in easily.'

'You'd better get back before Margaret realises you've gone,' I said.

We embraced, then walked together to the end of the alley. Jenny melted into the crowd, so slight that the men and women swallowed her up until she reached the corner of the square and turned to give me a wave.

Thank God for Jenny. She'd been a great help to me today, but if I was going to ensure the slaves got their money, I'd need my family, too. Would Jos help me?

Usually I would have said yes in an instant, but that was before we'd rowed over him going upriver and leaving Willa on her own.

Poor Willa. It had been an awful day for her, too, finding out what little regard Rowland Cherville truly had for her. Likely she was at home, still crying. The first thing I had to do was comfort her, and then repair our relationship. She'd said some hurtful things to me earlier. If that's how she really felt, then once and for all we must fix it. I had to tell her about Mama and her sister – Nyx and Artemis – and why what had happened made it all the more important that Willa and I stuck together. Once she knew what Gervaise Cherville had done to our family, it would surely extinguish any feelings she had for his son.

XXX

Dirty laundry

I walked up the path to the cottage full of trepidation, but when I opened the door I could tell at once it was empty. Jos would be halfway up river by now. Had my sister been home at all?

I pulled back the screen that hived off the corner of the living room we'd made into her bedroom, expecting to find the usual mess: piles of clothing thrown over her chair or dropped on the floor. Despite the discarded shifts and drawers, it seemed clearer than usual, did that mean she'd gone? I dropped down on to the makeshift bed, thinking of the brief moment we'd shared the other week when I'd found her in my bedroom, getting ready to go out, and she'd let me brush her hair. It felt like a lifetime ago, and unwilling to let my melancholia take hold I forced myself up and went into the room I shared with Jos. This was cleaner, tidier, yet its orderliness carried a reproach, an accusation that we hadn't made Willa and her messiness wholly welcome. I couldn't just sit there. I needed a friend.

Sal's place was quiet for a Saturday but it was early yet. The tables that were taken were occupied by men on their own, heads bent low over pints of bitter. The factory girls sat in what I now knew was their usual corner. They were less raucous than they had been last time I was in. The events of the afternoon had affected them, not because they cared anything much for Gervaise Cherville per se, but because he was their livelihood and if anything truly serious happened to him they knew they'd find themselves in trouble. It was no great surprise that Willa was not among them. If she really had left, she wouldn't have gone anywhere I'd think to look for her.

I made my way to the bar where Sal was straightening bottles of brandy, whisky and gin on the back shelf. She usually had a sixth sense for when anyone was waiting, but when she hadn't turned around after a minute or two I knocked on the shiny wooden surface of the counter to attract her attention.

'I'll have a glass of your finest perry, please.'

Had I imagined how Sal winced at the sound of my voice?

'One moment, Hester,' she called over her shoulder. 'A half all right for you?'

She sounded tired and no wonder when she worked such long hours. I'd told her before to look after herself better, and was thinking of which herbs she might find helpful, when she looked up and I saw it wasn't only fatigue that had distorted her words. Sal's bottom lip was cut, so swollen that it would be painful for her to fully open her mouth. Her left eye was closed, too, the cheek beneath varying shades of purple.

'What's happened to you?'

Sal stuck her chin out, defiant, not wanting my pity. 'It's nothing. Drink your drink, Hester.'

'Let me have a look at that eye at least. You have arnica? Calamine?'

'My wife's been her usual clumsy self, you see.'

It was Frank, the lock-keeper. I turned to see him striding in, his colour up, suggesting that a barge had lately arrived. It was unusual to find him in the Hind of an afternoon, or at all really. He generally left it to Sal. Frank crossed the room and stood behind the bar, placing his palms down flat on the counter. My eyes darted to his knuckles, red and raw as I expected. Sal gave a warning shake of her head. If she didn't want me to get involved, I had to respect that, at least while she was serving.

'I came to see if my sister was in,' I said.

'Not so far,' Sal said. 'Her friends have been here an hour already, I overheard there was a bit of a to-do at the factory. They'll be rolling out of here by tonight, I reckon.'

While Sal might feel awful, it was good to hear her sounding like her usual self.

'Cherville collapsed there earlier,' I said. 'Rowland probably sent them home early.'

'I thought I'd got it wrong when I heard. The way you spoke about him the other day, I'd assumed he was bed-bound.'

'He was, more or less; he'd started feeling better.'

'Thanks to your care, I'll bet. That has to be a good thing?'

'It's a long story,' I said glumly.

'Go and talk between yourselves,' Frank said indulgently. I couldn't smile at him. Not knowing what he'd done to her. Sal raised the counter and led me to a booth in the corner.

'Your usual clumsy self?' I said, as soon as we were out of Frank's hearing.

'Don't stir, Hester. There's no use can come of it. We can't all strike lucky like you did with your Jos. What's that face for? The two of you are happy, aren't you?'

'Mostly. I wish he was more accepting of Willa, that's all.'

'He was carping a little when he was in the other night,' Sal admitted, and I frowned, hating the thought that Jos would air our dirty laundry before his fellow workers. It was one thing if Willa got on his nerves, but to complain about her behind my back was disloyal to me as well as her and it hardened my feelings towards him. I'd asked him to look out for my sister while I was at Tall Trees and he'd chosen to go away for work. If Willa hadn't let it slip I doubted he would have told me at all. Now this.

'She'd try the patience of a saint, that girl,' Sal said, turning the anger I felt into tears. I put my hands to my face and Sal pulled them away.

'What's the matter? You don't think she'd run off again?'

'She might have gone already. You know she'd caught Rowland Cherville's eye?'

'Was it serious between them, then? I told you he'd been in a few times, but I wouldn't have pegged it as any more than a flirtation.'

'For her I think it was love. Today she found out she was only a plaything to him, and worse, she blames me for creating a wedge between Rowland and his father.'

'She came back of her own accord before, she will again,' Sal said, but I didn't feel reassured. Wherever Willa had been when she went missing after Mama died had changed her. At home with Jos and me she might act up, but before I'd gone to Tall Trees I'd begun to see flashes of the old Willa. If she went again, I feared I might not get her back at all.

'The whole reason I went to Tall Trees was to earn enough money so we could start again as a family some-where new. What if it's all been for nothing?'

'Don't think the worst. Not yet. It's only been a few hours. I'll keep an eye out for her and send a note if she comes in.'

'You never know, she could be at home waiting for me,' I said.

'That's the spirit. You'll always find her, Hester. Your mother wouldn't have asked you to protect her if she didn't think you could do it.'

What a good friend Sal was to me; only she would realise that my promise to Mama was what lay at the heart of all this. What she didn't know was why it now seemed even more important to me. Mama felt she'd failed to protect her own sister from the Chervilles. All these years later, I couldn't allow history to repeat itself.

XXXI

The horse bus to Westminster

When I woke on Monday morning, Willa still hadn't returned and I was growing ever more anxious. Two nights I could bear, no more than that. I needed to find her and make sure she was safe. The trouble was I had no idea where she might be. Once, I'd known her favourite haunts and who her friends were. Since she'd come back she was secretive. I saw now how that had led me to smother her, so desperate was I to take the second chance I'd been given to keep my promise to Mama. Knowing the fate that had befallen her own sister, I could no longer question why she had been so fervent in her plea that I take care of mine.

Smoke billowed from the chimney of the Cherville factory. Business continued unabated despite Gervaise Cherville's perilous state. There was something devilish in

Rowland that he could preside over so much misery and still speak to his clients, manage his staff and receive and approve payments. It was almost as if the ruination of the lives of Lady Raine and her daughter was a hobby he had undertaken in his spare time. In all the drama of Cherville's collapse and my concern for Willa, my worries for Lady Raine had been overtaken. Tonight I would go to the Lukeses' house to see if she had fled there as I suspected. Please God she was still in London and I hadn't missed my chance.

I lurked about five hundred yards from the front entrance, careful to keep out of sight of the watchman. Rowland was vengeful and I couldn't afford to have him catch me, but talking to one of Willa's friends within the factory was my best chance of finding her. Luckily, it wasn't long until I saw Maudie Clarke on her way home from her daily shift. I was glad it was her – she'd been the one to warn me about how close Rowland Cherville was getting to my sister in the first place, so I knew she'd help me if she could. I waited until Maudie had gone a little way down the towpath, and then when she'd turned on to Euston Road I fell into step beside her.

'Not for me, thank you,' she said, waving me away before I'd begun to speak.

She'd assumed I was a street trader, trying to tempt her with a bit of battered fish or a ladle of beef tea. When I called her name, she started. 'Hester, I didn't realise it was you.'

'I'm sorry, Maudie. I had to see you and I thought catching you on your way home was my best chance.'

'My Tom will be expecting his dinner. Will you walk with me?'

We continued on the tide of people.

'You're brave to show your face 'round Cherville's. Mr Rowland has put it about that you've poisoned his father.'

'It's not true!' I exclaimed. I'd gone to Tall Trees to help Willa escape from Rowland Cherville. If his father died and he managed to pin the blame on me, I'd not be able to stay at the cottage. I'd have to run from him on my own account.

Maudie shrugged. 'I wouldn't count on folk to contradict him. Not for you and definitely not for your sister.'

'Willa hasn't been home since Cherville collapsed.'

'She didn't come into work this morning, either,' Maudie said. 'We heard that Mr Rowland had thrown her over and there's not too many sorry for her. The other women were jealous when she took up with him and she rubbed their noses in it. Wearing those clothes he bought her and that.'

I remembered the green dress she'd worn to the Hind, how expensive it had looked. If only I'd been more frank when I told her to stay away from him. *She never would have, whatever you said*, came the voice in my head. That was Willa. Always having to choose her own path even if it was one that was strewn with hazards. How like Artemis she was. Mama must have seen it every day and feared for her.

'I need to find her, Maudie. Have you any idea where I should start my search?'

'She talked about his club a lot. I think that's where he took her.'

'Hackers?' I said. Was there any chance my sister could have been there with him these last two nights? At Lady Raine's he'd talked of the popularity of coloured whores among the club's clientele and the memory of his words chilled me. He couldn't have meant Willa, could he? The thought of it made my stomach crawl – that was all she'd ever been to him.

'You're not going to go there, are you? I think you'd have a job of it to get in and they wouldn't let her stay there anyway. Not without him.'

'I've got to try,' I said. 'She's my sister. Someone there might know where she's got to.'

'I wish you luck. If I see her, I'll say you've been looking for her.'

'Tell her I love her,' I called as Maudie continued in the direction of St Pancras. It was time for me to catch the horse bus to Westminster.

At sixpence a journey, the horse bus was really beyond my means, but to walk would have taken almost an hour so I gritted my teeth and paid out the fare when one pulled up alongside me. I was glad of the conductor's arm as I climbed on and sank into a window seat, training my eyes on the outside to avoid the furtive stares of my fellow passengers. I still hadn't fully recovered from all the running I'd done on Saturday – it was getting to the stage of my pregnancy when I'd have to be much more careful not to exhaust myself. As we trundled along I shifted to get a better look at the places we passed, how some areas thronged with street sellers, others with beggars or couples walking arm in arm. I spoke of getting out of London; what I really meant was getting out of King's Cross. I'd heard of some of the places the conductor called out – Kingsway, Drury Lane, Trafalgar Square – but never visited. My London, Willa's too, had only ever been the furthest we could walk before we grew tired. No wonder she had found Rowland Cherville, with his private carriage that could take her anywhere, so exciting.

The road where the conductor set me down was opposite St James's Park. If I hadn't known better, I would have said this was the countryside. There were fields along the towpath, of course, but this green was of another order entirely: not only grass but flowers and a lake. How was it that the canal had all the same ingredients and felt so different? Perhaps the distinction was that in one place the poor were expected to work while in the other the rich took their leisure.

Hackers may have been a so-called gentlemen's club, but it wasn't unlike Tall Trees in appearance: a huge house, with pillars at its front entrance. I hovered outside, watching the smartly dressed men who went in and out, wondering if I'd recognise Lord Raine or any of the others who'd witnessed Rowland's betrayal of his wife's secret. I'd not been there long when the man on the door caught my eye and beckoned me to him. His livery, white breeches and a quilted jacket, put me in mind of what Lady Raine's butler Bingham had worn. I had my explanations ready in case he tried to move me on, but he muttered from the side of his mouth, 'You need work? You've got to wait round the back, late. The head man comes out around ten o'clock. If he likes your looks he'll pick you, but I warn you there's plenty of girls who wants in.'

I'd not been sure what to expect from a gentlemen's club – but whatever else it may have been, if I could be mistaken for a streetwalker and told how best to secure custom, for all its fancy entrance it wasn't far from a brothel.

'That's not why I'm here. I came to find my sister.'

He looked at me pityingly. 'I thought you was a bit older than the ones I normally see, but it takes all sorts, don't it? The girls don't make a bad living.'

'She's not like that, she's . . .' Out of her depth, in trouble, desperate by now, having been away from home for two days with no bag, no clothes and, as far as I knew, no money. 'She'd have only been here in the company of a man. You might have seen her with him. He's tall, dark-haired, Rowland . . .'

'Cherville?' the doorman supplied. Was it a good or bad thing that he knew him? I was frightened to ask. He scratched at his face, thinking. 'Is she a slight girl? Wears a green dress?'

'That's her.'

'Now I think on it, she'd got to be quite a regular. He liked her to be waiting in his room of an evening. I haven't seen her these last few days, though.'

His words landed like a blow. For weeks she'd been lying to me, not just about how long he'd been courting her, but how far it had gone between them, too. When she'd come to Tall Trees, she'd quizzed me on the signs of syphilis. Had she already lain with him when I told her of the disease? Poor, poor Willa. If she'd caught it from him, she'd need treatment. It was more urgent than ever that I find her.

'You'll keep an eye out for her, though?'

'I will,' the doorman said. He looked like he wanted to say something more, but when nothing was forthcoming, I left.

He called out to me before I'd got three steps away. 'Some of the girls, when they no longer come here, you find them round King's Cross.'

I gave him a nod of thanks. I knew all too well where women who'd been ruined went when they were desperate. Many of them became my patients. I'd searched among them for my sister before, was convinced that it was one of them who'd persuaded her to come home to me. Could she have descended that fast? Of course she could. I'd heard enough stories in my time from the women as I examined them and bandaged their hurts. A day's work lost or a poorly child in need of medicine. Any number of reasons that should have been a mere nothing had ended in the worst for them and, following her affair with Rowland Cherville, Willa was further down the road to ruin than most. It would be one small step with no food and no shelter. *You can't be sure exactly how far it's gone between them, though*, I reminded myself. Faint hope, but it was something to cling on to.

'Good luck to you,' the doorman shouted. Maudie had said similar. It was a shame that my luck had deserted me long ago.

I made to leave, but there was one last thing I must ask. 'You haven't seen Lord Raine come in at all, have you?'

'He's here now. Has been since last night though he's not usually one to stay over.'

Few knew better than me what kept him from his home. I gave a final nod and walked over to a bench a short way along from the club to plan my next step.

It was a little too early for King's Cross, I thought. Most of the men came when the theatres closed and the pubs kicked out. Meanwhile, a steady flow of gentlemen went in and out of Hackers. One man took the steps at a run and in doing so caught my eye. On reaching the door he paused to let another man past and all my attention turned to him, for it was Lord Raine, and before I was aware of what I was doing, I was on my feet and accosting him.

'Sir, might you spare a minute?' He cast a quick glance over his shoulder and then, frowning at me, walked on. Was I doing more harm than good? I didn't know, but I couldn't lose the chance to talk to him and so I followed on.

'Sir, please, it's about Lady Raine and your daughter Cecily.'

He stilled, his shoulders slumped, and I ran in front so I could face him.

'You were there, at Lady Cecily's luncheon. You're Cherville's woman,' he accused.

'Never that. I work for Gervaise Cherville, but he knew nothing of what his son had planned, I promise you.'

Was I really defending Gervaise Cherville after all he'd done to my family? I had to, however uncomfortable it felt. He was not the same as his son, and he'd done enough to make me want to acknowledge the difference between them.

'Don't you want to know where they are, your wife and daughter?'

'I have no wife and daughter,' he said and strode off,

leaving me staring after him. I'd seen the loving way he'd looked at Lady Raine before Rowland had arrived at the party, but now she might as well have been dead to him.

'Move along, girl,' a peeler said impatiently, jostling me as he walked past, and, feeling deflated, I dug in my pocket for another sixpence to pay for the journey back to the cottage.

XXXII

Blue with cold

For the third evening in a row, I came down the towpath to see the cottage ahead of me in darkness. It was two days since I'd been dismissed from Tall Trees and Willa had fled – far too early to lose hope, and yet I could feel it dwindling. There'd been a moment as I'd sat on the horse bus to Hackers when I'd wondered if that one place held the solutions to the problems I'd run into ever since I'd become caught up with Gervaise Cherville and his schemes. Well, I had my answer now. I would not forget the disgust on Lord Raine's face when he'd declared he had no wife or daughter and the doorman's suggestion about Willa's whereabouts had been only that – just a thought, no guarantees. In fact, I was hoping he was wrong completely. I tried to summon some of Sal's positivity. She'd say that Willa might be with a friend, but she didn't have many – none I could think of that would put her up, at least.

Inside, I went straight to where Jos kept his bottle of brandy and took a quick swig to fortify me for the journey I would have to make into King's Cross. The one I had been putting off. I was pouring myself a glass when Jos appeared in the doorway and I started.

'When did you get back? I thought you weren't home until tomorrow,' I said.

'About five minutes since. Not even long enough to put the lights on.'

We were strange with each other. In the last two days he'd started a beard. It made him look older. Not like my Jos at all. Perhaps he wasn't any more, not if he could go off without telling me, not if he couldn't keep an eye on Willa like I'd asked.

'How come you're here anyway? Should you not be at Tall Trees?'

'I've been fired,' I said, and took a gulp of the brandy. Jos indicated I should pour him one and I slid it along the table to him.

'Are you going to tell me what's happened?'

I looked to the door – the longer I delayed, the longer it would be before I found Willa. And yet it felt as though I was against the world right now. I needed my husband in my corner. I sat down at the table and Jos took the chair opposite.

'The last I knew, you were looking for Nyx. Did you find her?'

'I found out who she is, which is sort of the same.'

Jos looked at me as I took another glug, silent, his eyes troubled, waiting for me to tell it in my own way. I sighed, reluctant to say it out loud, even to him. Speaking it made it true, but unless I did I could not begin to get used to it.

'Mama was Nyx, and her sister, Artemis, Gervaise Cherville good as killed her.'

Jos whistled softly. 'Poor Essie, you've had to bear this all alone,' he said as I brushed away tears with the cuff of my sleeve.

'It's not only that. There's Lady Raine. Rowland announced who she was to a room full of people, then Cherville collapsed, and then there's Willa.'

I looked him dead in the eye as I said her name, waiting for him to challenge me. *What about Willa, what's she done now?* I could almost hear him say it in that sing-song way of his that made me want to defend her even when I knew she was in the wrong.

He reached over to me and I stretched out my arms so our hands met in the middle. He gripped mine in his own, holding them tight.

'Tell me about Willa first,' he said.

'I want to, but I've got to go out now. She's missing and I must search for her.' I picked up my coat and shoved in one arm and then Jos was there to help with the second.

'Let me come with you. We'll bring her home together.'

It was so cold that the night air caught at the back of my throat when I breathed in. Enclosed within Tall Trees, I'd forgotten how raw, how bitter, it could be down by the canal and I huddled into my coat.

'Where exactly should we start?' Jos said, stamping his feet to stave off the chill.

'There's a side street where the women gather. It's where I used to meet them to hand out my medicines.'

'I'll follow your lead and there's some things I have to say to you along the way.'

My heart sank. This, then, was why he'd offered to join me. Ever since Willa had returned, it had been building up to this; on Saturday when I'd confronted him at the ware-house, he'd said we needed to talk – and now it had come to a head. Even after I'd told him of the tragedy that made Mama so insistent I protect Willa, he was going to force me to choose. On the journey to find my sister, I'd lose my husband.

'Does it have to be now?'

'Please hear me out,' he said, and I nodded.

'I owe you an apology,' Jos began as we crunched along the towpath in the direction of King's Cross. I looked down at the pebbles beneath my feet, across to the field where the heavy bargee horses were put to pasture for the night – anywhere but at him.

'You made a promise, to your mother. All you've sought to do is honour it and I have not helped you as I should. In truth, I've been jealous. Willa can be difficult and I did not want to share you with her. I saw the toll it took on you when she disappeared and I resented her for it. Overnight it felt as though you'd aged, you were no longer my Essie, you were her Hes—'

'I was always both,' I interrupted, coming to a halt, and Jos stopped, too.

'I know that now. Last night I sat up on deck rehearsing what I would say to you. I was angry but I kept coming back to the promise you had made. I remembered that I had made one, too. I promised to love you, Essie. To protect you. Most times you don't need it. You're strong, you always have been, but when we married the promise I made was not only to you. It was to your mother, to your father – I'm sure he was looking down on us that day in church – and it was to Willa, also, and this one.'

Here he touched my stomach and I covered his hand with my own and held it there. 'I want to do better, Essie. I want to keep my promise.'

His eyes shone with feeling and he blinked back the tears that had gathered. 'Can we start again?'

'Yes, let's, all four of us. The moment we find Willa will

be our new beginning,' I said and we kissed to set the seal
on it.

The strength I took from Jos's hand in mine was much
needed as we joined the main road. It had been quiet on the
towpath; now passers-by loomed out at us, hidden by the
fog until we were close to collision. Though we walked in
step, several girls called over to Jos, offering their services.
One, a little more desperate than the others, came right up
to us. She shrugged off her shawl to reveal a bare shoulder,
already blue with cold. It was intended to look seductive,
but there was nothing alluring about the scars on her face
and the sharpness of the bones beneath her skin.

'Here, take this,' I said, holding out the last of my coins,
but she turned from the pity in my eyes and walked away.
I wanted to go after her, persuade her.

Jos pulled me back. 'We're here for Willa, not her.'

'They're of an age,' I said, but it wasn't only that. The
girl had a look of Lady Cecily and the thought that Rowland's revelations might force her down this path brought
tears to my eyes.

Just before Euston Road became Pentonville, I steered
Jos to the left. 'The place we want is down here.'

He looked around, eyes peering through the fog to take
in the rickety tenement buildings. 'I had no idea this was
where you came each night before you started working
for Cherville. Is it always like this?'

'I'm afraid so, and it will be as long as they're here.' I nodded in the direction of a carriage that had pulled up a little way ahead of us. The glass dropped down and a gloved hand emerged, the index finger beckoning, and two girls jostled each other to be the first to respond. 'Come on,' I said. 'This is the group of women I was hoping to talk to.'

'Do you want me to wait here?'

I hesitated, fearful of what I might find out.

'You'd prefer to go alone?'

No, not that.

'Stay with me,' I said, hearing my voice as if it came from far away, and Jos pressed my hand and led me forward.

The building the women stood beside had once been a chophouse. I'd been inside myself on one occasion and dispensed medicines and advice from the serving hatch that still remained. I knew it to be cold, the air fetid, and so it was no surprise that the women huddled together outside rather than go in.

'Well, look who's remembered us,' came one voice, and there was some jeering as Jos and I approached, not all of it good-natured.

I looked about me. There were one or two faces I recognised, but the majority of them were new. I heard one of the old hands mutter, 'She's our doctoress,' and felt a burst of warmth that they still claimed me, even though I'd abandoned them to go and work at Tall Trees. Hopefully it meant they'd show their loyalty by telling me if Willa had become one of their number.

'I did promise I'd be back,' I said.

'What have you brought with you?' came the shout as they gathered around me. My bag was still at Tall Trees, but I'd collected some tonics when I was at the cottage and I handed them out with instructions for when to take them.

'Is this a punter for us, too?' one girl asked slyly, eyeing Jos.

'This is my husband,' I chastised her. 'We came together because we're looking for my sister.'

A few of the crowd melted away. Not many women that came here wanted to be found. Nor always was it people with the best intentions that were asking for them. It was rarely mothers or fathers or sisters who sought out the missing. Most often it was pimps or bawds, full of gifts and reassuring words, until they had the naive or desperate runaways in their clutches.

'Gill, you'd tell me if you'd seen her, wouldn't you?'

I addressed myself to one of the older women. I'd thought Gill might have had a hand in encouraging Willa back to me when she'd run before.

'Been no sign of her 'round this way.'

'You will tell me, though, if you see her? Won't you?'

'I'd try the clubs first. Girl like your sister would make

far more there than here if the gents have a taste for the exotic.'

'I've been to one already, but I'll try some others. Look after yourself out here, won't you?'

'It'll be better when you're back to do it for us. It's not easy times for the girls right now. The disease is running rampant and the greener ones among us don't always have the sense or ability to sniff out which men are rotten.'

Or the luxury, I thought. I'd been down here on other nights and seen women so desperate for food or shelter that they'd go with anyone who'd pay, even when they knew they'd likely get a beating or worse in return. Thanking Gill for her help and asking her to leave word at the Hind if she heard anything, Jos and I made our way back to the cottage.

At the table he reached for the brandy, and by the way his hand trembled I knew he'd been shaken by what he'd seen.

'Not for me,' I said. 'I had a glass or so earlier and I wouldn't want too much with the baby. Besides, I've got to go out again.'

'You shouldn't be out at all in your condition,' Jos fretted. 'Doesn't it make sense for me to come with you if you're going to try more clubs?'

'There's somewhere else I must go, actually,' I said. 'Off Oxford Circus.'

'On you go, then, and once I've eaten, I'll try the clubs myself.'

'Would you?' I said, so grateful that the search could continue while I visited Lady Raine and her daughter.

'Working together, just as we promised,' Jos said, embracing me tightly before I went back out into the cold.

XXXIII

A bloom that meant peace

I expected no good reception at the Lukeses' and nor did I receive one. When Mrs Lukes answered the door and saw me standing before her, she curled her lip – she knew what had happened and blamed me.

'I was hoping to speak to Lady Raine.'

'She's gone already.'

Mrs Lukes had every right to be angry. All along she'd been concerned for the woman she knew as Aphrodite, and because of my involvement not only was Lady Raine in trouble but her daughter was, too.

'I trust we won't see you here again,' Mrs Lukes said, but I couldn't let her slam the door in my face.

'I know she's here. Please, at least tell her I've come and ask if she will see me.'

Mrs Lukes wavered, but only for a second. She stepped back and the door began to close.

'Say I'm Nyx's daughter,' I shouted. It wasn't enough, and the door slammed shut. I hovered for a minute, wondering whether I should try again. I'd spoken to her husband – surely Lady Raine would want to know – and then I remembered what he'd said: *I have no wife and daughter*. There was no need for her to hear that. Feeling dispirited, I began the long trudge home.

Maybe it was time to call a halt to things. I'd found Lady Raine, only for it to ruin her life; I'd found Nyx and learned she was my mother; and I'd got to the bottom of what happened to my aunt, Artemis – but what good had it done? Was it better to know of all that pain and sadness, or of Bright's treachery? Hand on heart, I couldn't swear to it, so what did that mean for my intention to help ensure Cherville's plan to pay his slaves in Honduras was enacted? Even if I could get back into Tall Trees, how likely was it that, ill as he was, I could make him confirm his wishes to Wheeler? If Rowland objected, I couldn't imagine a court in the land that would take my part. I sighed heavily, thinking how much better it would have been if I'd never laid eyes on Tall Trees, when hearing my name called made me turn.

Lady Raine was running towards me and when she stopped we both started to speak at once.

'I'm sorry,' I tried again, feeling all the inadequacy of the word.

She shook her head, brushing it away. 'Is it true you're Nyx's daughter?'

'After I saw you, I went to Mr Bright and he confessed he was the abolitionist you spoke of. He said Cherville tricked him, and that he'd got me the job at Tall Trees to make amends. I don't believe he had any idea that speaking to Cherville of atonement would make him think of you, or my mother and aunt. He was against it from the start, said that the Honduran slaves must be the priority. Now I realise he was not concerned with doing the most good, but of concealing his part in what happened here on his very own doorstep.'

'At best he was naive, but in his determination to set aside what he did, I see no true repentance. Cherville, for all his faults, took accountability in the end.'

'How is Lady Cecily? I've been thinking of her.'

'Come back to the Lukeses' with me. You can meet her for yourself.'

When Lady Raine ushered me into the sitting room, I could see that Mrs Lukes hadn't yet decided whether she forgave me. It was understandable; there were so many threads to what had happened, yet I was coming to think that maybe it was not about blame after all, but doing the right thing when you had the chance to, as long as it was for the right reasons.

'Lady Raine has been very gracious,' I said when Mrs Lukes reluctantly handed me a cup of tea.

'Oh, don't call me that. I'm not her any more, I never was,' Lady Raine said. 'Nor am I Aphrodite. That wasn't my name, but a title forced upon me. From now on, I will answer only to Joy – that is what my mother named me.'

It suited her. For me there was no Nyx either. I'd known her only as Mama, but when they were alone together I'd heard my father call her Ada. She'd never spoken of her sister. It saddened me to think that my aunt was forever trapped in the guise of Artemis; even in death she was not wholly free.

Joy turned to her daughter. 'Cecily, I'd like to introduce you properly to Hester Reeves.'

We smiled and shook hands and she was perfectly cordial, but in her eyes I saw that she was lost. I'd feared that exposure had ruined Lady Raine's life; now I saw it had broken her final bonds. For Lady Cecily it was different. She'd grown up with every blessing and privilege showered upon her. How would she adapt to this new understanding she'd been brought to?

It was a question I needed to answer for myself also. Mama was not who I thought she was. It shamed me now that I'd not seen all of her, her strength and courage, and I fixed my eyes on my cup, so a stray tear rippled the surface.

'Hester, might we speak privately?'

I followed Joy into the kitchen and then out into the Lukeses' little garden.

'That is one thing I will miss about that life. My beautiful hothouse,' Joy said, as she bent down to pick a lilac-hued flower. 'When I met you there, I gave you a bloom that meant peace. This one means farewell.'

I turned the Michaelmas daisy over in my hands, my mind throbbing with questions that I did not know how to put into words.

'Where will you go now?' I said at last.

'To the Continent, I think. I have a little money of my own that I have saved, and when I am gone, Mr Lukes will deliver a letter to my husband. I will ask him for nothing for myself, but he loved his daughter. He will wish to provide for her.'

'He loved you as well; I saw it in his face on the day of the party before Rowland Cherville came.'

'It is sweet of you to say, but he loved Lucilla Raine. He did not know me at all.'

'How did you do it all those years?'

'Do you know, looking back, I couldn't tell you. I needed to survive; maybe it was as simple as that.'

'I should be getting home. My husband will be waiting on me and my sister is missing.'

'Your sister is not Artemis.'

'Is she not? A Cherville will ruin her life. Is it not history repeating itself?'

'It doesn't have to be. You will find her, I am certain of it. I know your mother felt guilty about what happened, but it was not her fault, and whatever your sister does, that is not your fault either.'

'I made a promise to Mama when she lay dying. She gripped my hand and made me swear to protect Willa.'

'Your sister is her own person, as Artemis was. Look for her, but do not lose sight of that along the way.'

She opened her arms to me and after we embraced she held me away from her. 'You are very like your mother. I am surprised I did not see it straight away.'

'I've been told I have her eyes.'

'Yes, that's right, and maybe something of her steadfastness. Go well, Hester.'

I turned to leave, but there was one final thing I wished to ask her. 'After he realised who you were, Cherville said he would change his will to free his slaves in Honduras.'

'I am glad he repented.'

'Is that true? After all that's happened, don't you think that some apologies are better left unsaid?'

She put her head to one side and considered for a moment. 'When Cherville spoke to my servant Patience, she wouldn't take the money he wished to give her. In the end he left it on the table. She told me she didn't want him to feel that it was enough to make amends for what he'd done.'

'Do you know if he actually said the word "sorry"?' Without it, had he really accepted the harm that he'd caused?

'Talk can be cheap. The action he has taken to change his will says it for him.'

'He was very excited that afternoon when he got home after he saw Patience, but it wasn't until the bazaar when you made that speech, and for the first time he saw who you were, that I'd say he truly felt remorse.'

'That was his second step; he could not have made it without the first one. I say: whatever you can do to help the slaves in Honduras, you should do it.'

Joy led me towards the house and we embraced again before I left her there. Back on the street, I set my face in the direction of home, my ears ringing with Joy's exhortation to help Cherville compensate his slaves.

XXXIV

Frown lines

Jos let himself into the cottage a little after eleven. I'd fallen asleep in his chair by the fire, not wanting to go to bed before he returned. He had not found Willa. I could tell by the frown lines above the bridge of his nose that deepened whenever something was perplexing him. Usually they appeared because my sister had given him lip or come in late for dinner or stolen a treat he'd been looking forward to – any number of the many things she did that got to him. How wonderful to think they were there because, despite all her flaws, he wanted her back home again. After our row at the warehouse, I'd been fully prepared for him to say I must make my choice between the two of them. He'd come instead to truly accept we were all one family.

'You're later than I expected,' I said, wincing as I stood and crossed the room to greet him.

'I'm sorry, love. I tried three different clubs and there was no sign of her, but tell me why you're limping?'

'The walk from Oxford Circus was a long one,' I admitted. 'My back has been aching of late and my ankles are swollen.'

'Is that usual?' he said and then before I had the chance to answer, 'Is there something I can do to help?'

'I'm lucky it's not been worse,' I said, smiling to reassure him. 'The baby is getting heavier now, my feet will feel better if I soak them.'

Even though he was still in his coat, Jos ladled some water from the bucket into a china bowl for me and set it to heat over the fire. When it was ready he brought it to me and I thought with a pang of Mama's bag, left behind at Tall Trees. If I'd had it with me, I would have added some ground chamomile leaves to the water to help soothe my soles.

'I thought you'd be distraught I hadn't found her,' Jos said as he sat down beside me.

'I am, it's just something that Joy said, about Willa being her own person.'

'Who's Joy?'

'Lady Raine – at least she was, and before that she was Aphrodite.'

He rubbed his eyes in confusion. 'I must be tired.'

'It's not only that. I told you it's been a strange few days.'

'That look you're wearing tells me it's not over.'

How well he knew me.

'I need to go to Tall Trees.'

He shuddered. 'I thought you said you were finished with that place – Cherville gave you the sack.'

'Actually his son did, but I must go there all the same. It's for the men and women he enslaved in Honduras.'

Jos pulled at his newly grown beard. I hadn't noticed before, but there were flecks of grey among the black.

'How can going to that place help people on the other side of the world?'

'It will if I can get Cherville to sign a piece of paper saying he fully intends for them to get his money when he dies.'

'Is it true, though, that that's what he wants?'

'It is. He's changed since I first went to work for him.'

Jos looked pensive. I could tell he still wanted to object, but our reconciliation was new. He didn't want to jeopardise it by browbeating me.

'At least let me come with you.'

'I was hoping you would.'

'How will you get in if Rowland Cherville doesn't want you there, though? And that housekeeper. You said she was against you from the start.'

'I'm not going to knock on the front door, am I? Jenny's going to let me in and, besides, Rowland and Margaret will be distracted. Rowland Cherville is hosting a special dinner tomorrow night to celebrate his engagement; they'll be too busy with that to notice me creeping in.'

'You've got it all worked out, haven't you?' Jos said, and I nodded. Though it was fraught with risk, it was the best plan I could come up with. Much would depend on me getting in unnoticed. It helped that Jenny already knew to expect me and I could keep out of sight on the back stairs. The only unknown was Cherville and whether he was in any fit state to be signing things. He'd looked awful at the factory, and near death according to Jenny by the time Spinks had brought him home, but that had been two days ago. Under Margaret's watchful eye, I could only hope he'd improved.

'We should leave around seven o'clock. That way, by the time we get there, the dinner party will be in full swing.'

'I'll make sure I'm in from work. You're certain there's nothing else going on?' Jos said, his eyes probing mine.

I shook my head. It wasn't dishonest not to say what I'd been thinking, because I hadn't made up my mind yet, but if Cherville was in his senses I was considering telling him who I was.

XXXV

Tinged red

From the very first, Tall Trees had exerted a strange pull on me. The pain and fear its walls had witnessed had stolen into my bones – and now I knew it was because Mama and Artemis, the aunt I'd never known existed, had been here before me. Tuesday evening had arrived and I tightened my grip on Jos's hand as we got closer. Outside the house, a carriage idled. Painted crimson, its crest picked out in gilt, I guessed it belonged to Miss Hawkins, which meant the engagement dinner had got under way promptly. I crossed to the opposite side of the road and beckoned to Jos to follow me. We stood with our backs pressed against the railings that lined the gardens at the centre of the square.

'I thought it was that one,' Jos said, pointing ahead to where Tall Trees lay behind its spiked railings.

'It is. I've never seen it with so many lights on.'

Murk – that's what I associated with Tall Trees, a combination of the gloomy insides and the secrets it held. The lights should have cut through, but somehow they only made it look more devilish, tinged red thanks to the heavy brocade curtains.

'We don't need to go in if you're having second thoughts. You've already done a lot.'

'Not as much as I can, and that's what I owe them. I'll be fine once Jenny opens up for me.'

'Come on, then.' Jos made to cross over, but I grabbed a handful of his coat and pulled him back.

'It means everything that you came with me, but I need to do this bit on my own,' I said.

'You'd put yourself in that danger?' I knew he wanted to say, *What about the baby?* and how much it cost him to bite his tongue. It was partly her I was doing it for. I couldn't give up now.

'I'll be fine if I know you're waiting outside for me and I won't be long. I know my way around, remember, and as soon as I've seen Cherville I'll come straight out.'

'You are telling me everything, Essie, aren't you? It's worth it, all this risk?'

'Please, Jos, you have to trust me,' I said, and though he wasn't happy he opened the gate to the gardens and slipped inside, looking back at me through the bars.

'I'll be watching from here. What floor is Cherville on?'

'The second. The third window along is his bedroom.'

'Well, I'll keep my eyes trained on that and if there are any problems all you need to do is wave and I'll come running.'

I kissed him on the cheek, but he reached through the railings and pulled me into an awkward embrace, so I felt the cold of wrought iron through my coat.

'I don't say I understand why you're here, Hester, but when you come out again, things between us will be different. We'll leave everything bad that's gone on these last few weeks inside that house. Do you agree?'

His eyes glinted with fervency and I kissed him again by way of answer. All the secrets and the hurt and the pain, I'd lock them up inside Tall Trees and never come back again.

I crossed back over to the right side of the road and, keeping to the shadows where I could, made my way down the side entrance to the house. When I was close to the kitchen door, I flattened myself to the wall and peeked inside. There was Jenny at the table, handing a sauce boat to a girl I didn't recognise. She must be one of the servants hired in by Margaret for the evening. I waited for her to stagger off with her burden before tapping my fingers softly on the glass. On the other side, Jenny cocked her head, then looked in the direction of the sound, her face lighting up at the sight of me. With a quick glance over her shoulder to check there was no one to see, she pulled open the door and flung herself at me, then stood back, dusting me down from where she'd covered me in flour.

'You came after all. When I didn't hear from you, I wasn't sure you'd make it. I was worried that rotten peeler had got you.'

'I should have sent a message. This last couple of days . . .' My voice trailed away as I stumbled over where to begin.

Jenny shook her head. 'You can tell me another time. Best thing for now is to get you in and out, quick as we can, is that right?'

'It looks like they'll be at their dinner all night,' I said, eyeing the kitchen table with the serving dishes readied and pots and pans smeared with sauces.

'All to impress Miss Hawkins. Do you reckon she'll be fooled by it?'

'I'd say not, but she can't have too much sense if she's accepted him already.'

We shuddered simultaneously at the prospect of marriage to Rowland Cherville and then Jenny gave herself a further shake as if to get the unwanted thoughts and images from her head.

'She'll have to look to her own concerns. You'd better get upstairs.'

'Is there any change in how Cherville's doing?'

'Not much. Mr Bright was here yesterday to give him

the last rites and he rallied a bit. This morning he was worse than ever; his breathing's all raspy and I'm not sure you'll get a lot of sense out of him. He barely seems to know who he is. I've been taking in his meals so Margaret can keep watch over him. His mind was wandering when I brought up the breakfast and when he spoke it sounded like gibberish. You'd left behind some of your poppy mixture, so I gave him that. I did right, didn't I?'

'You've done perfectly. It's exactly what I would have given him,' I said. Jenny beamed at the compliment, but inside my heart was heavy. If Cherville really was as bad as she said, there was no way I could achieve what I had planned.

'They're still on the first course so you've got a bit of time, but try not to linger.'

'What will I do about Margaret?'

'She's supervising the dinner. The footmen we got in were making all sorts of mistakes and she couldn't have the Cherville name brought into disrepute if they served from the wrong side. I don't think she'd have left him if the family's honour wasn't at stake.'

I could well imagine that, seeing as she believed so fervently in the Chervilles. I wondered if I'd ever know for sure if the whispers were true and she was really one of them?

'I've packed up this for you, by the way – save you having to go to your old room,' Jenny said with a nod towards the far corner of the kitchen where the bag that Mama had bought me was nestled. 'It's got all your things in it, all the herbs and the powders and the empty bottles.'

'I'll be glad to have it back again.'

'Good. Go now, then. I hope you get what you need.'

I couldn't quite believe that I was back inside Tall Trees. The house had been my home for a little less than three weeks, but as I jogged up the back stairs I still remembered where to skip over the creaking tread and where to lift my hand from the wall to stop the plaster from crumbling. As I passed the door that led out on to the ground floor, I heard the plink of harp strings and paused for a second. Across the hall, Rowland Cherville was sitting with the heiress soon to be his second wife and thinking he'd won. Not yet, though. Not if I could get to his father as I'd hoped. The door swung inwards and my heart jumped into my throat before I realised it wasn't Margaret, but the maid I'd seen Jenny send up with the gravy.

She put a hand to her chest with a nervous laugh. 'You startled me, standing there like that. I didn't see you when they were dishing out the instructions earlier.'

She looked me up and down and I drew my coat a little closer so she couldn't see I wore no uniform. 'I'm one of the live-in maids.'

'How did you manage to skip out of helping, then? She's a miserable old bint, that housekeeper.'

I nodded to show I agreed, itching to get away without wanting to be so abrupt that she mentioned me to Margaret. 'I'd best get on. Old Mr Cherville upstairs will need his bed bath soon.'

'I won't envy you that,' she said and tripped off to receive her next task. When I heard a creak followed by a brief burst of clanging pots, I knew she'd made it back to the kitchen and I continued on my way. Up the next two flights of stairs I ran and out onto the second-floor landing. There was no need to tiptoe past Margaret's room, not when I knew she was busy with Rowland and his fiancée, but I did it all the same. I'd made it and with a final glance over my shoulder at the empty corridor, I pushed open Cherville's door and went in.

Here was Cherville, but not as I'd seen him before, even after the night when he'd cowered on the third floor in the room filled with furniture. His breathing was uneven and there was a grey cast to his skin. My heart went out to him and I touched the back of my hand to his forehead. Clammy, but not feverish. When I'd raced here after my clash with his son Margaret had said Cherville was at death's door. It seemed she hadn't been exaggerating. The strain of what had happened at the factory had done for him, and from the way he'd set off it didn't seem as though Spinks had taken the necessary care when driving him home. It appeared as if Cherville had experienced a stroke as a result and I was surprised to feel my eyes brim with tears. Not for him. I wasn't crying for him, was I? Nevertheless I sat down in the chair by his side.

'I came here today to tell you who I am,' I said.

He murmured and his brow creased. Could he hear me after all?

'Do you remember a girl child you brought to England from Honduras? You called her Nyx because you said her skin was dark as night?'

Had his breathing become faster? I leaned in closer and spoke more urgently.

'Nyx had a sister, do you remember her? To you she was Artemis. All your property, but they escaped from you, they ran away.'

There was no denying it this time: his fingers flexed where they rested on the covers. Air whistled through his teeth, or maybe it was a word half-formed, but I couldn't catch what it was and now I was the one who breathed too fast and I realised I had raised my voice. I'd forgiven him, hadn't I? So why was I so angry?

'Do you hear me, Cherville? I want you to know that I am Nyx's daughter.'

Behind me came a gasp and I twisted around to see Margaret standing in the doorway. She was dressed in her usual austere style, but I saw at once she was not herself. She had the agitation borne of long nights spent watching and her pale eyes glittered unnaturally. She stepped in and closed the door behind her.

'Well, well, you managed to worm your way in.'

Her voice was strangely flat. Wary though I was, I refused to be cowed by her.

'Cherville hired me to look after him. I have every right to see if he's improved.'

'You think dragging up the past will help? You and that vicar are just the same. See what you've done to him?' I looked down and saw Cherville was weeping silently. There must have been a part of him that had heard me after all.

'Are you happy now? To see him so wretched in his final moments?' Margaret said. She walked over to the bed and gently brushed away Cherville's tears with a forefinger. 'I thought it would be enough if I broke up the furniture, if I helped Mr Rowland get rid of her,' she murmured half to herself.

'All I told him was the truth,' I said. 'If he is as close to death as you say, you should join me in honouring his final wish – to make provision in his will for the slaves that work on his plantation.'

'Mr Bright was always on at him about it, and then you. It was no wonder he gave way under all that pressure.'

'You know as well as I it was what he wanted. You heard him say as much when he came in from Lady Raine's bazaar.'

Margaret was conflicted. I could see it in her face. 'What of Mr Rowland?'

'He cares nothing for his father. You know that better

than anyone. His only interest is himself and if he wants money he will take it from the poor woman he's persuaded to marry him.'

My argument held sway with her. Yes, she loved the Cherville family as a whole, but it was Gervaise Cherville's portrait that hung above the table in her little room, not his son's.

'What is it you want?'

'I will write a note to confirm Cherville's final wish was to compensate the slaves. It might not be enough, but if Rowland tries to dispute his father's will he will have to explain away two documents that contradict his version of events. Will you help Cherville sit up?'

I left her to haul him into a sitting position while I went to the desk and wrote a brief statement.

I fanned it to dry the ink as I returned to Cherville's bed and knelt at his side. A strand of saliva clung to his chin and he would have slumped had Margaret not held him beneath the arms.

'Sir, this is a piece of paper to prove what we talked about. It says that despite what your son or anyone else might say, your wish is to compensate your slaves, do you understand?'

He turned his head towards me with an effort. His eyes were filmy, but I was sure I saw recognition within their depths and he made a jerking motion with his hands.

'A pen? Is that what you want?' I said, pressing one into

his grasp. The nib rested on the counterpane and an ink stain bloomed. It was no good. I wanted justice for the slaves, but now I felt I'd done enough. Margaret had been right, he was dying. I wanted no part of worriting him in his final hours, whatever the cause, yet when I reached to take away the pen, he refused to let it go.

'Here,' I said resting the paper on a book.

As Margaret and I watched he formed the letters 'G C'. No one who saw it could doubt his initials, shaky though it was, the hand was undeniably his. I added my own signature as witness and Margaret did the same. I'd got what I came for and it was time to go, but the doctoress in me would not allow me to leave without making him comfortable. I put the paper down on his bedside table.

'Here, help me,' I said to Margaret and together we eased him back into a reclining position. As we did so, his nightshirt gaped and seeing what the fabric had concealed made her cry out.

'What is it?' I said, but she'd covered her mouth with her hands, too shocked to say more. Well she might be. Around Cherville's neck was a ring of livid, finger-shaped bruises. He wasn't the victim of a stroke. Someone had throttled him.

The marks had purpled on Cherville's wrinkled skin. Margaret touched them gingerly as if to prove to herself they were there.

'Is this Rowland's doing?' I said.

'It can't be,' Margaret whispered. 'He wouldn't have, he couldn't have,' except there was no conviction in her voice.

As we stared down at Cherville, each of us struggling to absorb the depravity that would have allowed Rowland to do something like this to his father, there came the telltale creak of the floorboard outside Margaret's room.

'What's that?'

'It's him,' Margaret hissed. 'Get in the master's dressing room. Now!'

XXXVI

Broken glass

Margaret bundled me into the dressing room. It was only just in time, for a second later I heard Rowland walk in and shut Cherville's bedroom door behind him. My back to the wall, I held my breath for the best chance of hearing him, waiting for him to exclaim at the blankets pulled back and the strangle marks we'd left exposed. He didn't seem to notice and I slid to my haunches, weak with relief that we'd avoided discovery. Margaret was standing at the door, her head tilted so she could see through the tiny crack. I watched the side of her face and the emotions that ranged across it – the tightening of the jaw, the flicker of the vein at her temple – as Rowland began to speak.

'It's all agreed now, Father, my engagement. Are you

going to congratulate me?' Rowland paused for a moment, as if he genuinely expected Cherville to speak. 'What's that, Father? I didn't quite catch it. You seem to be having trouble with your throat.'

He let out a high-pitched laugh and I realised he was drunk again. It took me back to the last time I had hidden here, the night I'd learned of the suffering Gervaise Cherville had wreaked on my family.

'What's he doing?' I whispered to Margaret.

'I can't tell. He's sat down on the bed so all I can see is his back.'

'Where are his hands?' I said, thinking he'd come back to finish what he'd started, but she shushed me.

'I want to hear what he says.'

We waited in silence, straining to imagine what Rowland was doing, but then he resumed his strange monologue.

'That's two fortunes I'll have now. Hawkins's and my own. Lucky for me I found out your plans before you gave it all away, Pa. I couldn't have you stealing my inheritance like that.'

Margaret turned to me. 'That was your doing. This was your fault,' she hissed. I shook my head. The idea for atonement had been Bright's. It was him who had planted the seed, thinking to lift Cherville's gaze to Honduras. He'd not reckoned with his wanting to make amends to the slaves he'd brought to England in order to stop the cries that plagued him and as a result the vicar had been forced to confront his own complicity.

'You know what I'm going to do with the money?' Rowland continued, 'I'm going to rebuild our plantation in Honduras and refurbish this house and invest in the railways. The Chervilles will be one of England's foremost families. Two hundred years from now we'll be running companies around the world and making laws in Parliament and it will all be thanks to me.'

I dropped my head in my hands at the chilling picture he'd presented. I could see it, as clearly as he could, and with his father dead there was nothing to stop it. There'd been a chance for the Cherville family to redeem itself, but it would never happen now. Joy and Mama and Artemis: looking back on what had happened had been a turning point for the father. To the son, they were just so many stepping stones beneath his feet and he didn't care who he trampled on to get what he wanted.

At the door of the dressing room, Margaret shifted and gave a low moan.

'What is it?'

'He's just stood up, he's . . . oh my God, he's hit him.'

'Quiet,' I warned, but it was too late.

'Who's there?' Rowland called and Margaret stepped swiftly to one side as he kicked the door open.

Rowland's eyes were bluer than ever, the black at the centre reduced to a pinprick. This was more than drink. He looked half-crazed and his lurching movements as he grabbed at Margaret and hauled her from the dressing room only proved it. Once in the main room, she twisted from his grasp and ran straight to Cherville's bedside.

'What have you done to him?'

'The old coot's already on his way. What does it matter if I help him along a bit?'

'We heard your confession. Do you honestly think you'll get away with it?' I said, stepping out of the dressing room.

Rowland looked thunderstruck. In his intoxication he hadn't noticed me.

'You!' he spat. 'What are you doing here?'

'I came to ensure your father's wishes were honoured,' I said, adding silently, 'and to tell him who I am.'

Rowland's face cleared and his tone became solicitous. 'I'm terribly sorry. I think you'll find you're too late,' and out came that laugh again that set my teeth on edge.

In his bed, Gervaise Cherville groaned and began to shake, froth appearing at the corners of his mouth, and Margaret let out a low scream.

'You've poisoned him!' she cried.

'It was all taking too long – why not put him out of his misery?'

When Margaret had walked in on me, I'd been prepared to dodge if she lashed out. Rowland's reactions were shot by whatever brew of drink and opiates he'd taken. She set on him and it took a moment for him to thrust her off. She'd raked his face with her nails and he touched his finger to the scratch she'd left behind, then looked down at the smear of blood.

'You crazy bitch!'

Margaret panted, poised to strike again. There was a wildness in both their looks that said they'd each tipped past the edge of reason. I had to go, but first I must retrieve the statement that Cherville had signed. It was still on his bedside table where I'd left it when we'd helped to make him comfortable. While Rowland and Margaret glowered at one another, I edged slowly towards the bed. The paper was within my grasp if only I could get a little closer. I stretched out my fingertips . . . I'd got it, but as I pulled it to me Rowland spotted it.

'What's that?'

I put the paper behind my back.

'Hand it over.'

'This belongs to your father. He gave it to me.'

'If it's in this house, it's mine.'

I looked over his shoulder. Both he and Margaret stood between me and the door – could I get there? I took a step to one side and Rowland did likewise, meaning to block me. The only way was through him and I readied myself to barge him aside, when Margaret pushed him in the back and I saw my chance. I leaped forward, but Rowland recovered quickly and snatched the paper from my grasp.

He held it up before his eyes, face reddening as he took in what I'd written and his father's initials scratched beneath, along with mine and Margaret's signatures.

'You will not take my money,' he bellowed, wheeling round to encompass us all.

Margaret made a grab for the paper, but this time Rowland was ready. He dangled it just out of her reach as she strained to take it from him.

'You'd rather Cherville money went to these savages?' he said incredulously, with a jerk of his head in my direction.

'The money should go where your father wants it to,' Margaret said. She lunged for Rowland again and this time she got to him. They struggled back and forth then broke apart, both breathing heavily, but now it was Margaret who held the paper in her hand.

'Give me that,' Rowland said, his voice low and dangerous, but she shook her head. 'Don't be foolish. Give it to me, now.'

Seeing it wouldn't work, he changed tack.

'You're practically a member of this family, Margaret,' he wheedled. Did that mean he, too, had heard the rumours? More likely it was a cynical ploy to remind her of her loyalties – would she fall for it?

'Remember it was you who recognised this woman for the charlatan she is in the first place.'

I already knew the role Margaret had played in bringing

Rowland back home from the club. I had no doubt she regretted it now, but she wavered visibly and it was just what Rowland needed. He seized the paper from her hand and cast it into the fireplace. Immediately it caught light, its edges curling into ash. All the promises Cherville had made would be lost unless I could get to it.

In the same instant, Margaret and I both dived for the paper. With a strangled cry, she put her hands into the flames and drew it out. Too hot for her to hold, she dropped the precious statement to the floor where it began to smoulder.

'You're too late, don't you see. No one will be able to read that,' Rowland said.

'We still have the will,' I said.

'A document drafted by a lawyer who has been in the pay of my family for decades. If he knows what's good for him, he'll forget he ever set eyes on it.'

'I won't,' said Margaret. She staggered towards me to close the gap between us. At last, she'd chosen the right side, but then she gave a yelp. The paper had continued to burn and the rug beneath our feet had caught. Flames licked at its edges too high to stamp out.

Hastily, Rowland plucked Cherville's blanket from him. He threw it in the direction of the flames, but instead of smothering them it flared. The fire travelled along it and now it lapped at the corners of Gervaise's bed.

I crossed to the nearest window, threw up the sash and shouted into the night. 'Jos, there's a fire! Jos!' I expected my husband to come running, but there was no sign of him and the night air turned the flames into a blaze, filling Cherville's bedroom with acrid smoke.

'We've got to get out,' I said.

Margaret leaned down to lift Cherville from his bed. He was too weak to support himself and they stumbled to the floor.

Rowland moved towards the door, but instead of pulling it open he turned the key that locked it behind him and pocketed it. 'Neither of you will leave until you've helped me douse this blaze.'

It had taken several minutes for the flames to work their way across to the right-hand window. They shot up the drapes as if the heavy fabric was made of gas. From there they found the reddish wooden panelling and the smoke started to billow.

'It's taken hold. There's nothing you can do,' I said.

'It must be stopped. Fire took my plantation. It will not take my house!' he cried.

Rowland cast about him, but there was nothing suitable in reach. He swiped his hand across his eyes as sweat dripped from his brow. Dropping to his knees, he rolled up the carpet. Did he think he could beat the fire down? It was too far gone for that, but as soon as he'd entered the room I'd seen he was beside himself. His eyes were glossy with mania. Syphilis could do that to the brain. I skirted around him and touched the back of my hand to the door-knob, before snatching it back with a yelp. Blazing hot. To open it would take the skin off my hands. I tore the hem off my skirt and wrapped it around my palm ready to try again.

'Hester, are you in there?'

The door rattled in its frame. Thank God. It was Jenny.

'There's a fire. Can you open the door?'

The handle twisted back and forth, but the door refused to budge.

'It's stuck. Who's with you?'

'Rowland and Margaret and Cherville,' I called.

The door rattled again.

'Your husband's gone for help, and the dinner guests are safe. You need to find a way out.'

How could I when the door was shut fast? I looked beyond the flames licking the window frame. If I could get past them, I could jump. But they were only growing higher and it was a long way down.

'Kick the door, Jenny. Kick it,' I shouted. Alas, my words were swallowed by the smoke and I cradled my stomach as my body convulsed with coughing, terrified for the baby I carried.

I set about the door from my side, but the smoke had sapped my strength. My efforts were so weak and ineffectual, the thick mahogany did not even splinter. Sweat stung my eyes and I swung my leg ever more wildly, no longer able to see my target.

'Help me,' I croaked out. 'Help me,' and when I thought all was lost and no one was coming, I heard Jenny shout, 'Stand back, Hester. I'm coming in.'

The door burst inwards and there she was on the other side. Smoke surged out and I gulped down the clean air from the hallway.

'I thought you'd gone.'

'I went for Margaret's spare key. Even unlocked, I had to put my shoulder to it.'

She looked beyond me where Rowland and Margaret still beat at the flames. There was a crash and we both flinched as the glass in the left-hand window blew out and the blaze surged higher.

Jenny reached for my arm, but I shook her off.

'Margaret,' I wheezed.

She'd given up on fighting the flames and was dragging an unconcious Cherville to the door. I took his leg, trying to help her. He was a dead weight and all the while the flames were building despite Rowland Cherville's attempts to contain them.

'Help your father,' I shouted to him. The expression in his eyes was crazed.

'I must stop it,' he cried, redoubling his efforts to beat at the fire with the rolled-up carpet.

'It's too late.'

I made a lunge for his coat tails, but he dodged and left me clutching air.

'I will not let my house burn!'

'He's got a death wish,' Jenny said, hovering just outside, the flames too high for her to come in. Margaret and I could jump them, but there was no way we could get Cherville out, too.

'You have to leave him,' I pleaded with Margaret. She'd slumped down beside him on the floor, her hair hanging in limp strands from the effort of dragging him only halfway towards the door.

'I can't.'

'Margaret, he's gone. If you don't come now, you'll die here with him. Is that what you want? Please, Margaret,' I said, but she shook her head. And put her legs out in front of her, drawing Cherville up so he half-lay in her arms. His eyes flickered open.

'It's all right, sir, I'm here,' she said and he closed them again.

'Hester,' Jenny shouted, more frantic now. 'You must come.'

I stood before the doorway. If I took a running jump, I'd make it. I turned back, my eyes smarting at the smoke. I could just about see Rowland Cherville still beating at the flames. His motions were becoming feebler, and he coughed so violently I was surprised he remained on his feet. Back he went and back, but the flames were winning. He would not tame them now.

'Come on,' Jenny said again, and holding my hands to my stomach I leaped and reached the other side. The smoke was out here, too, and I pulled Jenny down to the floor so it bloomed above our heads.

'It's the panelling made the fire spread so quickly,' Jenny said through her coughing.

'You said all the dinner guests were out, servants, too?'

'Every single one. It's only us here now. The back stairs. If we can get there, we'll be safe.'

We crawled along the corridor on our hands and knees. There was a crash as the building started to collapse in on itself and I heard the fire crackle as it consumed Cherville-blue fabric and mahogany. The smoke was so heavy, I had to rely on Jenny's voice to find my way out.

'Hester, I'm at the door, where are you?'

I'd thought I was right behind her, but somehow in the smoke I'd got lost and now she sounded far away. 'Go on, Jenny. I'm almost there. Get downstairs.'

'I won't leave you.'

'Go!' I shouted.

I heard the door to the back stairs shut. Right – I had to go right. I stood and felt my way along the wall. Another crash and then the smash of broken glass as more windows shattered. Rowland must be overcome by now. The door, at last. I pushed it open, and half-fell into the back stairwell. The fire hadn't taken hold here. I tried to stand, but my legs buckled beneath me, and I stumbled before falling down a handful of stairs.

'Jenny, are you there?' I called.

No answer came and coughing took me over.

XXXVII

The language of forgiveness

The fire at Tall Trees commanded half a page in the *Standard*, with an account of the fatalities and how it had taken twenty men more than five hours to bring the blaze under control. A few days later, the *Morning Chronicle* carried an obituary of Gervaise Cherville, noting his accomplishment in building his mahogany business and furniture factory against a backdrop of personal tragedy, including the untimely death of his wife. Rowland's death received only a line to the effect that he'd not had time to achieve his undoubted potential. Margaret was not mentioned by name in either publication. I learned all this in the days after having sustained a concussion when I fell down the stairs. Thankfully, the burns I'd got were minor and, most importantly of all, the baby was safe. Jos had pulled me out and carried us away. I didn't dare think what would have happened had he not been there.

While he was at work, Jenny looked after me. With nowhere else to go, she had moved into the cottage. Of a night she slept in Jos's chair by the fire. I couldn't have had her in Willa's makeshift bed, not while my sister was still missing. It would have felt as though we were trying to replace her. Jos still carried on the search, but it was coming up ten days since she'd disappeared, almost as long as the time before, and neither of us held out much hope of her return.

I was sat in Jos's chair one afternoon when there was a rap at the door. I threw back the blanket that covered my knees, preparing to stand, but my growing belly made swift movement impossible and Jenny was quicker, jumping up from the table where she'd been reading one of her penny dreads.

'Stay there. Let me.'

It had been wonderful to have her by my side in the days since the fire. With few burns, she'd escaped the worst of it and made it her business to be indispensable. Any hope of moving out of London had died with Gervaise Cherville, who'd perished before he could pay me. Had he lived, I couldn't have left without Willa, but if we ever did gather the funds we needed, I would ask Jenny to come with us.

She opened the door and over her shoulder I could see that the man who had knocked wasn't the usual sort of visitor that came to the cottage. His black coat and broad-brimmed top hat gave him an official air and I felt a flash of panic. Before he'd died, Rowland had put it about that I was imposing on his father. It seemed to be accepted that the fire had been an accident, but if anyone believed I was a charlatan willing to poison a rich man, it wasn't a huge leap to think I would burn down his house. *It may not be anything to do with you, he may just be lost*, I told myself. All the same, I burrowed down in my chair so I wouldn't be immediately visible.

'Can I help you, sir?' Jenny said nervously.

'I'm looking for Hester Reeves,' the man replied.

'I don't know if . . . Will you tell me what it's regarding?' Jenny stuttered out and, despite my anxiety, the incongruity of it tickled me – that someone who lived in a two-room cottage would appear to have a maid to answer the door for them.

'Mrs Reeves is not in any trouble, I assure you,' the man said, seemingly guessing Jenny's hesitation, and I hauled myself up to speak to him.

'I'm here, sir. You'd better come in.'

While he took off his hat and coat and gloves, Jenny joined me at the fire to boil water for tea.

'He didn't give you his name, did he?' I muttered from the corner of my mouth.

'I thought he was a peeler at first when I saw that hat. It makes him look ever so tall.'

She was right – that had been my first thought,

too – but the peelers were a rough lot and this man was far more refined.

'I can't help but think I've seen him before, though, I'm sure of it,' Jenny said, throwing furtive glances in his direction.

Tall Trees. It was the only place she'd have come across a man like that. I swayed a little as a bout of dizziness came on and took me back to the smoke-filled corridor, how I'd clung to the wall to find my way out and known myself to be saved before I fainted.

'Here, sit down,' Jenny said, steering me into one of the chairs at the kitchen table.

'It was not my intention to inconvenience you, Mrs Reeves,' my visitor said. 'I see you are still suffering the effects of the smoke.'

So he was connected to the Chervilles, then, but now he was closer he didn't look so stern.

'Please sit down, won't you?' I said, and after bringing over the teacups Jenny joined us. He picked up a cup without seeming to notice that none of them matched and took a long sip.

'That's better. Forgive me, I have not yet mentioned my name,' he said. 'I am Mr Wheeler, solicitor to Gervaise Cherville. I am come to talk about his will.'

When Cherville had said he wanted to atone, I'd been suspicious, but you couldn't argue when there was money on the table. I was still grappling with what Lady Raine had said in the garden at the Lukeses' house – that when it came to slavery, cash was the language of forgiveness. I could see that, on their own, fine words of regret and sorrow were not enough but I couldn't help but feel that if truly meant, they were the start, otherwise there was no acceptance of wrongdoing. According to Mr Wheeler, Cherville had given his whole fortune to recompensing those he'd enslaved and I was to be given charge of ensuring that it reached them. I sat back, struggling to take it all in, while Jenny failed to hide her amazement.

'Can you believe it?' she mouthed.

I wasn't sure I could. I hadn't given much thought to Cherville's will since the fire, convinced that Rowland would have followed up on his earlier threat to prevail upon Mr Wheeler to change it.

'Mr Cherville did mention something of the kind,' I explained to the solicitor. 'I wasn't sure how much was real and how much a warning to his son of what he might do, but then just before the fire broke out he initialled a statement to say he wanted the slaves to have his compensation money when it came through. The paper it was written on got swallowed up by the blaze so I put it out of my mind.'

Mr Wheeler nodded gravely. 'Rowland Cherville had made an appointment to come and see me. He wrote that he was concerned his father had given me some ill-advised instructions, but Gervaise himself had explained his son was not in favour of what he was doing and might challenge it. In anticipation of any difficulties, he insisted on two additional witnesses to attest he was of sound mind when he came to sign the document.'

The fire at Tall Trees had begun when Rowland cast the initialled paper into the flames and Margaret, knowing it detailed her beloved master's true wishes, tried to retrieve it. To think it had never been needed at all. Did that mean I was in some way to blame for the blaze? No, I reasoned, if Rowland hadn't been so intent on thwarting his father and hanging on to ill-gotten gains he had no moral right to, Tall Trees would still be standing. This was not my burden to bear.

There was one last thing I needed to understand.

'Why do you ask me to hand out the monies, why not—'

'Mr Bright?' Wheeler supplied. 'I think he would have been Mr Cherville's first choice, but I understand that he is returning to the Indies. It's not a long life for an Englishman over there and Mr Bright is not as young as he was.'

'He is going back to Honduras?'

'Oh yes. I thought you might be aware of his plans. I assumed you were close, as it was he that recommended you for this task.'

'When?'

'Friday the fifteenth of November,' Wheeler said, tapping again at the document. The day I was due to finish my month at Tall Trees. I cast my mind back. Mr Bright would have put me forward after our confrontation about the part he'd played in Artemis's death. I wondered, if Cherville had not died when he did, would the vicar have told me himself before he left the country?

'A sad business all round,' Mr Wheeler said. 'I served the Cherville family for over thirty years, I hate to think of Gervaise in pain at the end.'

'He was already so weak I think the smoke would have taken him quickly. I know he felt loved as he departed this world,' I said, remembering how carefully Margaret had cradled him. 'He was with his housekeeper to the last.'

'That is a comfort,' Mr Wheeler said, before picking up his cup and taking the last of his tea. 'For now I will say goodbye and thank you for the refreshment. It will take a week or two to work through these papers. I would have waited, as it is always preferable to do these things in the office, but knowing you had been caught up in the fire, I thought it made sense to bring you the news in person and now I see your condition I am doubly glad. Congratulations.'

He rose and let himself out before Jenny or I had the chance to stir.

'Did you hear that? Did that really happen?' Jenny said.

'It absolutely did,' I replied. 'Justice has been done.'

XXXVIII

A watery smile

Autumn had turned into winter and, though my lungs were still weak from the fire, as soon as I was well enough to go outside, I asked Jos to walk me to the churchyard at St Hilda's. Wrapped up well against the cold, we made our way hand in hand along the towpath. The hedgerows were noticeably bare of flowers and even the duckweed had sunk from the surface of the water. The next few months would be hard canal-side, but things always improved with the arrival of spring. And we had the baby to look forward to.

I'd not visited Mama since learning she'd been enslaved and that Gervaise Cherville had brought her to Tall Trees. It saddened me that the only conversation we could have about it now would be one-sided, with me awaiting answers that would never come as I knelt by her graveside. I thought I understood why she'd never told me – it was a part of her life that she'd wanted to leave behind, but it had stayed with her always in her regret for what had happened to Artemis. It was that she'd passed on to me – not the knowledge of the events, but the attendant feelings – so desperate was she that my sister didn't share the fate of hers.

I was convinced Mama had seen something of Artemis in Willa. Their stories seemed too similar for there not to be some sort of wild or reckless streak that had driven them to believe the false promises of Cherville in one case and his son in the other. There was one hope that I clung to: Willa's story was not yet over. She was out there somewhere, I could feel it, and so even though there were moments when the sadness I felt at her absence threatened to overwhelm me, I told myself that one day she would come back. She might be angry now or scared, but deep down I hoped she knew that whenever she was ready to return home there'd be a place for her.

Jos sat down on a bench just beyond the churchyard gate to wait for me. I'd thought I'd have the place to myself, so it was a surprise to see a woman hovering by one of the monuments ahead of me. She had her back to me and was wrapped in a cloak with her hat down low over her face. In the early days I'd made many visits to the churchyard like that, hiding my tears behind a veil, and so

I hung back, not wanting to disturb her privacy. Down by her side the woman held a posy of bright red flowers.

After a few minutes I coughed gently, to let her know I was close. She started and, dropping her flowers to the ground, took off, weaving her way between the headstones. I stepped forward, realising it was Mama's grave she'd been paying tribute at. I bent to retrieve the blooms. Chrysanthemums. There were only two of us left in the world who knew they were Mama's favourite.

'Willa, please,' I called after her.

Would she stop? Unless she did, I wouldn't catch her, not in my condition. 'Come on, Willa,' I muttered under my breath. Slowly she turned around, walked towards me and, when she was close enough to touch, I flung myself on her.

'Careful, Hes,' she exclaimed, trying to wriggle out of my arms, but I refused to let her go and after a moment she wrapped her hands around my waist. As soon as I felt her return my embrace, I squeezed all the harder.

'Willa, thank God. You came back,' I hiccupped through my tears.

'You can let me go, I won't run,' she said, but still I held on tightly and, for all her words, I felt she wasn't ready to let go either. I'd told myself she'd return when she was ready, as she had before, but there'd been a part of me that worried some awful fate had befallen her. That it wasn't choice that kept her away, but death.

At last I stepped back with a sniffle. 'Let me see you.'

I was almost scared to look on her after she'd been missing for so long. From having held her in my arms I could tell she'd grown thinner. It made the angles of her face sharper and her eyes were warier than before, but she was my beloved sister all the same.

'I wondered if I'd see you here one day,' she said.

'Have you come to visit Mama often?'

'A couple of times. When I've had enough money to light a candle for her.'

'You've been inside the church?'

'Never for very long. Mama didn't think much of it, did she?'

I knew why now, because Bright had been the one to persuade Artemis to go back to Cherville.

'I heard Tall Trees burned down and old man Cherville with it.'

'And Rowland, too,' I said, watching her closely for a reaction. There was barely a flicker.

'And Rowland, too,' she agreed. 'You weren't there when it happened, though?'

'Yes, I was.'

'I thought you'd been thrown out? I saw a couple of the girls after I went; I've been staying with one of them these last two weeks – Caro, I don't think you ever met her. I would have come if I'd known.'

She looked distraught and I decided to believe her.

'You should have come anyway.'

'I didn't think you'd want me. I saw the trouble I was causing between you and Jos and I felt embarrassed about what happened with Rowland.'

I took a deep breath. 'Did you lie to me about how far it had gone with him?'

Willa looked down, mumbling into the ground. 'Sort of.'

I grabbed her by the shoulders and gave her a shake, fear overcoming my delight she'd returned. 'Did he take advantage of you or not?'

'No,' she said indignantly. 'I wouldn't have lied to you about that. Are you all right? Come, sit down here.' She led me to a bench for I swayed on my feet, light-headed with relief.

'Willa, I've been so scared for you. You cannot do that to me again, do you understand?'

I meant to stop, not wanting to spend these precious moments of her return in scolding, but holding Willa in my arms had broken something inside me, and all the hurt and anxiety I'd felt while she was missing bubbled up to the surface and spilled out.

'I've been worried sick, afraid you were lying in a ditch somewhere, or that the disease had got to you and you'd been shut up in a lock hospital. Now you tell me that all the time you were staying with a friend? You would have known I'd be thinking the worst. How could you do that to me?'

Her expression was mutinous and I braced, waiting for her to hit back with a few choice words of her own. Instead her eyes filled and she buried her face in my shoulder.

'I'm sorry,' she blubbed. 'I was angry, so angry. At Mama for dying, at you for not being able to give her something that would save her, at Rowland, at you for being right about Rowland.'

'That's a lot of anger, Willa,' I whispered, feeling weak now my own flash of temper was spent.

'I know it. And I could see you were angry with me, too.'

'Never with you. Only at the situation. That's why I went to work at Tall Trees. I knew if I could earn the money to get us away from here, we could start afresh and everything would be better.'

She sat back and wiped her nose on her sleeve, looking younger again. 'What about Jos?'

'Jos has been out every night he could looking for you. He wanted to find you as much as I did. You should give him another chance, Willa.'

'He did that for me?' Willa said, a watery smile brightening her face.

'Of course he did. We both love you very much. He'll tell you that himself. Jos!' I called and my husband appeared at the entrance to the churchyard.

He beamed to see Willa and, coming forward, he caught her up and held her tight. My eyes swam to see them so close, and when he put her down, I saw we'd all been crying.

'Welcome back, Willa,' Jos said.

'You'll always have a home with us,' I said. 'You would have known that if you weren't so stubborn.'

'I have been stubborn, haven't I,' she said.

'A little, but then you always were like that. Do you remember when Mama refused to buy you a doll at the market? You wouldn't come home then, either. We had to drag you in the end.'

'I just wanted something nice. I thought about that doll when I made the bunny for the baby – I can't believe how big you've got, I can't wait to see my niece.'

'Another one who insists it's a girl. I'll be outnumbered completely,' Jos grumbled.

I looked down to where my belly showed. There wasn't too long to go now.

'Why don't we go back to the cottage?' I said. 'I can show you the clothes I've been making for her.'

Willa nodded and Jos offered an arm to each of us. Willa, weaker than I was, leaned on him, but before I could link arms myself I saw that Mr Bright had come out of the vicarage and stood watching us.

'Go ahead. I'll catch you up in a moment,' I said.

'You're sure?' Jos said.

'I am, I won't be long.'

Mr Bright waited for Jos and Willa to disappear through

the gate and back on to the towpath before he walked over to join me. He looked gaunt, a little frail, not like a man who would survive long in the heat of the Indies. There was no chance he didn't know it himself.

'I was in the kitchen at the vicarage and saw you looking around. I thought it might be me that you were seeking.'

'I've just been reunited with my sister,' I said meaningfully.

'The woman in the black cloak is your sister? I have observed her once or twice, but she's always hurried away when I attempted to talk to her. I'm glad I was able to see you, though, Hester,' Mr Bright said. 'I don't know if you've heard, but I will be leaving soon for the Indies. I wanted us to part as friends.'

The last time we'd spoken he'd confessed to his role in the downfall of my aunt and I could never forgive him. Not because he'd persuaded her to return to Cherville. I believed he'd thought he was acting for the best, but he could have no excuse for encouraging me to enter Tall Trees without telling me of what horrors it had held for the women of my family.

'You won't return?'

He didn't answer but said, 'There was something I wanted to show you before I left. Will you come with me now?'

The *no* had already formed on my lips, but his eyes were pleading and I was curious.

'I don't have long,' I said grudgingly.

I followed him to a gate at the far edge of the church-yard, wrapped around with chains. When he realised I wasn't right behind him, he stopped.

'What you have to show me means going in there?' I said.

'Yes, I'm afraid it does.'

Mr Bright withdrew a key from his pocket and fiddled with the padlock. It sprung open and when he unwound the chains, they slithered to the ground like an iron snake. Only somewhere precious would be so well protected, or somewhere prohibited. Potter's Fields. That's what they called them and I could already feel the weight of desolation in the air.

'I'm sorry to have to bring you here, but once you know why, I hope you will understand.'

He led me out into an unkempt patch of grass. Far from the shelter of the church building itself, it was colder than ever and the few trees that grew were stunted and misshapen. Their twisted forms added to the bleakness and I shivered, knowing that with every step I would be walking over someone's grave. Beneath my feet lay the bodies of the nameless. Either the way they'd lived their lives, or the manner of their deaths, meant they'd been denied headstones, but for every murderer buried here, there were twenty people whose only crime was to be poor or desperate or both.

'If you walk in my footsteps exactly, you can be sure

you're not trampling on anyone,' Mr Bright called over his shoulder.

His boots had pressed down the grass, not just today but on other days, to form a pathway. Ahead of me, he'd come to a stop by a mound where the grass was healthier and green shoots burrowed up from the earth beneath.

'The village I'm from, they stick to the old ways,' he said when I'd caught up with him. 'My cousin wrote to me some years back of a young man who'd returned from fighting in the Burmese War. He'd been badly injured and it left him despairing. When they pulled him from a shallow river, they buried him at the crossroads with a stake through his heart. Was it not barbarous of them?'

'Is this where my aunt is buried?'

'Yes, Artemis is here,' he said.

We stood side by side in silence, briefly united by our love for her. Mr Bright murmured his prayers, but I couldn't join in while the church insisted that a woman who'd gone through so much pain must sleep in unconsecrated ground. At last he made the sign of the cross and ran a hand across his eyes. His voice was heavy with the emotion he'd been unable to suppress.

'I have brought you here because I am the only one who knows her resting place. There can be no stone, but will you remember where she is? Will you visit her?'

'I will. Every time I come to see Mama.'

'I loved her, you know.'

His voice was fierce, as though I might dispute it. I saw he had and I'd not given him credit for it. Since he'd admitted his role in her death, I'd felt betrayed. Now I realised that when Cherville had gone back on his promise not to punish Artemis, Mr Bright had been betrayed, too.

'You took a great risk burying her so close to St Hilda's.'

'I wanted her by me.'

'Lady Raine said you were naive.'

'I was. I genuinely thought that Cherville would take her back in and then, once we abolitionists had triumphed, he would grant her freedom. Instead he told her he would send her to Africa to be sold and so she took her own life. I struggled to forgive her at first.'

I looked up sharply and he had the grace to look shame-faced.

'I can see why it would offend you, the idea that I would need to forgive her, but I feared for her soul and I was making many sacrifices to be with her. I do not believe I understood the difficulties she faced.'

'She knew that if she were sold she would never have her freedom. The only choice left to her was death.'

'I brought her body into the church. I anointed it with oils and placed a scarf around her neck to hide the marks. She looked serene. No one seeing her then would have known how she died. But I did and ever since it has tormented me. I was angered when you said Lady Raine told you I might as well have tied the noose because the grain of truth in it burned me. I killed the woman I loved.'

He put his head in his hands and his shoulders heaved, but I couldn't bring myself to comfort him. When he stopped, I said, 'Will you go direct to Honduras on Friday?'

'Yes, to take the advice that I gave Gervaise Cherville. Thinking that Lady Raine was missing, knowing that your mother and aunt were dead, I knew there could be no true atonement anywhere but the place it started.'

To me that place was Tall Trees; now it was burned to the ground like the Cherville plantation before it.

'Mr Wheeler came to visit me and said that you'd suggested I be an executor of Cherville's will, to ensure the money gets to those he enslaved?'

'That's right. I'd hoped to be away before he told you, but I'm glad we've had this chance to speak. I'll rest easier knowing you will visit your aunt, that someone other than me knows where she sleeps.'

I looked around, committing the exact spot to memory, picking out markers among the trees and bushes that would help me find my way back here.

'I hope you see how sorry I truly am, but I will not apologise, knowing it cannot undo what happened. It is one thing that I have reflected on since last we spoke. For many years it has been something I have advocated, but I wonder now if some apologies do more harm than good?'

It was something I had pondered, too. When Cherville

had insisted on finding the woman he'd thought was
Aphrodite, there'd been a selfishness in his desire to
atone that denied true repentance. His sole motive had
been to assuage himself of guilt. Maybe when it came
down to it, all apologies were like that, even when they
were heartfelt.

I bid Mr Bright farewell and caught up with Jos and Willa
who'd waited for me on the towpath. Together we made
our way back to the cottage.

'Look who I found,' I called as I let us in through the
door.

'This is your sister, then,' Jenny said shyly, laying down
her darning on the kitchen table.

'It is. Jenny, meet Willa.'

The two smiled at each other.

'We met before, when you came to Tall Trees,' Jenny
said to Willa, reminding me.

'That place. I'd be glad if I never heard of it again,' Willa
said.

'I think we can manage that,' I replied, and beside me
Jenny nodded emphatically.

Still, I couldn't help going there one final time. I wasn't
sure why. Maybe to pay my respects to Margaret whose
body they hadn't been able to recover. The fire had burned
long and hot and I'd been told the smoke hung over the

square for days afterwards. Tall Trees' charred remains, the blackened rubble so stark against the white surrounds, would be removed in time; for now they bore witness to this strange chapter in my life. The night before the fire, what had Jos said to me? That all the pain that had been unlocked during my time in the house should stay there. Vain hope – even the fire had not cleansed it – but I was learning to shoulder the burden of the knowledge I now carried, and the understanding I'd come to of Mama's wishes.

When she'd exhorted me to take care of Willa, it had been Artemis, her own sister, she'd been thinking of. Mama hadn't been able to save her, but my fears that history would repeat itself were unfounded – Willa had come back to me. Every day she grew a little more open, a little easier with Jos and with herself. I watched over her as closely as Mama could have wished, but that was not the only way I would honour the vow I'd made. There were other girls like Willa and Artemis, and many of them would have caring older sisters, too. I would be a doctoress for them, for all the women who needed me; and for each one I treated, each one I nursed back to health, I would say, 'Yes, Mama, I kept my promise.'

Author's Note

House of Shades is a story about a woman driven by the promise she makes to her dying mother. It is also about reconciliation, truth and justice for the victims of slavery. For a long time it's felt as though the question of reparations has been framed as an American concern in much the same way slavery has been talked about as largely an American issue. In the last twenty years, however, there's been a growing albeit gradual acknowledgement of Britain's full role in the transatlantic slave trade. And for some it has come as a surprise that it is considerably more complex than what we've traditionally been taught at school or even university.

When I began writing *House of Shades* the conversation about reparations still felt somewhat one-sided but over the last two years there's been a definitive shift – the case for compensation is now getting a full hearing and the descendants of the enslaved are not the only ones in favour. I think we'll look back on this period and recognise key moments as the turning points they'll no doubt prove to be. The Church of England setting aside £100 million to address past wrongs; members of the Trevelyan family travelling to Grenada to make a public apology for their ownership of 1,000 slaves; the *Guardian*'s commitment to restorative justice having identified its founder's historic links to slavery through the textile industry.

Opponents of making reparations for slavery remain in full voice. They focus on the logistics of identifying and making payments to individuals and question the fairness of expecting people not directly involved to pay for the sins of the past, although British taxpayers were paying back the loan that compensated slave owners for the loss of their 'property' until around 2015. Perhaps when all is said and done the most important thing is that we're talking about it. And, while the conversation will be painful for all of us, it is most necessary.

London, September 2023

Acknowledgements

Thanks first and foremost to my wonderful agent Juliet Mushens and to Jenny Bent for all her help and support in the US. And to my editors Emily Griffin who believed in me even when I didn't and Millicent Bennett and their teams at Hutchinson Heinemann and Harper. Thanks also to fellow writers who cheered me on, especially Rosie Andrews who staged an intervention to help me find my path and my MA critique group who read too many early iterations to count. To my amazing family for bearing with me while I was writing and more importantly when I wasn't. And to friends and colleagues and random people I've shared my woes with whilst battling to get this story on the page. Finally, thank you to the readers for allowing me to share my words with you.